PALE MORNING

LIGHT WITH

VIOLET SWAN

PALE MORNING LIGHT WITH VIOLET SWAN

A Novel of a Life in Art

DEBORAH REED

Mariner Books
Houghton Mifflin Harcourt
Boston New York
2020

For information about permission to reproduce selections
from this book, write to trade.permissions@hmhco.com or to
Permissions, Houghton Mifflin Harcourt Publishing Company,
3 Park Avenue, 19th Floor, New York, New York 10016.

hmhbooks.com

Library of Congress Cataloging-in-Publication Data
Names: Reed, Deborah, author.
Title: Pale morning light with Violet Swan : a novel of a life in art /
Deborah Reed.
Description: Boston : Houghton Mifflin Harcourt, 2020. | A Mariner
original.
Identifiers: LCCN 2019045641 (print) | LCCN 2019045642 (ebook) |
ISBN 9780544817364 (trade paperback) | ISBN 9780358308973 |
ISBN 9780358311829 | ISBN 9780544817418 (ebook)
Classification: LCC PS3602.R3885 P35 2020 (print) |
LCC PS3602.R3885 (ebook) | DDC 813/.6—dc23
LC record available at https://lccn.loc.gov/2019045641
LC ebook record available at https://lccn.loc.gov/2019045642

Book design by Margaret Rosewitz

Printed in the United States of America

DOC 10 9 8 7 6 5 4 3 2 1

For Dylan and Liam

Defeated, exhausted and helpless
you will perhaps go
a little bit further.

—Agnes Martin, *Writings*, 1991

PART ONE

1

Shortly after dawn, Le cygne drifted from the Telefunken radio, and Violet's eyes grew moist at the rise and fall of the cello. She turned from her lamplit canvas to the windows, the sun radiating edgewise across the yard, the garden brightening with greens and golds. This too gave her heart a clench.

She stepped away, brush in hand, to the windows, where the air felt charged, expectant, in the way of spring. The wooden floor creaked and clunked beneath her clogs, perhaps loud enough to wake her son, Francisco, and his wife, Penny, downstairs, though in the forty years they'd lived beneath her, Violet had never asked about the noise, and didn't want to know. Speckles of pale ochre slipped from her brush to the dropcloth, and now to the fir floor. She was fond of the groaning planks, their bricolage of color and grooves running from one end of the loft to the other, crisscrossing from her workbench to the canvas, to her reading chair, kitchen sink, and bed, like a map chronicling her days.

She swiped her cheeks with the sleeve of her smock. The morning still held a promise like so many that had come before. The ides of March had arrived, and the Irish moss between the walkway stones was now a rich emerald green. At a distance, the soft shapes resembled parakeets nestled along the path.

Violet's emotions were tender as ever, humming close to the surface, her love for this world often seen through a swift convulsion of tears. But lately it felt as if the world was dismantling her into something puny and indecisive, and this was not how she imagined the end.

Ever since her diagnosis at the start of the year, the days felt squeezed and the nights stretched on, hours threaded with fragments of sleep and dreams that were fleeting and strange. Lungs full of spiders. Hands dissolving into dust. But this morning she woke to the gentle voice of her old friend Ada Dupré — *Bonjour, sweet Vio-lette* — as sharp as any memory that Violet had carried for decades. Ada's olive skin and freckled nose, her eyes the color of jade, lingered beyond the dream: *Dance with me, Vio-lette. Why don't we just dance?*

Violet had jerked out of bed and gone straight into a coughing fit.

Her concentration was slipping. The base coat on her canvas was only half finished, and still she remained at the windows, distracted by the light, the yard, and the thick forest beyond the grass, the warm sun drawing heat from the trees, an orange gas rising. Periwinkle crocuses streamed over the lawn like lightbulbs with golden filaments. Barn swallows flitted to and from phone wires, their steely-blue wings and mustard bellies flashing in the sun. The Oregon coast had finally thrown off its gray-sky cape and stepped into the fuller light of spring.

Violet coughed into a tissue from her pocket, catching rust-colored flecks against the white. She wiped her mouth, balled the tissue, tossed it into the wastebasket, and looked west through the opposite set of windows at the curved horizon where the sky met the ocean, blue against blue. The cool colors had a way of tempering the heat inside Violet's lungs.

She swiped her tears with the back of her hand and returned to the large canvas, braced on the wall by brass hooks. She painted vertical strokes in time with the music, and moments later, traces of ordinary happiness began to sift through.

The scars on her right hand appeared shinier, richer, through wet eyes and morning light. At ninety-three years old, nearly all of her was mottled in swirls of pink and red and honey brown of parched skin, the discolorations no longer assigned to the scars that covered her right side, from shoulder to foot. Her body resembled the leaves of the variegated shrub near Francisco's work shed—which he hadn't been spending enough time in lately, always watching the evening news or staring at his phone instead of creating something new with his hands, and she would tell him this, even when—

Something was happening.

Tin cans full of brushes and pencils began to rattle, skip across the workbench, and crash to the floor. Rulers, notebooks, and masking tape plunged into easels against the wall.

Violet's knees gave way beneath her. It seemed as if the house had come unmoored and was drifting out to sea. Walls trembled, floorboards heaved, and down she went, letting loose a throaty cry, a *mercy me*.

She was flat on her back when scenes from her past flickered like an old film crackling, in and out, in and out. Here was Richard reading her a poem, his voice so close she felt the heat of his breath on her cheek. " 'The world offers itself to your imagination,' " he whispered. "*Richie*," she said, but he was already gone, and in his place was a child. Seven-year-old Violet with her body set aflame.

She stumbled from the burning farmhouse with her mother, catching a breath in the snow while the blaze lit the night sky. Coughing, shaking the small birdcage clutched in her left hand—her sister Em's canary from Woolworth's, warbling, whistling, alive. *Wait till Em hears this song*, she thought, looking down to see her charred skin thawing a circle at her feet. She was naked, her nightgown just a collar, singed and ringing her throat. The right side of her body had melted, and was hardening like wax in the cold.

In a flash Violet was fourteen, taller than her mother, standing beneath the canvas tent of a revival, the scent of moonflowers, and floodlights on every kind of person swooning across the dusty Georgia ground. Her mother dragged her by her scarred arm and delivered her to the Holy Joe onstage, who slapped Violet's soft cheeks and hissed that she repent her wicked ways.

And then Violet tromping through rugged forests in a dress and oxford shoes, hungry, bitten, and scratching like the feral creature she had become.

Another clip and spin of the reel as Richard's young face appeared on a front porch with the Pacific Ocean glinting at his back. "Who are you?" he asked. "Why are you here?"

"I'm Violet Swan," she said. "And you'll know in just a minute."

2

The house settled abruptly. The Moonlight Sonata had taken over from *Le cygne* as if nothing had happened, even as Violet lay on the floor. She may have fainted. It seemed as if she'd been traveling for days and was relieved to find herself home.

Hanging plants swung like pendulums of asynchronous clocks above her head. Her paintbrush remained clutched in her hand, wide and heavy as a house painter's, especially when wet. Her large plastic measuring cup full of paint had flung across the dropcloth, and the pale ochre coursed between folds of fabric near her head.

She struggled to sit up, swiping the brush across the floor and her smock and rolled-up blue jeans. She glanced around the loft for Em before realizing that Em couldn't be in the house on the coast of Oregon where Violet had lived for the past seventy-five years. Em had never been here, or anywhere, since the fire. And yet the loss of her sister seared so deeply it was as if Violet had just received word. The left side of her body flushed with perspiration. The right, thickened by scars, remained cool and dry as ever.

The Emergency Alert System cut through the sonata on the radio. The tone was not a test. There'd been an earthquake, its epicenter fifteen miles inland. A 5.8 on the Richter scale. "Well, heck," Violet said.

She'd never felt such a thing in her life. Her grandson, Daniel, worked as a film editor in Los Angeles, where earthquakes happened all the time. This was no way to live. She would tell him so the minute they spoke.

Her breath was thin, inadequate, her lungs tickled and pulled. The taste in her mouth was unpleasant, like the night of the fire when she'd stuck out her parched tongue to catch the icy snowflakes, but it was ash she'd caught, warm and chalky in her mouth. Maybe it hadn't been snowing at all. Those days could be difficult to recall.

It was important not to rise too quickly, not to get ahead of herself by jumping up before her heart could hoist fresh blood to her head. It didn't help that the past had brushed so closely up against her, and continued to billow like gauzy drapes around the room. Little Em with sweaty curls and big-eyed joy, the shimmer of a moth's coated wings smeared on her palm.

The landline rang until voicemail shut it off, and after that Violet was surrounded by heavy quiet before the ringing began again. Her trembling hands had calmed, but a swaying within her continued for a time that couldn't be measured. Neither Francisco nor Penny appeared to be on the way up to see about her. Violet pounded the handle of her paintbrush against the wooden floor, to let them know, she supposed, that she was all right, though it could be read either way. She heard Francisco through the vents, calling for Penny. Penny was yelling something indecipherable from the direction of the backyard.

Another wave of dizziness, and Violet closed her eyes and thought of rain collecting in the barrel for the garden during the driest days of the year. She was suddenly greedy for summer, for the sound of bees tip-tapping the windows, the feel of reading on the porch while the air smelled of lavender and brine, the evening sun glowing rubescent and gold. She had already lived longer than most people, longer than anyone she'd ever known, and for years it seemed as if she might live forever.

She opened her eyes to tiny fissures in the lath-and-plaster ceiling, minor cracks added to others from the house forever settling into the ridge. A chalky film dusted her lips, and she brushed and spit it away, coughing again as if some of it had slipped down her throat, though she was certain it hadn't. The line Richard was reading came from a poem that was written long after his death. There was no sense to be made. He had been gone for twenty years and she was still here, and this had always seemed the most unlikely thing to have happened.

She unfurled herself bit by tender bit, floating upward to stand as if rising from the depths of a dream. She made her way around tin cans and photographs thrown from the shelves. The shattered glass distorted the faces of people she loved—Richard, Ada, Francisco, Penny. But the one of Daniel as a boy at the beach was unbroken; the grin he still had to this day beamed up at her from the floor.

A tsunami watch was issued. The house stood high on the ridge, far above the danger zone, but the town of 571 people, with its bookstore, bakery, small grocery, tavern, and lumberyard, would be gone in an instant if a wall of water came ashore.

Violet dropped her brush into the sink and gripped the counter's edge. From here she could see Penny through the window, wandering between alders in the backyard, her hands cupping her ears.

"What in the devil?" Violet said, and rubbed the light feeling in her forehead.

The chifforobe against the wall had rolled across the floor. Violet's breath steadied, and she was clear-eyed, and the chifforobe, tall as Violet at six feet, had her attention. It was mahogany, and robust on tapered legs, with rusted metal wheels that still turned, as was plain by the way it had trundled at least a foot across the floor with the entirety of Violet's clothes, along with the sweater Richard was wearing the day he died, all folded inside. There was something about the earthquake and her sister Em and the chifforobe that she couldn't quite articulate. A triptych just beyond her reach.

If the world was asking Violet to pay closer attention than she'd already paid, the world was asking too much. She'd spent a lifetime navigating her observations. Back to her first pencil shavings and the scent of vanilla and sugar, her mother baking and teaching Violet to write her name. Violet yearned for her mother even as she stood two feet away in their kitchen, with its grasshopper-green tiles and Dutch-orange bread box, her mother's sheer yellow hem shifting with the swish of her hips. "Like this," she said, stretching her arms into a giant V, before offering Violet a slice of lemon cake. The composition of this life, its scale, shapes, and colors, gave way to interpretations that Violet didn't always understand. She held tight to everything, even in the middle of having it. She missed her father while listening to him beg Dolly, their hairy mule, to *plow, today, if it would please Your Highness.* When the scent of straw and dust reached Violet through their kitchen windows, she could see and feel the lines of pale umber, chalky reds, and blues of her father's and Dolly's work across the earth and up into the sky, and its beauty confused her. She made drawings of forks and shoes and her mother's apron before she could spell her own name, and sometimes when she saw what she had done, she was moved in ways she didn't understand, and she hid in the back of the barn to let loose her gulping tears.

Violet crossed the loft and opened the door to the outside balcony. The air swept in, a mix of damp soil and sweet daphne at the foot of the stairs. Gulls cawed, chickadees zipped in and out of trees, and Violet felt all of life at once in her bones. The steps were slick with dew but sturdy.

"It's all right," she called out, but her voice was hoarse and broke in midsentence. She made her way across the spongy yard and finally embraced Penny, whose head barely reached Violet's breasts and whose arms dangled at her sides as if she were walking in her sleep. Her blouse was damp with sweat, her copper hair a series of unwashed ringlets. "Are you hurt, Penny?"

Penny shook her head with a dull expression. The tips of her bangs clung to the freckles around her wet eyes.

"Where's Francisco?" Violet asked.

Penny pulled loose and paced between the thin white alders, shaking her head at the ground. She had a thing about trees, and Violet shouldn't be surprised to find her out here among them, but she was. Violet caught her when she looped back around, and she took hold of Penny's shoulders the way her own mother had taken hold of hers, and she jostled Penny until their eyes met with recognition. "Where *is* he?"

Penny came alive, as if seeing Violet for the first time. She grabbed Violet's hands and squeezed so hard that Violet pulled away. "Oh, God. You're a right, aren't you?" Penny gripped Violet's shoulders and held her at arm's length to look her over.

"What about Francisco?" Violet asked, and Penny, as if struck by a new realization, pointed toward the kitchen at the back of the house.

When Violet opened the back door, she was thinking the worst, though she'd heard her son's voice moments ago. An ancient trembling inched through her body as she stepped toward shrieks from their old cat, Millicent.

The kitchen shelf, loose for too long, had busted from the wall, and each shelf collapsed onto the one below it until everything they'd contained had crashed to the floor. Dozens of spices gave rise to colorful plumes; brick reds and burnt oranges, like the dusty old roads of Georgia.

Francisco was sitting on the floor in the corner near the oven, his face covered in powdery spices and a slick sheen of blood from a gash in his forehead. He seemed to hear Violet stepping over the mess and held out his hand. "Penny?" he said.

"It's me, son."

He quieted and retrieved his hand. Violet told him he was all right, that it was going to be all right. She looked out at

Penny, then back to her son, took the dishrag from the oven door handle, and dabbed the cut while he hissed. A sliver of white bone repeatedly shone through the skin. "You're going to need a few stitches. It's not that bad. Just a few. Hold this tight against it."

"Are you all right?" he asked, holding the rag to his head.

"Don't worry about me."

An odd sensation that began this past winter came over her again, as if she were arriving at a familiar destination at the end of a long drive. Something brand new and familiar at once. Last month she'd felt it when a raven flew past the window, and she'd called out the time of day, the way her mother began to do after the fire—a superstition to stave off sorrow. Violet had never done that before, even as it felt as if she had. The sensation returned the following week when she discovered that the fairy fort on the corner had been destroyed. The tiny village was a gathering of pinecone angels eating out of acorn bowls at a miniature driftwood table and chairs. At the center was a cubby house made of hemlock twigs. Toadstools and delicate ferns flourished in the shady little garden that had been there since her grandson Daniel was born thirty-five years ago. Fairies would congregate at that split knot of the giant fir, if fairies were real, and what did Violet know? Perhaps they were. They certainly could have been on that tiny corner of the world that her neighbor had maintained for decades, and coming upon its ruin was like coming upon a desecrated grave. Who would do such a thing? It appeared to have been crushed beneath a foot. Or bashed with the large volcanic rock that lay nearby. Violet had stared at the massacre as if she had seen it before, but of course she had not, so what was this feeling of living in more than one time and place at once? Maybe it was a lack of oxygen to her head. There were times when she felt a little drunk.

Francisco lifted his free hand and squinted at his wristwatch. His hair and shoulders were dappled in dry clouds of what appeared to be cinnamon and cayenne. He hissed again.

Violet sneezed twice in a row.

"Bless you," Francisco whispered.

"Are you hurt anywhere else?" Violet asked.

"There's broken glass . . . be careful. No, I don't think so. Just dizzy when I try to get up."

Violet retrieved a fresh cloth from the drawer and wiped the blood from her son's face. He was slick as a newborn, his lashes thick and wet. Her hand trembled as she cleared his eyes to see. When Francisco was born, she was afraid to hold him. He was so quiet she thought he was dead, and she jostled him just to see his arms rise and fall on their own.

He glanced up, and Violet was certain he was about to cry. She hadn't seen his tears since he was a young boy, and she reared back, wondering what to do. Among all the unexpected things of the morning, this seemed the most peculiar.

Millicent was a ball of orange without the spilled spices, but now she was dappled in streaks of tangerine and amber like a hybrid tiger, and she began howling from a slab of cherry wood near Francisco's face. Whether it was a show of concern or a furious protest of the wreck she believed he had caused, Violet couldn't say. "Stop it, old girl." Violet clapped her hands. "Go on, out of here."

Millicent bolted past the open door toward Penny.

Another wave came over Violet, and she blinked to free her eyes of the colors of the Grand Canyon — scarlet bursts of fire as if the sun had melted upon the rocks. The landscape had resembled Violet's scars — ruddy, ridged, and cleft. Richard was telling her about the crimson- and caramel-colored map of the Grand Canyon that his parents had given him as a teenager. He'd fallen in love with the place long before he ever saw it because of that beautiful map, and perhaps this was why he'd so easily fallen in love with Violet, too. He was joking, of course, but the thought that his parents, who weren't exactly pleased by Richard and Violet's marriage, could have fated it into being with a map that resembled the right side of Violet's body made them laugh.

Violet covered her mouth, but it was no use. She snorted and gripped her knees to keep from falling over. Shock had dissolved her constitution. Her emotions had broken down and built back up in too short a time. It was all peaking now with the full-body relief that her son was safe and alive. Even so, she regretted the laughter. It was the kind of thing that Francisco would find difficult to forgive.

"What?" Francisco said in between Violet's laughter and cough, which was mild, and she thanked the heavens. He was looking at his phone, or trying to, blinking through the blood. Even now, he couldn't seem to leave the gadget alone.

Violet finally calmed. "The radio said it was a 5.8. And a watch has been issued for a tsunami, but there's no warning. Is that what you're looking to find out on that thing?"

He scrolled his thumb up and down. "There's no WiFi."

"The radio just said . . ."

The landline in his office rang, stopped, and started again. A cell phone was going off somewhere in the house. Violet wiped her runny eyes and called for Penny, but Penny had her fists against her ears.

Maybe they could use some help. But whom should Violet call, and what exactly was she asking for? She and Penny could drive Francisco to the clinic themselves, and anyway, everyone in town would be dialing the volunteer fire department right about now, an outfit of four men and one woman who were surely dealing with their own families. Could be that whoever was calling was trying to offer a hand.

"Wait right here," Violet said. "Don't get up just yet." She passed through the dining and living rooms. The walls had lost a small painting, and a portrait Richard had sketched of Francisco as a boy. Lamps on either side of the sofa had crashed to the floor, though the potted succulents in the windowsill remained in place. Violet lifted a broken frame containing a photograph of Richard and his brother, James. She carried it with her, and blew tiny shards of glass from the surface into the wastebasket in Francisco's office. A wave of dizziness from dispensing too much breath passed through her, and from seeing Richard and James with their arms around each other —young, happy, and alive. She placed the photograph on the desk with the intention of reframing it and hanging it upstairs, to help her remember and, perhaps, as a reminder to be brave.

3

V*iolet reached for* the ringing phone on Francisco's desk, glanced down to catch a breath, and noticed the receipt for her most recent painting, titled *June*. The painting now hung in a museum in Reykjavík, the translucent blue and venetian-green palette of grids at home among Iceland's rolling grasses and the grays and blues of fjords. For a moment, Violet was transported to waterfalls and lagoons. And then she halted at the price, in bold.

Seeing the numbers had a way of sharpening her breath. She didn't come from such sums of money, and still didn't understand how so much had come to her.

She lifted the receiver, but couldn't think of what to say.

The voice on the other end was her grandson Daniel, asking who was on the line.

"Oh, honey," Violet said. "We've had a bit of a rumble up here."

"*Grand*," he said. "*Finally.*"

"Hi, little bear," she said.

"What took you so long to answer?" His voice was so much like Richard's that Violet had to lower herself into the desk chair and get her head straight. The photograph of Richard lay beneath her hand.

"Listen," she said. "Getting knocked around like this . . . it's no way to live."

"It's all over the news," he continued, as if he hadn't heard.

"Are you all right? What took you so long? Were the phones out?"

"This is no way to *live*." Violet glanced at fallen books and binders, tiny cracks in the wall, a mug of coffee broken on the wooden floor. "A few things fell," she said. "But it's all right. We're fine, sweetheart. The phones are working just fine." She pushed herself up and retrieved a white hand towel from the half bath across the hall, came back, and dropped it over the spilled coffee. The creamy-brown stain spread across the fabric like walnut ink on paper. She lowered herself back into the chair.

"Hold on a second," Daniel said. "There's something else on the news . . . They're saying, oh, it's nothing, just that the tsunami watch is still in effect."

"Well."

"It's not a warning, Grand. It's probably OK. But you need to . . . Can you get Dad? You should shut off the gas and water just in case something's cracked. I don't know about that soil on the ridge. It's made from volcanic ash and clay. I have no idea if that matters with the foundation of the house. Can you get Dad? Is he already shutting stuff off? *Nobody's* hurt?"

"Let me hop off here and we'll take care of it. Let us call you back in a bit. We're fine. We're all just fine."

"You don't sound fine," he said.

Violet filled with emotion, as if his acknowledgment of her feelings was all it took to make them real. He didn't sound fine either, and she couldn't tell if it was the quake that had him upset, or something else, or both. It seemed like both. She hadn't seen Daniel in over a year, none of them had, and lately he'd been calling less and less, cutting ties with his old life, and as much as Violet wished to respect his independence, she wanted to reach out and snatch him back against her. She loved him like no one else on God's green earth.

Her forehead was damp with sweat, and her heart banged around the thin cage of her chest, and she wondered if she should mention that she didn't feel so well. *God's green earth* was a phrase her mother had used, and one Violet had never thought to use before.

And now a loud, thundering roll, a pressure on the air, and then a resounding boom.

"What in the Sam Hill?" It took a second to realize it was the fighter jets running drills all the way from Portland. They had gone supersonic, releasing booms, which seemed careless, if not cruel, considering what everyone down here had just gone through.

Francisco was cussing in the kitchen.

"What's that *noise*?" Daniel asked.

"You can hear that?"

"It's *loud*."

"The fighter jets. They put your father in a mood, which he certainly doesn't need right now."

"Where is he?"

"In the kitchen."

"Can you put him on the phone?"

"At least once a week with these things. But letting loose the supersonic? Now?" She cleared her throat. "Ridiculous. Just give us a bit, will you, honey?"

"I'm going to come up, Grand. Can you hear me? I was planning to come up very soon anyway, so . . ."

"Well, there's no need . . . I mean, of course. But we're all fine . . . Honey, let us call you back."

He sighed and told her he loved her and that he'd be waiting by the phone. He said, "I was planning on calling. There's something I want to talk to you about."

"OK, but honey, if it's about the documentary again . . ."

"No, Grand. I mean, yes, I wish you'd change your mind about that, but—"

"I'm a private person, Daniel."

"I know, Grand, but listen, it isn't about that. Can you call me right back?"

"We will."

Violet told him three times that she loved him, and then

she hung up with a tightening toward the boy he used to be, a pull on the tether of some bygone innocence that Violet had no time to address.

Back in the kitchen, she saw Penny still wandering outside, now with Millicent clutched to her chest. Penny's sedan and Francisco's pickup in the driveway appeared untouched by debris. There was no way to tell if trees had fallen in the road, but she guessed they would find out shortly when they took Francisco for stitches.

And then music. Perhaps Violet hadn't heard it a minute ago, or perhaps it had just returned after a brief silence, but either way, it sifted through the vents. Violet peeled away the dish towel Francisco was holding to his head. The white of his skull still flashed as before, but not quite as much blood rushed in. "OK, son. Let's get you up. And that was Daniel on the phone."

"Where's Penny?" He scrolled again through his phone as if he might find her there.

"He wants to visit. I told him we'd call back shortly. Right now I need to shut some things off."

"Those damn jets."

"I heard them."

"Where's Penny?"

Violet glanced through the window. Penny stood with her face to the sky, eyes closed, as she sneezed. Millicent leaped to the ground.

"She'll be right here," Violet said.

The music became clearer when Violet crouched closer to Francisco. "Son," she said, and suddenly he set down his phone and began to sob, openly, deeply from his chest. The sound caught in Violet's throat, her own agony set loose as much as his. She tried to stifle a cough, but the spasm won out. "Son," she said in between, and patted his hand. "Everything . . ."

She wedged herself down next to him, gripping his arm, her ear now inches from the vent on one side, her son's cries on the other. His tears were unbearable, gasps of old miseries. Her presence seemed an intrusion. She wasn't meant to see this private moment, but she didn't dare gesture in any way to stop it.

Her coughing subsided.

Francisco lowered his head. His shoulders continued to jerk.

After a moment he began to calm, and lifted his face. "Sorry," he said, wiping his snot on the dishrag.

"There's no need to apologize," Violet said.

He blew his nose into the dishrag with the blast of a trumpet, and this made them laugh, and the laughter wound into a weepy string of halfhearted cries.

In the seconds before Penny found them on the floor, Violet's mind wandered off into fragments of memories that were unclear, leaving a ball of discomfort in her gut, before returning to her son, and to the radio program she'd listened to every day for decades, now coming through the vents from upstairs. For the first time she understood that the show was recorded, not live. What the host had said this morning he'd also said last week, and what he played, she suddenly realized, seemed to be in the very same order, if she wasn't mistaken. For years she'd believed that she was listening to it in real time, that the man at the station was speaking into a microphone forty miles to the north, speaking and playing what Violet wanted to hear in the moment she was hearing it. How did she not catch it before today? Somehow this mattered in a way she couldn't sort out right now, because her only child, an unshakable man of sixty-five, had been brought to tears by something beyond an earthquake, and because the piece that was playing—Chopin, Nocturne in E-flat—which had always struck her as hopeful, now seemed mournful, pitiful even, to her ears. She didn't know if it was due to the state everyone was in, or if the music somehow lost its finer tones of affection when it echoed through the vents and entered the part of the house that belonged to Francisco and Penny.

4

Francisco *rode up* front in Penny's sedan.

"Hold that rag tightly to your head, sweetheart," Violet said from the back. "It might help with the scarring."

The leather seats were the color of creamed potatoes beneath Violet's rosy hand. The air was sharp with artificial mint from the cleaning kit Penny used for the mats. The pine tree air freshener was meant to hang from the mirror, but Penny felt the dangling object was a hazard, so she left it in the tray between the seats, and now the vents blew air from front to back and the fragrance concentrated in Violet's face. The car closed up like a capsule, sealing off the noise of the world, and the rest was like wintergreen on Violet's tongue.

A mood rose in the tight space. It prickled the downy hairs on Violet's left arm, her senses pulsing the way an animal sensed fear. She didn't know what to say. She didn't know what Penny and Francisco were doing when the earthquake hit, and was hesitant to ask. It seemed clear that Francisco was in the kitchen, but where was Penny? How did she end up outside? The thought of her son crying on the floor stung Violet's eyes all over again.

She turned her face to her window as they passed the marina, the Crab Shack, boat docks, and Jimmy's Jetty Bar. Even with the car closed up, smells of the sea sifted in, until the acrid scent of pine, both real and replicated, swept them back out, and all Violet could see behind her lids was green, green, green. Like Ada's eyes.

Maybe Penny and Francisco were acting strange because they'd been wrapped up in one of their arguments when the earthquake hit, and didn't run the cycle to the end. *You always, I never, that's not true, that's not what I meant, I'm sick of doing this, you don't listen to me, I don't listen, you're the one, no* you're *the one.* Slam a door. Slam another. A pattern that appeared with such frequency that it inspired one of Violet's geometric abstracts, a painting with horizontal graphite lines spaced closer to each other as the eye traveled from the bottom to the top. The lines appeared to repeat ad infinitum against a backdrop of smoky, Egyptian blue that faded into chalky white. Violet titled it *Until Kingdom Come,* as it seemed their bickering would never end. The painting hung as part of the permanent collection of a London museum, and a British art critic claimed that, unlike Violet's other works evoking harmony and joy, this one evoked a feeling of eternal unease, and to that, Violet agreed. But then he claimed that when the work was coupled with the title, and with Violet's fundamentalist upbringing in the southern United States, the sentiment was most certainly a rejection of religion. Violet never responded to critics. She believed life was better lived when one left open the gate, so that whatever had wandered into the corral could just as easily wander out. But she bristled at assumptions about who she was and where she came from. People back in Rockwood, Georgia, had been interviewed about her over the years, some who had known her mother, others whose mothers had known her mother, but no one who had known Violet. Books and articles had been written about her life and art. Violet rarely gave interviews, and never spoke of where she came from or what she'd lived through, and none of these books and articles knew what they were talking about.

I'm a private person, Daniel.

I'm your grandson and I barely know a thing about you.

Come now.

Who better than me to tell your story?

What's the point?

Your legacy.

My work is my legacy. You are my legacy.

It's one thing to be private, Grand. It's another to hide the truth.

Penny flipped on the car radio long enough to hear speculation about what a tsunami *could* have done to the coast had one struck, now that the watch was canceled. She sighed and shut it off. "Well, it didn't strike," she said, "and no one needs your doomsday entertainment right now."

Francisco gave a small nod.

Violet's sigh turned into a cough. She held a tissue to her mouth and searched for resolve against a spell, found none, or not enough. Her eyes watered as she coughed into a tissue. The tiny flecks began a week ago and immediately brought to mind Jackson Pollock, which made her laugh. Violet had only ever been mildly interested in his work, let alone his person. She'd preferred his wife, Lee Krasner, in both instances, and had had the occasion to tell her so over whiskey at the Neahkahnie Tavern, back when they were all so young.

Crowds of daffodils along the roadside were bowing their bonnet heads in the breeze as if to say, *Yes, indeed, what you recall is true.*

Penny bobbed side to side, trying to locate Violet in the rearview mirror, telling her that she needed to see Katherine again about that cough. Or someone else at the clinic. "It's been, what? A month? Several? I've lost track, but surely it should be cleared up already."

Violet hadn't found the right moment to tell them, though closer to the truth was that she had so little time left, and wished to spend it painting, being in the great outdoors and taking in its scents, listening to music, reading books. What she wanted was to be ignored. If she told her family the truth, death would get on everything, become the talk of the house, or its opposite, the quiet weight bearing down on the room, sucking the remaining life out of Violet faster than cancer ever could.

If Francisco was aware of the conversation, he didn't show it.

Violet's cough subsided, and she swallowed from the bottle of water in her bag. "These respiratory things take time to heal," she said. "Especially at my age."

All these years and Violet had never mentioned what she could hear downstairs, having decided long ago that it would only embarrass them, or worse, interfere with the flow of their lives, as if she were hovering, judging. And, like Violet with the creaky floor, they'd never asked how sound traveled, and maybe they thought her hearing was worse than it was, but after a day of cross words between them, they exchanged looks at the dinner table as if wondering what Violet may have heard. Those meals were full of compensation, side-eye glances and hamming up the good cheer. It seemed to Violet like an overcorrection, careening a car off a cliff just to avoid a squirrel.

Violet had never once heard the sounds of making love.

She leaned her head back on the headrest. What a thing to be sealed off from the world and at once woven so deeply into its seam. When she returned home she would take a walk on the garden path behind the house to capture fresh air inside her lungs and all the corners of her mind, and in this way reclaim the day and the work she'd set out to do. She could already hear the crunch of pebbles beneath her old boots. She'd return to the canvas waiting for her amid the loft's familiar scent of pencils and acrylic paints and the faintly sour smell of masking tape that lay in rolls on nearly every working surface and shelf, or had, before they were knocked to the floor. When the days became warmer, as now, the raw aroma of wooden floors lifted into the mix of stone and glass and the moss-stained skylights above. The house, tucked into a rain forest on a cliff with views of the Pacific Ocean, was her sanctuary, and Violet missed it when she was away, even for an hour.

She closed her eyes and drifted off on a thin vibration, some peculiar lingering from whatever it was that the earthquake had shaken loose, like the chifforobe rolling across the floor. That heavy piece of furniture hadn't moved since they built the house and placed it upstairs seventy years ago. Richard's parents had given the chifforobe to them for their wedding, filling it with bolts of raw cotton fabric that Richard's mother meant for Violet to dye and sew into dresses for herself, into shirts for Richard, and into a baptismal gown to be used by all the children they were supposed to have, according to Richard's mother. The war had just ended and fabric was scarce, yet Violet had cut, stretched, and nailed squares of the fabric onto wooden frames she'd built herself, and from this came twenty-five canvases. She exchanged ten of them with another artist for a palette of paints and various-size brushes, and Richard could not have been more pleased. He looked at her the way she looked at art, possessed and obsessed, infused with deep chasms of love. There would be no brood of children and no need for a baptismal gown. The only child they would ever have was Francisco, though they made every effort not to have any children at all. When he was still in diapers, they affectionately called him Oops. Their little mistake. Baby Oops, they said, which made them laugh. But by the time he was old enough to walk, his resemblance to Violet's sister Em was so uncanny that Violet could barely stand to look at him, and there was nothing funny about that.

5

The warm car hummed, and Violet slipped back in time, back to the days of racing through piney woods where the trees and animals were known to her by name, and where she'd ventured across the Alabama border within days of running away from home. She was fourteen, and the Second World War was raging, a devastation thick in the air. Newspapers wrote of bloodshed in Germany, internment camps for Japanese Americans, stories of life obliterated at every turn. The faces around town were set like carvings, drawn and anguished, shoulders hunched in despair.

By then, Violet had already lost two people she loved, three if she included her mother, which she did, and now the horrors of the war seemed a backdrop, a dark story that her own dark story continued to play out against. When the sun went down that first night she ran away from home, the forest turned black and cold as onyx, and she couldn't see what stood before her. But she knew that parasites and snakes settled down with the drop in temperature, and she shivered against the dry husk of a fallen pine where she covered herself in strings of moss she'd yanked out of a cypress tree. Without soap, the dirt beneath her nails wouldn't wash clean in the creeks, and the blackberries she foraged stained her fingers like ink, but Violet tried to clean herself, splashed her face with icy river water, and after two days on her own she reared back on her knees in the rough grass, taking in the bright morning sky, and she understood what it was to be saved. The opaline streaks across the heavens, the flock of cerulean warblers migrating over the forest like pieces of moving, frenetic blue sky, caused Violet to weep the way the country preachers had always wanted.

All she'd owned when she left home was the dull brown paisley dress she was wearing, three ripe peaches and a block of cheese she'd stuffed into its pockets, plus the underthings she had on, and her oxford shoes, which soiled easily in the damp heat of summer in the woods. It wasn't until she had passed through town that she realized she'd run out the door with a book in her hand—a novel given to her by a traveling preacher. For the longest time it served as a reminder of the book she'd left behind, the one her father had given her after he was dead. It had survived the house fire like a miracle, wrapped in paper beneath a Christmas tree in flames. When Violet was released from the hospital, her mother silently drove her to the place that used to be their home, and Violet didn't dare speak the entire way. It felt as if she had gotten into the car with a stranger and anything she might say could lead to something worse than the pain she was already suffering. When they arrived, her mother stumbled out of the car and dropped to her knees on what used to be the back porch, and she pounded her fists into the frozen ground and cussed Violet's name together with God's name, because wasn't all of this Violet's fault after what she'd said to Em about the still? Violet was seven years old. "Mama," she whimpered, but her mother didn't seem to hear, and Violet stepped away long enough to spot a charred square among the ruins in what used to be the living room. The blackened wrapping paper around the book turned to dust when Violet brushed her fingers down the front and uncovered *The Good Earth*.

In the years before running away from home, Violet read that book repeatedly, and it never stopped smelling of smoke, this story of famine and floods and ruined crops, of families trying to make a better life for themselves, and in this way Violet carried this story from her father in all of her senses when she fled the house where she'd lived into her early teens with her mother and old Annie Burke, who'd lost her husband to the First World War, a house run by pious widows where traveling preachers dropped in for shortbread and dimes and, every once in a while, for the feel of a young girl's thigh beneath her dress.

6

"Violet?" Penny said. "Are you all right back there?"

Violet opened her eyes and saw the river she loved, the smooth boulders lining its edge like immense vertebrae discarded by giants. She covered her mouth, felt the lines of her old face, saw that she was in the car with her son and daughter-in-law, two people she loved more than they would ever know, which was no one's fault but her own.

A blue heron lifted off the water like the black-and-white snakebirds of Georgia. "I am," Violet said. "Fine."

"You just made a sound. Like a gasp."

"Well. Look at that bird."

Francisco seemed to see the heron too, his head shifting slightly with the arc of its flight.

Penny searched for Violet in the rearview mirror while Violet slumped to the side.

Francisco didn't acknowledge anything anyone was saying. He appeared to be as lost in thought as Violet had been, and Violet leaned forward and patted his shoulder, and he patted the top of her hand in return. When he was four, the same age as Em when she died, Violet no longer let him sit on her lap or hold her hand, though in the next moment she might clutch him to her chest and kiss his entire face while fighting back tears. Her love for him was a fierce battleground where sides were never established, their aims never quite made clear.

7

The *waiting room* was overheated, though not as crowded as Violet had expected. Two middle-aged women sat together, twins it appeared, wearing rubber boots caked with mud that smelled faintly of chicken manure. They wore matching green floppy nylon hats and blew their noses in a nearly synchronized way. It seemed from all the activity down the hall that everyone else had already been taken back.

And there was Quincy Rhodes in the corner, their neighbor who lived down the hill on their street, the young woman who owned the bookstore. Her right foot was bare, her ankle swollen as a burl on a spruce. She'd propped it onto a nearby chair.

"Oh, heck," Violet said, crossing the room toward her.

Quincy appeared out of breath when she spoke, which seemed to thicken her otherwise trace of a Florida accent. "Hello, Violet. Penny. Oh, God, Frank, what happened to your head?"

"A shelf," he said to the floor, as if still half dazed.

"What happened to your ankle?" Penny asked.

"I slipped on the stairs when the earthquake hit. I think I sprained it, but I'm a little worried it might be broken."

"Quincy. Honey." Violet sat next to her, leaving Frank and Penny across the room.

Quincy leaned into the back of her chair, her mouth slightly open as if in pain. Violet didn't know her well, but she liked her more than she liked most people. She bought books from her nearly once a week, and thought her gentle, and perhaps a little odd. Quincy was a few years younger than Daniel but had the presence of an old soul, and her mind was often given over to wonder—*how does that work, have you ever seen anything so beautiful, I once read about, oh, will you look at that.* She lived in the carriage house halfway down the hill, and Violet had known her aunt Elin and Elin's dog Fluke, who lived there before Quincy, and Violet had been fond of them, too.

"And what about you?" Quincy asked. "Are you hurt?"

"Not at all," Violet said. She patted Quincy's arm. "You look like you might be in a good deal of pain."

"Well . . ." Her curly hair was pulled into a knot at the base of her neck. Bright strands floated around her face and caught in her mouth, though she seemed not to notice or care. "Quite a bit, actually. I've never broken a bone in all of my thirty-one years—if, in fact, it's broken. But the pain . . ."

Violet took the liberty of hooking her finger on the strands and tucking them behind Quincy's ear. Quincy smiled in return, though weakly, her face paler than usual.

"Have you ever broken a bone?" Quincy asked.

"My nose. A very long time ago."

"I never knew you broke your nose," Francisco said, perking up.

"What happened?" Penny asked.

Violet swiped the air. "It was a long time ago."

Quincy gazed at Violet with a look that seemed to go through her and out the other side. It was only now, in Penny and Francisco's presence, that Violet remembered: Quincy was the only person in the world, aside from Dr. Kath, who knew that she had lung cancer. Violet had wandered into the bookstore after her appointment, and the words sort of fell from her mouth.

"I was planning on coming to the store today," Violet said, although she had made no such plans; she needed to finish her painting. "I'm guessing you may not be going in . . ."

"We'll see. I hope to get down there and at least check on things. I imagine plenty has been knocked off the shelves."

After all these years, the bookstore's worn wooden floors continued to creak in the same places, to the same chorus, with the same scent of thick paper and ink mixed with the light fragrance of lemon polish used to dust the shelves. It was one of Violet's favorite places on earth, and Quincy was one of her favorite people. It probably wasn't a coincidence that Violet had wandered in there after hearing the bad news, drawn to a place of solace and sympathy. "What novels are worth my time when one considers there is so little of it left?" she'd blurted.

Quincy had started to laugh, but then stopped and eyed her. "You're not joking, are you?"

"No." Violet glanced at the shelves of books, feeling the rush of stories, as if surrounded by a roomful of people, and every kind of person Violet ever was, or might have been, had things gone differently in any direction. She'd looked at the ceiling and remembered her first kiss with Richard, upstairs. In some ways her life had begun there, and now she was delivering the news of its end. "I've just come from Dr. Kath's office. It's not good, but it's not as if I didn't know . . ."

Quincy lowered herself onto her stool behind the counter. "Violet. I'm so sorry . . ."

"Don't be. Sooner or later . . ." What else was there to say?

With barely a hesitation, Quincy had said, "So, then, what will you do with the rest of your one wild and precious life?" She was earnestly quoting the same poet that Richard was reading from in Violet's ear when the earthquake struck this morning.

"I don't think I'll *do* anything," Violet had told her. "Differently, that is. No bucket list business. Just carry out the rest of my days as they are. That's enough. It's plenty."

"Is your house OK?" Quincy asked, breaking Violet's reverie in the waiting room.

Violet stared, gathering her thoughts, caught in the chiffony light that seemed to radiate out around Quincy. Even now, when Violet could see she was in pain, there was something about her that transcended one's expectations of what a person could be.

"It appears so," Violet said. "Yours?"

"A mess of things fell, a few broke. I'm lucky it wasn't worse."

"Do you live alone?" Violet asked, and it sounded funny, if not intrusive, to hear it out loud. "I'd heard something about a breakup between you and that fellow from Wheeler."

"That was months ago. I'm alone, yes. And happier for it."

"You enjoy the solitude?" Violet couldn't seem to mind her own business. She noticed Penny's ear turned toward the conversation.

"I do," Quincy said.

Penny looked down at her hands in her lap.

In the silence that followed, Violet thought about what she'd said to Quincy in the bookstore, about not changing anything in the remaining days of her life—it wasn't entirely true.

When Violet first moved to town in 1946, she'd rented a small apartment above the bookstore, and she recalled those days with a distinct warmth for the work she created in that tiny space. That smell of hot radiator and acrylics and salty air, the rippling sound of birch leaves outside her open windows in summer, and Richard, dear Richard, courting her by secretly leaving baskets of cheese and bread and jam.

A nurse appeared. She was short, with dark hair and pale skin. Her feet seemed a little large for her height. Violet had never met her, which was unusual in this cluster of small connecting towns.

Penny immediately suggested that Violet ask to see someone about her cough.

"I'm fine, thank you, Penny." She held up a hand to halt the fuss, and asked the nurse to go ahead with Francisco and Quincy.

The nurse said, "Are we sure we're feeling OK?" That patronizing tone, a condescension reserved for children and the elderly. She touched Violet's elbow, and Violet lifted her arm in a circle so that the woman's hand fell away.

"I don't know about you," Violet said, "I don't even *know* you, which is strange, but *I'm* feeling OK, and my daughter-in-law is feeling OK, but my son and our neighbor here could use some quick attention."

"My name is Clare. I'm new."

The twins were coughing again, harder than before, and Violet was certain that her immune system was no longer built for other people's germs. "Can you ask them to put a mask on? I'm old enough that a cold could kill me."

"Violet," Penny said.

"Well?"

The nurse glanced at the women. One wiggled an apparent itch from her nose with the palm of her hand. "It's allergies and asthma," she said. "The pines," the other said. "We aren't contagious. We're short on inhalers."

Clare turned to Violet and Penny with a look that Violet didn't care for. "The rooms are full, but it shouldn't be more than a couple of minutes. I'll be right back with a wheelchair for you," she said to Quincy.

Violet shrank from bad manners. It wasn't like her to snap at people. She was usually good at keeping her mouth shut.

Francisco looked toward the window, and Violet looked too, a view of hills covered in evergreens, the river cutting through to the bay, and beyond, the ocean—blue upon blue upon blue, though none like the other. She wanted to say to her son, *Look how pretty,* as if he were still a boy seeing it for the first time. But he was far from the child she once knew. All he did now was watch and read the news. It was crushing him, diminishing the person he used to be. He muttered and paced, and Violet was pretty sure that the noises she heard in the night meant that he wasn't sleeping any better than she was. He spoke to the television more than he spoke to anyone in the house. "Why isn't anyone taking to the streets?" he'd say.

"All they do is scream at each other online. I give money to *this* cause, *that* politician, *those* people over there, and I might as well be throwing it down a well."

But now he turned in the direction of the twins and spoke like a man she'd never met. "Do you two sell something to keep critters out of gardens? I've been in your store but don't remember."

So that's who they were. The women who owned the garden shop down here. Violet was even more embarrassed by her behavior.

The twins nodded in unison. "I'm Jessie and this is Jan," the one on the left said. Her voice was scratchy, nasal.

"I'm Frank. I thought you were the same person."

"We've heard that once," Jan said. "Or twice," Jessie said.

Frank smiled. There was blood in his teeth. "My garden is going to need some help," he said. "I've got a rabbit that's been eating the buds."

"Get a dog," Jessie said.

Penny sat straighter, alert. "I've been thinking about getting a dog."

Everyone looked at her.

She glanced around the room. "*What?* I have."

This was the first Violet had heard about rabbits and dogs.

"A dog would be nice," Quincy said without looking up.

In the silence that followed, Violet thought to break up the strange mood by mentioning the obvious fact that they'd been spared something worse. Sure, they were shaken, she could say, that was true and expected. But aside from Francisco's head and Quincy's ankle, which would be fine here shortly, no one was seriously hurt. None of them had lost a thing. Everything remained as it was, and wasn't that something to be grateful for?

But Violet didn't say any of those things, because those words were not what Penny and Francisco needed to hear. She wasn't even sure they were true.

She said, "Daniel wants to come up."

Penny leaned forward. "*Oh*. He said that? Did he say why? Is it just because of the quake?"

"We didn't get a chance to go over it," Violet said.

"Is he bringing Macy?" Penny asked. "He hasn't said much about her lately. He hasn't said much of anything these days. Remember when he used to call every Sunday? Now it's been like, I don't know, weeks? A month? More? It *has* been more. All they do down there is work and drive around in traffic."

"He didn't say."

Quincy flipped through the pages of a magazine, and for a time it was the only sound in the room.

"I mean, he has earthquakes every other week," Penny continued. "It's not like . . . such a worrisome thing. Did he sound worried?"

"He did."

"Oh, God, I would love for him to come home. But for this, I mean, we're all fine. There's no emergency. Did you tell him?"

"Yes, all of that."

Francisco stared out the window.

"Son?" Violet said.

"Hmn?"

"They'll take you back in just a minute."

He smiled at Violet in a way he hadn't done in years, with a gentleness in the corner of his mouth. She sensed he was remembering that he'd cried in front of her, and seemed aware that she was remembering it, too.

Penny said, "I don't understand why Daniel never calls. Quincy, do you call your mother often?"

Before Violet could open her mouth to try to correct what was about to happen, Quincy said, "Actually, my mother died when I was very young. But I do call my father quite often, yes."

Francisco finally turned to Penny, looked right at her.

"Oh, I'm so sorry." Penny's face flushed. She covered her

mouth and quickly dropped her hand. "I didn't know. Did I know that? I forgot, I guess, or not *forgot*, I just wasn't thinking."

"No, no," Quincy said. "Honestly, it's fine." She swiped the air, and then her expression fell flat when she turned to the view through the window, and Violet wondered if she was thinking of her mother, the way people do when they're in pain.

Violet recalled the hesitation in Daniel's voice on the phone. What was it he needed to say? Why *did* he want to come up? What did he mean by all of that? For years he had been asking her to allow him to make a documentary about her life, and she had heard a similar register of need in this call. In the middle of trying to do what had to be done, Violet had rushed him off the phone, and now it pained her.

Daniel's love had been one of the greatest privileges of Violet's life. He'd entered the world smiling beneath soft copper hair like his mother's, round chestnut eyes like his father's. When freckles began to appear on his face and arms, around the time he started school, the rusty constellation caused people to stare, to look twice, which made Violet feel as if the boy had something of hers, even if the reasons for staring were not the same. He was beautiful. An easy child born to an anxious mother and a stoic father, though Daniel was neither of those things, even as his parents believed he was both, and that was how it was for parents, seeing what sometimes wasn't there, but within themselves instead. From the moment Violet first held the warm quiet of Daniel's body to her chest, she felt and saw something familiar, an achy nostalgia of missing him the way she'd missed her mother and father while still the center of their love and care, and she couldn't stop crying for days.

Clare returned with a wheelchair for Quincy and beckoned Francisco to follow them back. Just before he rounded the doorframe, he turned and lifted a hand to Violet as if he were a boy again, headed off to school.

A small peck in her heart. "There you go," she said, her eyes starting to sting.

"Are you that woman who paints?" Jessie asked, and it saved Violet from crying, but somehow made her aware of just how tired she was in her rumpled wool sweater and jeans, her worn leather boots spattered in paint. She'd been wearing the same kind of clothes, sporting the same haircut—blunt at the chin—for nearly eighty years, and suddenly, God, she was tired of everything. "I might be her. There are plenty of women who live on the coast and paint."

"I know. I mean *the* woman who paints in Nestucca Beach."

"My name is Violet Swan. It's a pleasure to meet you."

"You too," the women said.

Violet continued, "I'm sorry for being rude. The day is turning out a little differently than we thought, isn't it?"

Everyone nodded as if she had said something profound. Being well known came with an authority that baffled Violet. Sometimes people approached her in a way that resembled fear. She'd been placed into an order of things she didn't claim to understand, in a way she'd never asked to be, and she wished to remove herself, but couldn't, as none of it was her doing. She'd spent a lifetime never saying more than was necessary, and for the most part it had served her well.

It's one thing to be private, Grand. Another to hide the truth.

She was thinking now of the doctor who had taken Richard aside to tell him that, as Violet's husband, he could force her to undergo shock therapy. It was as simple as declaring her unfit. Richard had shoved the doctor against the wall, took Violet's hand, and stormed out. In the car on the way home he promised her that he would never do such a thing. But Violet stared at his profile, his eyes intent on the road. His strong hands gripped the wheel while her own shook in her lap, and she was frightened by the power he held over her, even if he never chose to wield it.

The day is turning out a little differently than we thought, isn't it?

Violet held her hand up to the clinic window the same way she had done that day in the car with Richard, watching sunlight sift through her fingers, a composition of shapes and colors filling her mind. Memories she thought long gone tugged at her once more. When Francisco was a boy, memories of Em used to catch her unaware while standing at the sink or her canvas or soaking in a running bath. They seeped into her dreams and preyed on her with a graphic sort of charm —Em dashing across the living room with bouncy wisps of dark hair, offering Violet a dead moth from her hand. Christmas lights reflected in the windows that dripped with steam. She could feel the muggy house on her skin, the vapor from her father's copper still in the basement. The sharp air reeked of fermented corn. The last time she saw Em was when she'd opened her fist to show Violet how the powdery pink glitter of the moth's wings had smeared across her damp palm.

She hadn't recalled her father's whiskey still in years, or the glitter of the moth on Em's hand. So much of her past had been thinned out, like trees, making room for other things to grow. But perhaps her fuller recollections had never really gone away, never quite been wiped out, after all. Perhaps they were instead driven underground, dormant as daffodils, waiting to reappear once conditions had changed.

8

Violet *became agitated*. The feeling traveled throughout her body and culminated in a restlessness in her legs. She stood, balled her hands into fists, and crossed the waiting room to the window, where a set of blinds lay on the floor near thin slivers of glass. A frame appeared to be missing from the wall, shards glittered in tiny lines near Violet's feet as if swept in haste. She thought of the new nurse navigating a broom on the carpet. Clare with the large feet. Young and nervous, the world and this work still new. Violet should have been more kind.

A giant cedar partially blocked the view. It resembled the cedar just outside Violet's windows to the east. It too was nearly two hundred feet tall, weeping like a willow, forming a dark shelter of fragrant shade around its base. Richard had buried their old dog Lady Bird beneath that tree forty years ago, and Violet had wondered ever since if the cells of the dog's body were absorbed into the cedar, and if so, how they might appear in the branches and leaves. When Daniel was four years old, Violet mentioned that very thing to him, and while he stared up into the vast branches with a look of wonderment, Violet said, "Maybe we can find something in its bark." She didn't expect him to get the joke without an explanation, but he did, and he laughed so hard he grabbed his crotch to keep from peeing. "You're not like any other child," Violet had said, and she lifted him up and kissed him while he laughed, and she felt a love for him, a *freedom* to feel such love, in a way she'd never been able with Francisco.

The dull western sky above the ocean was misting on a zephyr—as her mother used to call a western wind—and Violet gazed at the sea and craggy cliffs, her memories splintering between views of junipers clinging to sandstone the color of autumn blaze. Green-glass curls of spindrifts—the color of Ada's eyes—spun repeatedly, and Violet felt the flow of time, the day pulling away, far gone. She was too tired to paint. She had never been too tired to paint.

She would have to update her will. She hadn't looked at it since Richard died.

"What are you looking for out there, Richie?" she'd asked when he stood on the porch and stared at the ocean with a cigar and a tumbler of whiskey.

"All that I want to see. And not a thing that I don't."

Richard had his own past to lug around. He had been close-mouthed, too. Their generation, Violet supposed. These days everyone blabbed everything, and they did not seem the better for it, if you asked Violet.

Small fishing boats bobbed in the distance. At home, Violet often watched the crews of men and women through binoculars, dressed in their stiff orange jackets, spooling clusters of nets in their wake. All work was beautiful in its own way, especially as it made a difference in the lives of others.

There was a time when Violet was paid to scrub grease from factory aprons, rags, and smocks in a steel mill not far across the Alabama border. Her first job after running away. Back then it seemed unlikely that better times would ever return. The mill was supplying the war, and Violet worked long days, her skin itching those first weeks from the chiggers in the woods, her hands red and cracked through all the months she remained, made worse by lye soap. Her hands were raw appendages at the ends of her arms, especially her right, as the skin didn't have a way to recover, and she bled so badly that she kept a rag in her apron pocket to sop it up. She recalled the shift boss, a soft-spoken young woman, handing her two blue shirts and two pairs of trousers on credit. "Man yourself," she'd said with a laugh as she slapped the pile into Violet's arms. It was only a matter of time before the trousers wouldn't button all the way, but Violet said nothing about that. She barely spoke to the women who worked alongside her, kind as they were. Those women had known each other all of their lives —friends, sisters, mothers, cousins, and daughters. Their conversations were long and intimate, stories all wrapped up together, continuing from one day to the next. Sometimes they were snappish and nonsensical with each other, using shorthand or code that Violet didn't understand. Other times they spoke loudly over the machinery, wept openly when bad news arrived, and just as quickly turned to laughing, with brash talk in between. "And then he puts his hand on my backside and grins that grin, and what was I supposed to do with him getting me all worked up like that?"

After three months of work, Violet had earned enough to pay for the clothes and her rent, for a sketchbook and pencils and ink, and for a train ticket to Houston. Her body was changing, her breasts swollen and sore, and she was readying to leave the steel mill without giving notice, certain she'd be fired once her secret became known. Sometimes the shame seemed worse than the thing itself. She wondered what her mother and Annie were doing at the exact moment she was thinking of them. They'd be saying grace over supper come five o'clock, and the smell of buttermilk biscuits and ham would be rising, and Violet would second-guess the abrupt decision to leave home. She was fourteen years old, though taller than most women, and plenty of men, and it was ham and biscuits she was thinking of in the steel mill when she fainted on the concrete floor, and woke to a pain in her cheekbone where she'd struck the edge of her washbasin. Voices drifted all around. One woman was telling another that she had guessed right: "That kid is carrying some man's child. I *told* you so."

The next morning, Violet boarded a train, her hands slick with witch hazel, given to her by the woman who'd guessed correctly, along with a pea coat and sea bag from the woman's dead brother, Wesley, and a five-dollar bill. The woman's name was Mary Jackson, and *W. D. Jackson* was stenciled on the lining of the coat and on the outside of the sea bag. The coat fit well over Violet's dress. She set off for the West with the look of an exhausted young widow, dedicated to the loss of a man she never knew.

But how good it felt to sit for hours on a train, filling a new sketchbook with scenes of Mississippi and Louisiana, murky bayous and giant cypresses and strings of hairy moss. Violet recalled all of it so clearly. How the air smelled of diesel and raw tobacco and now and then coffee or cooked beef. The open land flew by the windows like abstract paintings, strokes of green, blue, and golden yellow. It was a luxury like nothing Violet had ever known. She drew Greek columns of Mississippi estates and swirling iron railings of art nouveau balconies in Louisiana, and even then her renderings slanted toward the abstract, not least because of the accidental smears of glycerin from her hands on the pages. She drank coffee with milk and ate buttery pound cake and potato soup, though she barely slept, afraid that someone might steal what little she owned. Once, when she had closed her eyes, she'd quickly sprung to her feet and slammed the heel of her shoe on the foot of a man whose hands had slipped inside her coat. Her height seemed to take the white-haired man by surprise as she rose abruptly above him, and sent him cussing about damnation down the aisle. He was dressed in a woolen overcoat and black felt hat, like someone's kindly grandfather.

Switching trains in stations, she drew stares. It seemed as if Violet, alone in a pea coat, reminded women of what they might face, or already had—abandonment by the men they loved. How else to explain their averted eyes? Soldiers on their way to war often stared as if thinking of the women they were leaving behind, women who might someday walk around in their coats under the gaze of the men who made it home without them. Violet felt their eyes on her when she read the travel boards and searched for a place to sit and wait for the next train. Some men smiled and tipped their hats. Others approached and asked if she needed help. *With what?* she'd wondered, shaking her head no, realizing this was just a way to start a conversation, and then realizing too that it was meant to convey how vulnerable she was, a girl alone in the world. She didn't know if they could tell she was pregnant. Her belly barely showed beneath the shifting fabric of the dress, and she was thin to begin with, but maybe there was some other way adults knew about these things that she did not. This was the farthest she had ever been from Rockwood, Georgia. When a group of young girls drew hopscotch squares on a station's concrete platform, it took everything Violet had to keep from asking to join in. She was not a child. She was not a woman. But as she watched them jump and snicker and squeal, a huge grin formed on her face, which she'd only realized after a man sat next to her and offered a cigarette and she felt her mouth go slack. "No, thank you," she said, flushing hot. "How about a steak?" he said, and Violet stared at his pocked but handsome face, his blond hair neatly combed back, and she guessed he was a decent enough young man, but maybe she was just woozy with hunger and couldn't judge. "No, thank you," she said in a way she thought was polite, but then he stood and spit on the ground and called her a whore before walking away.

9

"*Your boy is* all stitched up, Violet." Lindsey Hanrahan stood before her. A nurse, and Violet had known her all of her life. Her parents lived on the corner by the fairy fort, which was placed there by Lindsey's grandmother Julia, who was no longer alive. "You can come back now," she said. "We'd like him to stay around for a bit, in case he's got a concussion."

Violet didn't understand why Lindsey was telling her and not Penny, the grown man's wife, standing there like an uninvited guest with her jacket draped over her arm.

"Thank you," Penny said.

For as empty as the waiting room was, the rooms in the back of the clinic were crowded with people whose voices were familiar, talking behind curtains about being nicked and broken and bruised, as if everyone had been thrown from a horse.

And here was her son with sixteen stitches, on a bed behind one of those curtains, and it was a terrible sight to see. Lindsey, she guessed, had wrapped gauze around his skull to hold the bandage in place. Her son resembled a wounded soldier. And women, one of whom was Violet, stood on both sides of his bed, like a photograph for making history.

His face was washed, and it looked worse. Swollen, vacant eyes staring straight ahead. He barely lifted his hand in their direction, as if the smallest movement filled him with pain.

"Hello, son," Violet said.

"Hi."

Lindsey chuckled, checked his pupils, and said how lucky

he was that the shelf missed his eye. "We've given him a good dose of pain meds. He might be a little out of it. Right, Frank?"

"I think so."

Violet looked away and quickly turned back. Another wave of agitation rushed through her. "Do you know what happened to the fairy fort?" she asked Lindsey.

"*Oh*." Lindsey rolled her eyes. "No. And everyone in town is asking, so if you hear something, tell me. My grandmother must be flipping in her grave."

"Who would do such a thing?" Penny asked.

"Probably some obnoxious teenager from out of town," Lindsey said. "You know, *having a good time* at the beach."

Penny and Violet shook their heads as they sat on either side of Francisco's bed.

His disfigured face reminded Violet of works by Francisco Goya, her son's namesake, in particular *Saturn Devouring His Sons*. She thought again how she should never have let Richard name him after an artist with so many problems—and really, it did seem odd that Goya was deaf and Francisco so often did not hear things, or just refused to take them in.

"It was me," Francisco said.

Violet glanced at the damp, wispy curls at the back of his ear. He was sweating, his cheeks flushed.

"What?" Penny asked.

"The obnoxious teenager," he said. "Right, Mom?"

Now Violet began to sweat. All these years and she remained acutely aware that it was only down her left side.

Lindsey laughed. "Like I said, the pain meds are a little strong."

"What did you say, Frank?" Penny asked.

He smiled with closed lips.

Lindsey laughed again.

Violet cleared her throat, disturbed by all of it. He had indeed been an obnoxious teenager.

Time, like a wizard, continued to transform her child

before her eyes. From an infant to a boy, to a sullen, angry teenager, to a young man, to a father, who grew quieter with the years, and finally to the sixty-five-year-old before her, whose stoicism wasn't thick enough to hide his outrage and pain at an ever-changing world. For his entire life Violet had been forced to exchange him for another, watching as each disappeared. Letting go, letting go, letting go.

Jessie and Jan were coughing nearby. A child named Bo cried while his mother tried to convince him that a shot might hurt for one second but it would take away the other hurt that was worse. "Listen, Bo, listen." Moments later came an awful shriek, and shortly after, Bo was quiet, the whole clinic silent, as if everyone felt relief for the boy.

Violet stared at Francisco's swollen face, saw the future move into the room and squeeze her out. Maybe it was the same for him, watching her grow old, exchanging one mother for another and another. Violet had never seen her parents grow old.

Violet was getting sleepier beneath the harsh fluorescent lights. It was so quiet she could hear the sound of her own faint, shortened breath.

And then the wall clock revealed that twenty minutes had passed, while Penny looked at her phone and Violet may have fallen asleep.

Francisco broke the quiet. "Where did you go, Penny?"

Penny glanced at Violet across the bed. "I'm right here."

"Are you dizzy?" Violet asked. "Do you feel sick to your stomach?"

"Before, I mean. In the kitchen." His gaze appeared fixed on his shifting toes beneath the blanket. "I counted eight minutes. I'm just wondering where you were."

Penny leaned forward.

Violet felt her eyebrows rise, and made an effort to bring them down.

Penny took Francisco's hand between hers. "I was knocked to the floor. I wasn't sure at first what was going on. It just took me a minute to get to you."

Violet dropped her sights to her lap, to the flecks of paint in the folds of her right hand, her fingernails crusted with it, too.

"What were you saying when the shelf came down?" Francisco asked.

On the other side of the denim-colored curtain, a male orderly in black, thick-soled shoes pushed a wheelchair next to the bed. Violet recognized Quincy's coral sneaker as it came into view. Quincy hopped toward what Violet assumed was the bed, and then her foot disappeared.

"The doctor will be right over as soon as he looks at the x-ray," the orderly said. "Did you fall during the earthquake?"

"Just the last step at the bottom of my stairs. I don't think it's broken. Could it be broken? It's just so swollen I thought I should come in."

"Well, I'm glad you did."

Was he flirting with her? Violet didn't care for his tone.

"Is the pain relief setting in?" the orderly asked.

"It is. Thank you."

And then Francisco said, "I checked my watch." His right eyelid was nearly shut, his left bloodshot and ghoulish. "I picked glass and seeds from my lashes, trying to get a look for *eight* minutes, which felt like an hour, because I didn't know where you were. I didn't know if you were, you know . . . *OK*."

The curtain slipped sideways. "Hey," Quincy said, "how's it going over here? Oh, looks like you've got some stitches, Frank."

"Sixteen," Penny said, and gripped the edge of her hard plastic chair. "He's lucky it didn't hit him in the eye." Penny patted his thigh. "What about you?"

"Still waiting on the doctor to read the x-ray," Quincy said.

Penny crossed and uncrossed her legs.

"OK!" Dr. Bill Maynard appeared, an old classmate of Francisco's who owned the clinic, though he had been threatening to retire for years. He looked from one patient to the other.

"You feeling all right, Frank? Nauseous or anything?"

"Hey, Bill." Francisco's cadence was slow. "I'm ready to go home."

"Just give us a minute for the paperwork. Penny, Violet, good to see you both. You keeping an eye on this guy? Maybe stop him from getting into more trouble?"

"We'll try," Penny said. It was an inside joke. Francisco had never been in trouble—outside the house—in his life. Once a source of pride, it suddenly irritated Violet. He'd only ever acted out at home, with her and Richard, throwing things, becoming sullen.

"Well . . ." Bill turned to Violet. "I read about your work in that Chicago show."

"Oh?"

"Seemed a big deal. It was in the Sunday *Times*."

"Yes, I guess it was. In the *Times*, I mean."

"I don't claim to understand the abstract stuff. I'm more of an impressionist man myself."

"No, that makes sense," Violet said.

Bill nodded as if faintly puzzled.

Violet had lived a lifetime with comments like these. If she had a dollar for every time someone, usually a man, told her he didn't really get her *big-deal work*, well, what did it matter? She had plenty of money, so it wouldn't change a thing.

Her mood was plunging. The bleakest edges of who she knew herself to be were beginning to win out.

Bill turned to Quincy. "Looks like you've got a fine break in that ankle of yours."

Quincy groaned. "*No.*"

"Darn it," Penny said. "We can wait for you, Quincy, if you need a ride home."

Quincy rubbed her eyes as if the news exhausted her.

"Should we call your father?" Violet asked, mostly to create a diversion, because as soon as Quincy disappeared behind that curtain, Penny and Francisco would return to their conversation.

"It's OK, I've been texting with him," Quincy said. "I'll be all right. And listen, if you guys want to go on home, I can get a ride from someone around here. In fact, my next-door neighbor, Jameson, is here. He was sawing some wood trim when the earthquake hit and had to get a couple of fingers stitched."

"Are you sure?" Penny asked.

"We don't mind waiting," Violet said, even as she badly wanted to go home.

Quincy met her eyes. "Go home. You'll be glad you did."

"Well," Violet said.

"Come see me at the store this week. And Frank, take care of yourself. Penny, you too."

Bill pulled the curtain closed and asked what color cast Quincy would like.

"Just plain," she said matter-of-factly, and Violet had the sensation of missing her, as if she'd left long ago.

"Let's head on home, then," Violet said.

"I don't think you can leave without the paperwork," Penny whispered.

"What are they going to do? They know where we live. They've got his insurance."

"I think they're still monitoring the concussion," Penny said. "Or to see if he has one. It's not really clear."

"You never answered my question," Francisco said.

Violet's eyebrows rose again, and this time she let them do as they pleased.

"Oh," Penny said. "I just got a little tangled in the mess of the kitchen. I don't think it was *eight minutes.*"

"It was exactly eight minutes."

Penny gave Violet a look that made her queasy. Was she trying to let Violet know that she'd been caught in a lie, and that she knew *Violet* knew she was caught in a lie? And now the two of them were in cahoots?

Penny tapped Francisco's hand, gently at first and then a bit rough, just short of slapping him, and he didn't pull away, and Violet guessed the drugs must have numbed his senses. Penny sighed. "It's over now, Frank. Your mom and I . . . we're *all of us* just fine."

"I wanted you to know I was worried," he said.

Penny caught Violet's eye again, and this time Violet understood that with the clear implication that *Violet* was all right too, Penny was trying to convey an apology for the fact that Francisco's concern had been for Penny when the earthquake struck, and not for his ninety-three-year-old mother. But maybe Penny was conveying more than that. Maybe the shock and the pain medication were causing Francisco to say strange things.

Penny said, "I really should give Daniel a call. I'll go out in the lobby, let him know you're OK, Frank. I've been texting him and I can tell he's worried."

"Would you mind giving me a moment to use the ladies' room?" Violet didn't wait for an answer. She stood quickly. A mild suffocation filled her throat. There was something about pretending things were one way when it was clear they were another that propelled her to flee the room. Another coughing fit took hold, and with every step she was surprised she didn't fall.

"Violet," Penny said. "We're at the clinic. Can you please ask someone about that cough?"

The heavy hydraulic door, built to brace against disasters, slammed like a thunderclap in her wake.

10

At dawn the following morning, a woodpecker drummed the rain gutter outside the window near Violet's bed, and the galvanized metal reverberated like a jackhammer splitting the house in two. At first everyone thought another earthquake had struck. Violet heard Penny cursing through the vents. But unlike when the actual earthquake occurred, this time Francisco and Penny came running up the interior stairs and banged on Violet's door and called out her name.

When Violet saw their morning faces, she didn't understand how they had aged so fast. Years were somehow gone, and all these worry lines set in place. Francisco was not only old, he was somewhat puffy in the gut, his face swollen and bruised. A small patch of dried blood remained in a crease of his neck. They seemed like strangers, intrusive and awkward at her door, and Violet did not know how to ask them to leave.

"It's just a northern flicker," Violet said, pointing toward the speckled bird perched on the gutter. She pulled her rose kaftan tighter around her waist, crossed the room, and smacked the window. Penny and Francisco watched as the bird flew away.

"For crying out loud," Penny said.

"Have you tried ice on your face?" Violet stepped toward Francisco, but he was already heading down the stairs with Penny. "It's fine," he said with his back to her. The mood between him and Penny remained strained.

Later that morning, Quincy phoned to say she was doing

well with a walking cast and cane, and that she looked forward to seeing Violet at the store. It didn't feel like a reason to call. And it wasn't. Before hanging up, she said, "Violet? I'm wondering if you've told your family the news."

"You know . . . I keep looking for the right time . . ."

"I just didn't want to say anything if they didn't know. I assumed they didn't know."

"No one does. Except you."

"Oh. Well. Thank you for . . . That's strange, Violet. Don't you think . . . ?"

"I do. I hardly know you, but I do—*know* you, I mean. The truth is, I trust that you being informed of the truth won't make my life more complicated—what there is left of it —if you get what I mean."

"Yeah. I guess I do."

"I appreciate that."

"You remind me of my grandmother. I feel like I know you, too."

"Oh, honey. That's good to hear."

It was common to meet people who knew that Violet was a well-known painter and never said so, but didn't need to. They gave off something, a feeling for which Violet had no name, but it reminded her of a spaniel yearning, just wanting to be near, that need to please while taking something away. Whatever it was, it was the opposite of what came off Quincy. She needed nothing and no one to stand in for who she was, and somehow she managed to speak directly into the cradle of Violet's soul.

"Violet, it's none of my business, but I think you should tell them."

"Yes, honey," she said, "I should. I will."

But for now, she would paint.

The following morning, the northern flicker returned in the same way, but this time no one came running to see about Violet. The bird woke her from a dream that was not a dream, but something of a memory drifting through her sleep. She'd been standing in the hospital bathroom just as she had two days before, staring at her reflection, and was shocked that no one mentioned that her face and hair were covered in dusty white plaster, her cheeks the bright pink of high blood pressure beneath the white. She resembled a pork chop dipped in flour, and no one said a thing. Even Quincy hadn't let on. Perhaps she was a caricature now, a white-haired fool on the hill, and no one cared if she looked strange in the world, because it was half expected that she should.

Violet had stared at her reflection in the antiseptically cold bathroom in real life as she did in her dreamlike state, thinking of pork chops in a freezer and wondering why it was it so cold in there. Like a morgue. Richard had never enjoyed a pork chop before Violet made him one the way Ada had taught her, and she recalled the smell of burning fat in an iron skillet, and she could feel her husband's hand on her shoulder, and then the scratch of his wool sweater behind her ear as he placed his arm around her, drew her close, and put his lips on her temple.

"Please stay," Violet said, but the sound of her voice made him vanish once again.

When she had stepped out of the bathroom, Muzak was streaming through the sound system. She'd only half noticed it going in. "Georgia on My Mind" by Hoagy Carmichael. Again that feeling descended on her, a convergence of time and space, as if she existed everywhere at once. She'd reached out her hand as if to touch her father's gramophone, with its oak horn sprouting like a giant hollyhock filled with crackling tunes. If the world was asking Violet to pay closer attention, the world was asking too much. The thing about time was that no matter how Violet had changed on the outside, on the inside she had remained every age she ever was. She wondered if Francisco felt the same. She could hear her father's voice cutting through the music as clearly as a trumpet's flare. As clearly as if he had never gone away. *Listen to this, Violet. It's a dandy. Go get your mother. And don't forget to grab Em.*

11

A *week had passed* since the earthquake.

Every day began with the northern flicker announcing dawn by bombastically hammering his beak into the rain gutter. The noise echoed off the trees, came back to the house, and again smacked the trees, until it sounded as if they were under attack by an entire flock of woodpeckers.

It became the talk of the house, especially between Francisco and Penny. All menace and worry surrounding this bird. And then the slow repair of the roads. When would everything go back to the way it was? Daniel couldn't visit until the cracks in the highway along the cliffs were safely repaired, and he insisted on driving up from Los Angeles instead of flying— two days of travel versus two hours—for reasons he'd refused to explain. The Little Grocer had run out of apples, pickles, canned baked beans, and bread. The shelves were being filled in by the locals—cartons of free-range eggs, butter lettuce, and marionberry jam and syrup. Susan's pie shop had received a large order of flour, apples, berries, and fruit pectin the day before the earthquake hit, and the lights were on over there at all hours. Pies were the new loaves of bread.

"First time for everything," Penny had said last night at dinner when Violet joined them downstairs for the last of a thawed-out Irish stew.

The flicker. The earthquake. Daniel insisting on driving up with a secret, everything culminating in something that was still unclear, but Violet could feel it moving toward them just as fast as they were rushing toward it, whatever *it* was.

"I think that bird is lonely, and hammering for a mate," Violet said.

"I think he's trying to scare off rivals," Francisco said.

"I don't know," Violet said, "but I'm certain that whenever he gets what he came for, he will move on."

"Someone should fasten a plastic owl up there just in case," Penny said. "But which one of us is going to climb that high with an owl? Or hang from an open window with tools? And anyway," she meandered onward, ending with "the new coffee machine makes way better coffee than the old one, so I guess that worked out."

Penny's old coffeemaker had crashed to the floor in the earthquake, and though she liked the new one better, she didn't care for the noise it made. "It reminds me of that gurgling sound Daniel made when he had those bouts with pneumonia. I have to leave the room until the coffee finishes dripping. Which reminds me again, Violet. Your cough is not getting any better."

"Oh, I don't know," Violet said.

Penny sighed and cleared the plates.

Francisco had replaced the kitchen shelves, but the wooden planks of the floor remained stained between each slat, and no amount of scrubbing would make it go away or stop the room from smelling as if something was cooking on the stove. Francisco had also been complaining of headaches, and as soon as Penny got up to clear the dishes, he spoke about the white rabbit he claimed was eating the flowers and tender new buds in his garden, and he said his eyes ached when he raised his voice. Neither Penny nor Violet had ever seen a white rabbit in the garden in all the years they'd lived in this house on the hill. And Francisco wasn't known to raise his voice. Penny stopped halfway between the sink and the table, and said, "Where and when have you been *raising your voice*?"

"Oh, not really raising, I don't know if that's what I meant."

"You don't know?"

"I think it was good that you spent some time in your work shed rebuilding those shelves," Violet said. "Didn't you feel better making something with your hands again?"

Francisco glanced up at her, then down at his plate, which was empty, though he held the edges as if to keep Penny from taking it away. "Why do you suppose those jet fighters are having drills every week instead of twice a month like they used to?"

Penny resumed her stride to the table, picked up the salt and pepper shakers and two water glasses, and returned to the sink. "Probably because of that nutjob across the ocean."

"Which nutjob?" Francisco asked. "Because that's the thing . . ."

Violet tuned out, pushed herself from the table, and retreated upstairs.

It was one o'clock in the morning when Violet felt a sharp stitch beneath her ribs. She lay awake, checking her breath, staring through the skylight at constellations appearing and disappearing behind wispy strings of clouds.

The wind softened. Every so often bats fluttered near the eaves.

Then a movement outside triggered the motion sensor light behind the house, and Violet rose from bed and went to the window, where she saw a raccoon scurrying across the backyard into the woods. This was the hour of predators. Violet recalled nights spent in the woods, where even the smallest creatures feasted, like chiggers on skin. She didn't care to look into the dark, but here a distant streetlight breached the hill and shadowed the trees and yard with a midnight blue, and the telephone wire cut a silver streak across the center of the window frame, and it was beautiful to look at.

A strange vapor rose from below. Violet knew instantly that it was not the marine layer rolling in from the sea. It billowed upward like smoke. She leaned her head against the glass and spotted Francisco pacing the wooden deck below in his underwear, the small mound of his gut lit by the light of his phone as he smoked a cigarette. Lately Penny claimed that roast beef and steaks and cheeseburgers would put meat on Violet's bones, and she'd been trying to feed her the way Violet had fed Lady Bird toward the end, offering a special reprieve from canned dog food, though Violet understood that Penny didn't intend it that way, and anyway, the meat was working on Francisco's bones instead.

It couldn't be over 50 degrees out there, and the soft drizzle would make it feel even colder. But it was the red tip of her son's cigarette moving in the dark that Violet found most strange, the faint fog rising above his head. Had he spent a lifetime hiding this habit from his mother? Had he just now taken it up?

She watched until he stubbed the cigarette out against the lava rock and then cupped the butt in his hand. She guessed he would tuck it in the trash where no one would see.

Violet had given up smoking decades ago, and at her age, who knew if the cancer had anything to do with what she'd done in her past? She'd gone on to live a very long life in spite of everything. And a grown man smoking outside his own house in the night shouldn't seem such a terrible thing. After all, Richard had smoked cigars right up until the moment of his death, when the one between his fingers dropped onto his chest and burned a tiny hole in his sweater before Daniel had a chance to knock it away. So why was Violet so angry?

She crawled back into bed, mad at the world in a way that surprised her. She had been in love with it for so long she'd forgotten what it was to come up against it. Maybe this is how it works at the end. Like raising a teenager. A rush of ill feeling sets in, making it easier to throw up your hands, step away, and say goodbye when the time comes.

The stitch in her side burned brighter.

She pulled the blanket over her head to shut out the images behind her eyes, but the memories continued to flare. A doctor's large mouth slowly enunciating words through straight white teeth. "I can help you."

Violet had glanced up from chewing her nails. "I'm afraid of it. And that's saying something. I'm not afraid of much."

"Flooding the brain with electricity has a way of nurturing the parts that are suffering." He leaned back and sighed as if exasperated. "It will make you a better mother."

Richard's face turned red with rage. "She's *not*—"

"No," Violet said, "let the doctor finish what he has to say."

12

Violet jerked awake at the woodpecker's jackhammering. She covered her eyes against the morning sun pounding into the room and the glowing lamp she'd left on atop her bedside table. She reached to shut it off and knocked the book she'd been reading during the night to the floor.

Don't you ever, ever let the Bible touch the floor, Violet May.

She hadn't thought of that in years.

The book was not the Bible. It was a novel Quincy had recommended about a dying preacher and all the wisdom he wanted to impart to his son before leaving the boy behind. Even so, allowing the book to lie on the floor made Violet feel as if she were being disrespectful, as if reading, of any kind, was divine.

She'd been dreaming about Francisco as a frightened little four-year-old, with dark, messy hair and large, flat brown eyes. His bottom lip was trembling, and as Violet reached to soothe him, he backed away from her scarred hand, putting up his soft pink hand to stop her, as if he were deaf as Goya himself and couldn't hear her words of comfort. Violet thought now that she may have been reliving scenes from when Francisco was that age, when she would reach for her paintbrushes and disappear inside her work, leaving them both miserable and in tears. If she wasn't working, she might have been recovering in the hospital that barred children from visiting. Either way, she was frequently out of his sight, and in her dream he was the same boy, always in need of her attention, her love. Violet didn't know what age she was supposed to be. She didn't feel any age at all. It occurred to her to turn to Richard in bed to say, *I saw Francisco smoking in the yard.*

But Richard was long gone, and they would not be starting their day with him sounding off a weather report from the window with his warm body wrapped in a soft gray robe. She would not hear him say, "Coral sky, thin feathery clouds, crescent moon near Venus like the Turkish flag. We've got ourselves a day." Not today, not ever, except, perhaps, in her dreams.

Twenty years of widowhood and still Violet ached at the loss. He was the only person in the world that she had wanted to absorb into her life from the moment she'd laid eyes on him —she, Violet Swan, whose time alone was its own heaven on earth. After each of her treatments in Portland, when she'd curled up in a hospital bed with a headache and sore jaw, Richard would overstay his visit, crawl into her narrow bed against the rules, and hold her until someone pulled them apart. Violet took in his woodsy outdoor scent and kissed his shoulder with her stiff mouth. No more than two miles away, Ada was playing with Francisco in her backyard in Portland, and later telling him bedtime stories in French when he was too exhausted to care that he did not understand. Ada, who so loved children, and would never have any of her own. And all the while Violet lay at peace in a hospital bed with Richard, thinking how the life they got to share was like an afterlife, a reward for the terrible one she had lived before, so blessed and so unlikely as it had turned out to be.

13

The *little town* of Nestucca Beach was beginning a new day, throwing open wooden shutters like some centuries-old village. The scent of dark coffee carried on the breeze. In the center of town sourdough bread and cinnamon rolls from the bakery filled the air. Flour had been delivered again. The roads were repaired. There was bacon and plenty more eggs.

Over the next few hours, the shop owners would unlock their doors and wave to each other across the only street of commerce, like another place from another time, but that was how things were, here and now, on the coast of Oregon. For decades, Violet and Richard had gotten out early for a morning stroll. Back in the 1940s, when the town was just a fraction of what it was now, visitors rented oversize canvas tents above the high-tide line, equipped with rugs and real beds and a potbelly stove, all tended by young women who worked for the Neahkahnie Tavern, which had a limited number of rooms and was too expensive for some. Visitors rose from their tents into the morning light, stretched, waved hello to Richard and Violet, and looked around as if they couldn't believe their luck, and Violet and Richard would glance at each other with the same happy stupor. Sometimes it was true what people said about remembering something as if it were yesterday.

Soon Quincy would be hobbling around the bookstore, turning on the stained-glass lamps. She'd flip over the sign to COME IN, so that a day like so many others could begin.

Violet, it's none of my business, but I think you should tell them.

Except today Daniel was coming home, and in spite of her terrible night's sleep, the air felt charged with excitement. Some of the best hours of Violet's life were early Saturday mornings when she'd gather up young Daniel in a jacket and boots and they'd lumber down the hill for hot chocolate and a cinnamon roll. They'd pick out a dune to sit and eat with sticky, sandy fingers and watch the waves and talk about how the shoreline and water and sky were never, ever the same shape or color from one day to the next. They'd find chunks of agate and shells and sand dollars, as one would expect, but also strange things like the tail of a disembodied beaver, soda cans with Japanese writing, and mermaid's purses that had housed the eggs of sharks. More than once they were lucky enough to witness a baby seal, brought onshore to rest by its mother while she hunted for food, this spotted blob of tender sleep rocking gently at the end of each wave, like a child rocked by its mother. Violet and Daniel often played a one-sided game of hide-and-seek, where Daniel hid and Violet had to find him. The thrill each felt toward tucked-away spaces brought them closer still. The energy rising off of Daniel's concealed little body was like a beacon guiding Violet to the place where he'd disappeared, and when she discovered him crouched behind a dune or giant log or charred remnants of a bonfire, he burst forth with a squeal, arms stretched into the air, giggling. Violet sensed that the exhilaration had something to do with anticipation, but also with knowing he would always be found. It was Daniel who had rounded out her understanding of the ways in which love and beauty and happiness all lived inside the body, thriving within the hidden spaces of the mind and heart. If only she had known with Francisco what she had come to know with Daniel, motherhood might have been easier, her expression of love for her son more casual with joy.

The screws of time were tightening. And Violet had a 7 a.m. appointment with Dr. Kath, who always agreed to see her outside of normal business hours. It was a small town. People talked. Best to have all the facts updated before she presented them to her family. Her condition had worsened much faster than she'd expected, and than Katherine had led her to believe.

Violet drew a breath and the sharp stitch poked her ribs as she hoisted herself up to sit. She blinked at the amber highlights that the sun pulled from the fir floor. They appeared like algae blooms in a lake. Looking down made Violet dizzy.

She cleared a cough from her throat. Her eyes watered and she glanced at the canvas braced on the wall, drawn to the color, its energy stirring, awakening her further. The work was a third of the way finished.

The flicker thrummed again, testing Violet's patience. She untangled the eiderdown and linen sheet from her legs, and the bedding no longer pricked with winter static, and she was glad for that. She bent with crackling knees, picked up her book, placed it on the nightstand, and took her time getting up. No matter, she was glad, once she did, for the feel of her old body in motion, a series of aches and lightheadedness, but she was still here, tall and rangy as a teenager, though her spine was somewhat bent, and a dull discomfort filled her bones as never before when she crossed the room to smack the window with the flat of her hand. The glass gave off a resounding pop and bounce. The flicker took flight through the trees.

From this side of the room snippets of conversation sifted through the vents.

"I'm telling you, someone needs to put an owl on the roof," Penny said.

"Maybe Daniel," Francisco murmured.

"I don't like asking him to do chores when he's home. We have so little time—"

"Then he can wake at dawn with the rest of us."

"But we don't even know what he's coming to tell us. What if it's bad?"

"What if it's good?"

"He could have told us good news over the phone. Why the secrecy?"

"You always think the worst."

Penny *did* have a way of thinking the worst, but if you asked Violet, there was a place for everyone in this world, and maybe it was Penny's place to worry. Several weeks ago, when a milky-blue discoloration appeared around Violet's eyes and mouth as she was feeling out of breath, Penny noticed and told her to sit down, to call a doctor, and Violet had refused. She told Penny not to worry, that she was old, after all, and then she realized that this was unkind of her to say. She should apologize. She would apologize. Penny worried about everything and everyone all the time, as was her nature, her love, fixed in a way that couldn't be changed.

"I guess I'm up," Penny said.

"I'm going to sleep in," Francisco replied.

"There's got to be someone in town. Surely someone can . . . even from out of town. There are people who do that kind of thing with plastic owls. Don't you think? I'll get the coffee going. Are you already asleep? Jesus. You stay up too late watching all that awful stuff on the news."

Violet switched on the radio. The host of the morning show was telling listeners about the classical pieces that had just aired and those that were coming up, and Violet recalled him talking about the same ones last week. And then he said, "How beautiful the day is, on this, our left coast," his cadence like a gentle sermon, and maybe this was why Violet had never caught on to the fact that the show wasn't live. She was lulled by his voice as much as she was by the music, and her mind transcended to a realm without judgment. All these years she'd imagined him in Astoria, looking out across the Columbia River from his studio, headphones to his ears, connecting directly with listeners as they did their work of life, up and down the coast, symbiotically. But he was not there, at least not now. He could have recorded the list of music anytime from anywhere on earth, an attic in the Midwest for all it mattered, and this irritated Violet all over again, as if someone she trusted had been lying to her for years.

She dressed and brushed her teeth and let the radio play as she closed the door behind her, stepping quietly down the back stairs and into the damp, cool air. The sun reflected the dewy lawn like a pool of quicksilver, and the earth gave off a fungal smell, more pleasant than one might think. Violet's breath released vaporous puffs as if she were made of steam, chugging along like a slow train straining toward the end of the line.

She put some distance between herself and the house before the crisp air was no longer a match for her lungs, and she let loose a long cough, perhaps the worst-sounding yet, but that could be the trees and sea air echoing the awful hack in all directions.

What used to be a twenty-minute walk a year ago was now thirty, and Violet was no longer sure she would make it on time to her appointment, though it was downhill the entire way.

And yet she stopped at the site of the fairy fort. No one had made an effort to replace it. She crouched and lifted the rock nearby to inspect it underneath. Pieces of shell and pinecone stuck to the bottom. It was a deliberate and strangely vicious attack. The fact that no one in town had taken the time to rebuild this sacred spot felt like a black mark on them all. Perhaps she could re-create it with Daniel. This suddenly struck her as a wonderful idea. She would ask him before anyone asked about putting an owl on the roof, and she was certain he would agree. Maybe she could get Francisco to build a new cubby house in his workshop. But then she remembered. "I did it," he'd said at the clinic, about destroying the fort. Violet shivered and the hairs on her left arm stood up. She pictured him smoking in the dark, staring at his phone. She pictured him crushing everything to pieces.

She groaned to stand, put one foot in front of the other, noticed thin cracks in the road from the quake, and trekked onward. Past Quincy's tidy carriage house, past the Sitka spruce with the giant burls, and the meadow where elk often gathered, though not today. When Violet first moved here, the meadow was three times the size, and sheep had wandered loose all over. Since then the land was divided into parcels, and homes were built on each by moneyed people, as Violet's father used to call them, though nearly all were used as second homes and stood vacant most of the year. When Violet passed one, as now, she couldn't help but feel the emptiness, the sense of waste. "I turned out to be a moneyed person myself, Daddy," she said, like a confession, an apology into the wind.

The open span of the Pacific before her glistened in the morning sun, and Violet stopped to catch a breath, uncertain of what had taken hold of it, the sickness or the beauty or the nagging worry over her son. Everything. It was everything at once.

When she finally reached the office, Dr. Kath had just arrived, too, and was unlocking the door. She took one look at Violet coming up the walk and her expression fell, her hand dropped from the door.

"Did you walk here?" she asked.

"I could use a place to sit down."

"My God. You look awful, Violet. Why didn't Frank or Penny drive you?"

"Hello to you, too, Katherine."

Dr. Kath helped her inside while turning on the lights as they passed switches, flipping on the intercom radio to the same station Violet listened to at home. She pulled up a chair in the room closest to the waiting area and asked Violet to sit down.

Violet lowered herself and tried to steady her breath. She coughed into a tissue.

After listening to her chest and heart, getting her pulse and blood pressure, Katherine walked her down the hall and took an x-ray. Back in the room, she palpated Violet's ankles and then sat in a chair across from her. "How do you feel?"

"Not the best."

"Come on, Violet."

"Fairly unwell."

The doctor was in her eighties herself. They had known each other a lifetime. Violet could read her face. "Your heart sounds weaker," Katherine said. "And your lungs . . . well."

"It seems as if things have sped up," Violet said. "When you gave me the news a few months ago, the symptoms seemed milder. At least compared to now. You said, maybe a year? But . . . I don't think so, Katherine. I don't think . . . can you give me . . . a more accurate update?"

"You've lived a very long life."

"I'm well aware. And that's not what I asked."

Katherine nodded. Her expression turned dark as she pulled up the digital x-ray on her computer screen.

"Daniel is coming home today," Violet said.

Katherine stared at the image, turned, and perked up. "That's wonderful news."

"How long do I have?"

Katherine leaned back and crossed her arms. She glanced at the x-ray, which appeared side-by-side with the previous one on the screen. Violet could see the difference for herself. The white masses were larger at the center of her lungs.

"I may have exaggerated the year." The doctor squeezed her hands together in her lap. "As we discussed before, you didn't want any chemo or radiation, and at your age, and the time it may or may not afford you, I think that's the right decision. In my experience, I would be surprised if you made it through summer."

Again Violet had the urge to laugh when nothing was funny. She shook her head. "Thank you for being honest."

"Are you in pain?"

"Some. There's an ache in my ribs. The cough is starting to produce some . . . stuff."

"What color?"

"Rust."

"I'm sorry. That's to be expected."

"Well, now that you have me checking myself over, I guess my bones have been a little achy, I mean, aside from being old. It's a different sort."

"That's also expected, I'm afraid. How's your vision?"

"I haven't noticed any change, just dizziness."

"You may start to experience some blurring."

This, above all, caused a prick of panic. Part of the reason Violet chose not to have chemotherapy was because it would prevent her from spending the rest of her days painting. But if she couldn't see straight, what difference did it make?

"Who destroyed the fairy fort?" Violet asked, because suddenly she felt cursed.

Katherine edged back in her chair and shook her head. "I have no idea. But if you find out, tell me. You're the third person this month to ask, and everyone seems a little sicker than usual. Not to mention the earthquake."

"Was your house OK?"

"Mostly. A pipe broke in the kitchen, but it was already in need of repair. Henry and I have been eating a lot of pies."

Violet smiled, hesitated. "Well . . . What now? With me, I mean."

"I can give you some medication to make you more comfortable. To help alleviate the symptoms to some degree." Katherine stood and rummaged through a drawer. "I've got a few samples to get you started. I'll call the rest in to the pharmacy."

"I've never needed any medication in my life," Violet said, though there had been the shock therapy, which Katherine knew nothing about.

"Yes, I know. It's your badge of honor, Violet. But it shouldn't be. This will help you breathe a little better. It will help Penny and Frank, too. It can't be easy for them to see you like this, to know that you're struggling."

Violet glanced at the floor.

"What? You still haven't told them?"

"Not exactly."

"*Violet.* Are you pretending you've got a goddamn cold?"

"Is that kind of talk allowed by the Hippocratic oath?"

Katherine groaned, looking through more drawers.

The front bell rang, signaling that Katherine's receptionist, a young man named Jack, had arrived. "Good morning, good doctor!" he called from the other room.

"Back here!" Katherine said.

"Would you mind giving me a ride?" Violet asked Katherine. "I mean not all the way, but mostly. They don't know I'm here."

Katherine shook her head and snatched up her keys. "We need to talk about end-of-life stuff, Violet. I'm sorry. Will you come back soon, and bring your family?"

"Sure."

"Sure?"

"Sure."

"Oh!" Jack said as they passed him at the front desk.

"Jack, I'm going to give Ms. Swan a ride home. I'll be back in five minutes."

"Good morning, Ms. Swan."

Violet raised her hand and smiled. Jack had a lot of energy.

Katherine and Violet didn't speak on the way up the hill, but when they stopped several houses short of 1907 Blueberry Lane, they faced each other, eye to eye. "Will it be like drowning?" Violet asked.

Katherine hesitated. The anguish in her face was clear, and Violet thanked her again for being honest. "I'm sorry for dying on you," Violet said. "It'll be bad for business when people find out."

Katherine laughed just enough to ease the tension.

"Well?"

"It *would* be like drowning," she said, "if we didn't interfere. But we will. We can make you comfortable. It will be
more like drifting off to sleep."

"My sleep is full of bad dreams these days," Violet said.

"That's not unusual. I've seen this happen. I believe it's a
kind of clearing of one's conscience toward the end. Pay attention to what you see."

"I've spent a lifetime paying attention."

"I know, Violet. But this is something else. A different type
of awareness. The heed of another kind."

14

V*iolet stopped and* stared as the house came into view. The lights downstairs glowed from every window, as if a party were under way or about to begin. It was like a home from a dream, as familiar as it was otherworldly. The hemlocks and firs steamed out around it, their trunks like bodies putting off heat, leaves and moss like hair, creatures as alive as Violet, though much older than she would ever be.

Penny had surely made coffee by now, and was no doubt pacing the rooms, chewing her nails, waiting for Daniel. Anticipation seemed to leak out past the drafty doors and windows, and penetrate the ground beneath Violet's feet. Frogs near the small creek croaked loudly, as if touched by the humming, too.

Violet made her way up the back stairs, wondering how many more scenes there might be like this, how many more hours she had left to paint. If she were to die by summer's end, what would the days look like just before? Would she take to her bed for long hours? Or just fall over with a brush in her hand when she was unable to catch that next breath? She guessed this was the kind of thing that Katherine wanted to speak about.

Every step up seemed more of a strain than it had only days before, but perhaps that was because Violet now carried a certainty of what was to come, and certainty carried a tangible, corporeal weight.

Once inside, she locked the door behind her, which was not

unusual, but then she double-checked that she had bolted it, giving it more importance than necessary. She started the kettle for tea, and instead of waiting at the table for it to whistle, she remained at the stove, not quite trusting the fire underneath. Shubert streamed from the Telefunken.

And for the first time in years, Violet reached up and changed the station. She rolled the dial all the way to the bottom, where she found a baseball game. It was recorded, not live, but nobody was pretending otherwise. It was first thing in the morning, after all. Violet liked the announcer's voice, the familiarity of it, something of the past that soothed her, as if the same man who spoke from the corner of his mouth had been doing the play-by-plays since Violet's father had propped the radio in the kitchen window and listened to games with her mother, while the two of them ate berry pie in the shade.

She liked the rumble of cheering fans, the satisfying crack of a bat hitting a ball. One man was safe. Another man struck out. Another had stolen a base.

The kettle whistled and Violet made her tea, taking care not to drop the beautiful stoneware mug in her hand, careful to feel the texture against the palm. Glazed sand. The world seemed a miracle. Paint and dishes and linen bedding and the stitching on a leather baseball. Her eyes filled with tears.

She sat at the table, wrapped her hands around the warm mug, and listened to the rhythms of the game. After a moment, her tea had cooled some, and she swallowed the pill from Katherine, closed her wet eyes, and thought how this moment was all there was. It was all there ever had been. Each second its own kingdom of time. The game roared through the speakers, a quiet, ordinary happiness sifting through.

15

Penny had said that it wasn't just the coffee machine making noises. Ever since the earthquake, the house clicked and chimed with an assortment of sounds, and the small, needling ones in particular were getting on her nerves. Creaks and flushes, little snaps of wooden panes. "I think we're settling faster into the ridge," she told Violet, "but Frank won't hear a word about it."

As the days had passed, Penny told Violet that she believed the plumbing had slowed, because sometimes she had to flush the toilet twice. Violet replied that upstairs everything worked as it always had, but Penny seemed not to hear, as she was already talking about the shower drain being clogged, though she allowed that maybe that was just her hair, because it had been a while since she'd cleaned it out. "Even so," she told Violet, because Violet would listen, "I'm worried the pipes under the house may have cracked or come loose during the quake."

It seemed to Violet that something other than the quake and the house was troubling Penny. "And I don't know, but the house sounds a little like it's sighing, don't you think?" she asked Violet.

Violet considered that this was possible, and might be true.

An hour after her appointment with Katherine, the baseball game was tied in the ninth, and Violet stood at the window where Richard once stood, gazing as he had gazed toward the western sky. *Ultramarine on the horizon, a layer of peach above*

*the sea. It's stunning, Violet, just like you. Seagulls floating in the
foreground, screwing around in the world, just like me.*

Violet dropped her head, smiled at the memory, and wondered, as she had over the years, what it was like to cross over
to the other side, and whether she would ever see Richard
again.

She startled at a shape on the front porch below, someone
gripping the banister the way Richard used to, looking toward the sea. It was Penny, of course. The scent of coffee rose
through the vents. Maybe she had gone out there to get away
from memories of her son struggling to breathe.

When Violet turned back to the sky, a wave of loneliness
turned with her. Penny was like a barometer. An emotional re-
actor to things unsaid. Violet guessed this was why she talked
so much, as a way to fill the air, temper the world's volatility,
smooth everything over, and put herself at ease.

But the placid scene in the sky suddenly broke apart. An
eagle swooped through the center of the gulls and snatched
one of their young out of midair. The rank of white wings split
in all directions, a zigzag of flapping, hurtling confusion. The
eagle was now gliding north with the small gull clutched in
its talons.

Violet covered her mouth. She looked down at Penny gripping her hair. Violet pushed open the window and stuck her
head out.

Penny looked up. "What the hell? Did you see that?"

"I don't think I've ever seen such a thing in my life."

"Me either, and I could have gone without it and done just
fine."

From the corner of her eye, Violet saw that her own foot-
prints had darkened the silvery sheen on the lawn, coming
and going from the back of the house to the street. Penny
need only look over to begin to panic over someone who had
walked through the yard while they slept.

Violet looked again in the direction of the birds. The large,
velvety span of the eagle was far to the north, the gulls hap-

hazardly turning back. She felt a chill. "You're out early," she said. "For you, I mean. Eight o'clock?"

Penny ran her fingers through her hair and dropped her hands. "I didn't sleep well. And anyway, I thought I'd wait out here until the coffee was ready, find some peace with the trees and the waves, but I mean . . . Jesus. Anyway, it's better than in the kitchen with that gurgling machine, not to mention Frank snoring down the hall."

"Ahh," Violet said. "I imagine it's worse with his nose still a bit swollen."

"He wants to sleep in." Penny held her hips. "*Today*. With Daniel coming."

Violet was overcome with fatigue. She didn't feel like sorting through trouble, and anyway, soon she'd be gone, and what then of this trouble?

Penny was saying, "Violet?"

"I'm listening," she said.

"I don't know, but him sleeping in feels dismissive, as if he sees no need to get going here and have the house ready, you know, in a comfortable way, in case Daniel's news is bad."

"And if the news is good?" Violet asked.

"Well, it's all the same. If we have something to celebrate, it would still be nice to give the house another tidying up, and to check that there's a bottle of champagne and, I don't know, something to make a cheese board this afternoon. *Something*. Frank could at least prepare *himself* to greet his only child. We haven't seen Daniel in a *year*. That's the longest we've ever gone. He never even calls anymore. It's hard. I don't understand what's happened."

"What does Francisco say?"

"Ha." Penny swiped the air. "That I'm overthinking it. That Daniel is off in the world becoming a man, and I should try a little harder to let him go."

"Well."

"This, coming from a man who lives with his mother."

Violet's face got hot.

"I'm sorry," Penny said. "I didn't mean it like that. It wasn't a judgment or anything. You know what I mean."

"I guess I do."

"Honestly, Violet, I didn't mean—"

"I know you didn't. But listen, I need to get to work, Penny."

"I'm sorry. Of course."

"But I will tell you this, even though it's probably no consolation . . . I agree with you. I think whatever Daniel has to say is going to be a challenge."

"Thank you for saying that. It *is* a consolation. But Frank sleeping in depresses me."

"Well, his head . . . And I mean, you know, none of us seems to be getting any sleep."

"It's just, I know you have to go, but I want to say this one thing . . . It's like ever since the earthquake, and Daniel's phone call afterward, the world feels a little too sudden, like it's coming for me in a way that I'm not prepared. Like I can't quite get enough air—not really *air*, I don't need more *oxygen*. But even out here, surrounded by forest and a giant ocean, and everything charged with negative ions known to lift one's mood, I don't know, Violet. Maybe I'm depressed." Penny stuffed her hands into the front pockets of her jeans and lifted her shoulders as if bracing against a wind.

Violet leaned farther out the window. "I can tell you one thing. The shape of our days is off from the start with that flicker jerking us out of sleep."

Penny lifted her arms above her head. "That's what I've been saying! Every morning I say the same thing and I look over and Frank's snickering with his head still on his pillow. What is that about, anyway? I don't know if he's laughing at the bird or at the way I jerk awake confused, asking, What is *happening*? Day after day, I forget before I remember. And by the time I think to ask what he means by laughing, I'm pulled along by the next thought, by the day starting too soon, the lack of sleep, the feeling that I can never accomplish the growing list in my head, and all of that before the sun has even had a chance to rise."

"I . . ."

"Oh, shit. I was going to bake soda bread. Maybe it will get that smell out of the kitchen. I don't understand how the combination of all of those spices makes it smell like onions all the time. I need to get inside."

"All right, honey. I'll come down when Daniel gets here."

"Do you think that puffy redness in Frank's stitches is caused by an infection? When I mentioned it yesterday, he waved me off. I don't plan to mention it again, no matter how it looks."

"It's likely. And I'm sure you will mention it again, too." Violet smiled.

"I know," Penny said. "I'll mention it, and I know it and he knows it and we'll both be bad-tempered with the outcome. It's so predictable and unavoidable at once." Penny laughed at herself and repeated that she needed coffee. "I can't believe I forgot to bake the bread, after leaving the butter out to soften overnight right next to the coffee machine."

"Daniel will appreciate it. We all will." Years ago, when Penny was working in real estate, she said the smell of baking could turn even the most beleaguered house into a place of calm and comfort, and fill people with a yearning to be there and nowhere else on earth. She had seen firsthand how baking bread or cookies could convince clients that the place they were standing in was suddenly, heartbreakingly, undeniably *home*.

"OK . . ." Violet started to close the window, but then Penny looked up.

"Did you see Katherine this morning, Violet?"

Violet felt a sinking in her chest.

Penny looked out at the ocean when she talked. "I saw her drive past. And then you walking across the lawn. So I figured . . ."

Violet glanced at the shadows in the grass. "Yes. I suppose I did."

"What did she say?"

The silence squeezed Violet's throat. She made every effort not to cough, and for once, it held. "I've been better, Penny."

"I know, Violet."

"I'm sorry. I don't want to cause any more trouble."

"Any more? *Trouble?*"

"Than there already is."

"What are you referring to?"

"I think you know. There's something going on in this family. It's not exactly what it seems. I don't know why, but before the earthquake it seemed easier to dismiss or hide or just live with. But now it's as if things won't fold back up and fit into the box they came in."

"Is it cancer? My grandfather died of lung cancer. Your symptoms . . ."

Violet didn't say yes. She didn't say no. She sighed. "I always imagined I'd just fall over, you know? The way Richard did. No fuss, just *go* . . ."

Penny nodded at the ocean. She crossed her arms, then just as quickly unwound them, and covered her mouth. Her head fell slightly into her hand, and Violet saw that her back was trembling. She dropped her hand and looked west. "I don't think there's any good way to go, Violet."

"I think I should come down."

"No. Please don't." Penny raised her hand in the air behind her but didn't look up. "I understand why you haven't said anything. I do. And I won't say anything to Frank or Daniel. That's for you to do, and I don't envy you having to deliver the news. Oh, God. Poor Daniel. I mean, poor Frank, too. That's not what I meant."

"I know what you meant."

"Daniel is young. He hasn't had as much time with you as Frank has, or as *I* have, for that matter." She swiped her face with her fingertips. "Daniel worships you, Violet. It's going to break his heart something awful."

"I don't care for it much myself."

Penny let go a single laugh. "Eh, no, I guess you wouldn't. I'm sorry. God, I'm so sorry." Her voice cracked. "I don't want you to suffer. I saw my grandfather—"

"I'm glad Daniel is coming. I was going to ask him to come up. I was just waiting. I don't know what for. It's not like things are going to improve."

"I understand, I do, about putting things off."

Violet didn't know, but she guessed this had something to do with whatever was said just before the earthquake hit.

"Katherine said I wouldn't suffer."

Penny lifted her chin and appeared to wince.

"I trust her."

"Of course."

"She wants to talk to us about, you know, end-of-life stuff."

Violet was thinking of how, if the worst should ever happen —hurricane winds and landslides and busted-out roads cutting them off and restricting their lives to the hill— Penny had stored a three-month supply of canned goods and water filters and a tent in the airtight room at the back of the garage. Francisco had purchased a two-way radio and a gas-powered generator.

Violet had stored several small canvases and a simple tin of paints.

After a long pause Penny said, "I hope you won't take this the wrong way, Violet, but I just want a minute with Daniel when he arrives. One minute when nothing interferes. You know what I mean? I just want to see my son and enjoy him without reservation for just one clear minute before everything that is descending on us falls."

"I understand. Don't worry."

Penny looked up. "There are so many kinds of wrong, but only a couple kinds of right. Do you know what I mean?"

"Honey, you should go inside and bake the bread."

"Did you used to smoke?"

"Yes."

"Funny. I can't picture it."

"No, I don't suppose you could."

"There's so much I can't picture anymore."

"Honey?" Violet said. "I wonder too if you might be depressed."

Penny swiped her cheeks again. She gave a small nod, a sniffle, lifted a hand toward Violet, and disappeared inside the house.

PART TWO

16

Penny ran a knife through the top of the soda bread dough, carving the shape of a cross, *to cut out the devil*, as her grandmother used to say. A tear slipped onto the loaf as she slid it into the oven.

She'd wanted to stay out there talking to Violet, even as her feet carried her away. She felt compelled to talk, just talk, all the time, though she sensed it was a nuisance. But thinking she was a nuisance made her even more self-conscious than she already was, and the more she perceived that people were tiring of her, the more she talked in an attempt to draw them in. Penny was a hamster on a wheel, running toward and away from herself at once.

She sat at the table, her coffee gone cold, certain that by the end of the day she would not be the same person she was at the start. She was already transformed, and it was not yet noon.

In the quiet, Penny could hear the faint sound of a baseball announcer coming through the vents. The last time she heard baseball on the radio was when Richard was alive.

If she couldn't talk, she would clean. She snatched up her yellow rubber gloves, filled the sink with soapy water that smelled of rosemary and lemon, and for the third time this week, scoured the floor with a brush and sponge. She opened the windows and back door, smelled the overpowering sweetness of hyacinth and daphne at the base of Violet's stairs, and it seemed as if all lingering evidence of spices had finally disappeared. But when she closed everything up again, the scent of onions returned, even as the bread began to golden.

The thought so loud in her head she nearly spoke it out loud: how in the world was she going to leave Frank now?

In her frustration she thought of the recent call with Daniel, the way his tone had dropped as it used to when he was young and trying to pull something over on her. What was going on? She'd felt like handing his words back to him in exchange for ones of candor, for a tone that conveyed the truth. Daniel had sounded like he was on a busy street, or perhaps outside in his yard. "Where are you?" she asked.

"I'm home. I'm here. I'm in LA," he'd said, as if correcting himself each time.

Now lung cancer flashed like a blinking sign catching the corner of Penny's eye. She turned as if there were something to see, but there were only shadows from hemlocks waving in the breeze. She was dazed, absorbing the news, and she felt it best to keep moving, even if moving was just another way of talking.

Penny forgot to buy lemons.

She gathered up a cloth shopping bag and her wallet and rushed out the door and down the street to the Little Grocer. The moment she stepped through the screen door, voices called out. *Hello, Penny. Hello, George. Hello, Graham and Marisa and Cheryl. Hello, Penny. How's Violet?* How many times had she run down to this store in a pinch to throw together something for her family? Over how many years? "Daniel is coming home today," she called out to everyone and no one as she piled lemons into her basket. "Tell him hello!" "Tell him to come say hi." "Tell him he still owes me ten bucks." Who said that? Penny turned to see Quincy with a deli sandwich and a bottle of iced tea.

"Just kidding," Quincy said. "I hopped over, *literally,* to get something for lunch. Daniel doesn't owe me any money."

Penny looked down at the cast and cane, then up at Quincy's face, and she laughed louder than was called for, as if the joke had grown during her slow response. "Oh, of course. How's your ankle?" She set the lemons on the counter.

"A few more weeks lugging this thing around and I'll be good as new."

Penny greeted the cashier, Cheryl, by smiling and handing her a twenty, thinking of Violet and Frank and how she'd left the oven on and the bread would be done any minute. She handed Cheryl the cloth bag. "I'm sorry I'm in such a hurry. Daniel . . ."

"Yes, he's coming," Quincy said. "I'm glad you'll get to spend time with your son."

What a bundle of nerves Penny was. Quincy's words sounded so sincere that Penny felt like hugging her. "Thank you."

"Please give my best to Violet," Quincy said, and Penny felt a tightening in her chest. Did she know? How could she know?

"I certainly will," Penny said. There was something about that young woman that Penny couldn't place. And there was no time to consider it as she rushed up the hill with a head full of imagined catastrophes. Fires and leaks and Violet unable to breathe and Frank alone in the world and Millicent dying and Daniel arriving on the scene, while his own mother was nowhere to be found. Was it normal to think this way? Did other people do this?

She blasted through the kitchen and found that nothing had been disturbed. No one was hurt. Millicent was flicking her tail in the sun by the door. Everything was as Penny had left it.

She clipped lilacs from the yard and placed them in the living room and kitchen. The house quickly absorbed the fragrance, blending with the warm, buttery scent of bread. And then she washed her hands and sliced the lemons, and still there was no sign of Frank. All the twisting and cutting improved her mood.

What on earth was Frank's life going to be like without

his mother? Penny didn't think he understood how much he depended on her. She'd watched the two of them interact for decades, this strange vying for attention between them. A volleying dynamic of push and pull. Like a need for . . . what? Forgiveness? It felt like forgiveness. Penny had no clue.

The only time Frank had lived away from Violet was when he went to college in Eugene, and that was an afternoon's drive from Nestucca Beach, and he returned home often. His mother was famous, and this house had stunned Penny at first sight. She was wooed, dazzled by the whole of it. Richard was surprisingly warm, accommodating, a funny man who enjoyed the company of others, while Violet spent nearly all of her time upstairs. With Frank away at school, Richard focused on their dog, Lady Bird. Sometimes over an entire weekend Violet never came downstairs, and Penny and Frank would play poker with Richard while Lady Bird slept by the fire in the living room, and the ceiling would creak with Violet's footsteps in front of her canvas, the pipes would rumble in the walls as she cleaned her brushes. When Violet did come down, it was as if she were emerging from a trance, and Richard would pour her a shot of whiskey with ice. It felt like an occasion. Everyone was glad to see her, and she reached for Richard's hand and smiled around the room as if she too was glad to find them gathered together in one place, and she spoke as though in a stupor, if she spoke at all.

Penny's first summer here was one of the most untroubled of her life. Fresh berries and peaches and barbecues on the lawn. Playing horseshoes while the sun went down, a campfire in the pit. The future was still unknown, her love for Frank and his family like a burgeoning superbloom, spreading in ways she could not have imagined. Holidays were spent reading by the fire, she and Frank and Richard, and sometimes Violet, everyone contentedly quiet with a book and a warm drink, thick socks on their feet, while rain crashed on the roof and chugged the gutters, and the smell of cinnamon and oranges drifted in from the very kitchen that now belonged to

Penny. Back then, she and Frank were in their early twenties and had sex nearly every night. They couldn't wait to get each other alone. They eyed one another across the tops of their propped-up feet, counting the minutes until Violet and Richard went to bed.

Now the house creaked and popped like the burning wood they'd once gathered around. Varied thrushes whistled out back, doves cooed from tree to tree. The hollow crack of waves smacking volcanic rocks at the north end of the shore was loud enough to hear with the doors and windows closed, a sound that Penny always loved, like thick, unbreakable balls of glass tumbling one against the other. Nestucca Beach was made up of emerald forests and cliffs jutting into the churning sea. Most people could only dream of living in such a place.

Penny poured a cup of sugar into a pitcher, added lemon juice to that, and watched as the white sugar turned gray.

How was a person supposed to feel gratitude for the life they had even if they didn't really care for it anymore?

How did it come to this?

She'd studied business in college, met Frank in her second year, moved to the coast when they graduated and married, and became a real estate agent, which was not everyone's idea of a good life, but it had been Penny's. She got a kick out of playing a role in someone else's dream to live on the coast. She loved hearing people's stories, meeting their children, seeing their faces when an offer was accepted, and again when she handed over the keys. Back then, Frank had managed the lumberyard in town that was once owned by his grandfather, and this was also not everyone's idea of a good life, but it had been Frank's. At the end of each day, his skin smelled like resin, his hair was full of sawdust, his palms held the scent of metal tools, and Penny loved every bit of it. She loved the way his shoulders were strong and broad from lifting and hauling and working on his feet. He taught shop classes, too, one evening a week at the community college in Astoria, and sometimes weekend workshops for seniors at the art center in town.

He told her stories about his students, and she told him stories about her clients, and sometimes they turned out to be about the same person. Back then, Frank had little interest in the news, but it also didn't run on a twenty-four-hour cycle the way it did now, with every hour "breaking" with something worse than the hour before. Back then, he and Penny fussed over the vegetable garden, hiked the coastal range, took picnics on the beach, and studied the stars. They had Daniel to raise, and the house was always banging with the racket of boys. Though they seemed to have bickered with each other from the start, it didn't seem nearly as bad then as it was now. She supposed that Frank had liked the way she smelled and looked during those years, washing and styling her hair every day in soft fragrances, putting on silk blouses, wool skirts, and a fine pair of leather boots.

And then Richard died without warning, collapsed on the front porch in the middle of speaking to Daniel. Among the many complications of his sudden demise, the most immediate seemed that there was no one to take over Violet's business affairs. Frank and Penny couldn't imagine a stranger stepping into Richard's role of managing the acquisitions, the money, the decisions about licensing, not to mention the role of managing Violet herself. She would not be pressured, cajoled, or talked into anything she did not want to do under the best of circumstances, let alone while in the middle of her grief. There was no question but that Penny and Frank would share the job, and in this way still have time to pursue other things. Except it never happened that way. They turned complacent in their own grief, lazy in their interests. They spent too much time within the same walls, going over the same issues of work, and so they got on each other's nerves. Before long, Daniel moved to California for college, and when he finished, found work as a film editor, and hardly ever came home.

Was that the story? Was it all so simple?

It was not a terrible life, but the rattled distress Penny carried around seemed to signal otherwise. She'd thought about keeping a diary, a journal of some kind, as she'd heard that a person's life could be more fully understood, or even turned around, by writing down what one was thankful for every day. But she wasn't that kind of person. The idea embarrassed her. Even if no one ever read it, even if no one so much as *knew* that she was writing in a diary—the thought alone filled her with a shame she didn't quite understand. She had heard people swear that journals produced results, that words of thanks on a page had the power to unlock the ways in which the universe worked in one's favor. Penny felt fine about that for other people. *Good for them.* She really did feel this way in her heart without sarcasm, but *good for them* sounded disingenuous and patronizing, or at least it had during those times in her life when it was said to her by teachers and bosses, and especially her parents, rest their souls. Even Frank used to say it, before she stopped him from saying it again. Was she just being stubborn about keeping a journal? Was she afraid of her own thoughts? *I wrote my dreams on a page. I'm trying to change my reality. Good for you, Penny. Good. For. You.*

The earthquake felt like a punishment. Without it, Frank might have agreed to let her go when she told him she wanted out of the marriage. Without the earthquake, she might have moved into her own home by now, and gotten a dog. But instead the earth shook like the devil, and Penny ran out of the house, feeling as if she'd been physically struck because of what she'd said in response to him telling her, once again, how the world was going to shit. "You know what's gone to shit, Frank? Us. You and me. I'm done. Finished. Do what you like, but I no longer want this life with you."

Now she and Frank behaved as if the words were never spoken. They pretended that Frank couldn't recall what was said after being struck by the shelf. They pretended she didn't leave him bleeding on the kitchen floor.

The smell in here was going to be the death of her.

17

Frank *wandered into* the kitchen with a dress shirt in his hand, opened the cupboard, and retrieved the iron. He was still wearing his rumpled, blue-striped pajamas. He squinted into the sun. Penny immediately felt sorry for him. His hair was slightly oily and pressed to his head, his jaw smoky with whiskers. The worn and needy look in his eyes reminded her of Daniel when he was small. On top of everything, Frank was about to lose his mother, and he had no idea.

The timer for the bread went off, and Penny swore to God. She slipped her hand into an oven mitt and retrieved the hot pan from the oven.

"Smells good in here," Frank said.

He was always tidy, clean-shaven, professional-looking, and a little over the top for someone who worked from home. But he considered himself a businessman, and he *was* a businessman, though he claimed to understand very little about art. He liked to say that he knew how to act around numbers without getting them wrong. But Penny had seen the way he gazed at the roselike petals of lettuce and cabbage, his eyes filling with an awareness of something beyond vegetables as he turned the pretty poms in his hand. He'd built the raised beds and wooden gates around the garden and yard by hand, using red alder planks placed in horizontal lines, with hinges and clasps made of hand-forged brass. He planted blue flowers next to orange, purple next to yellow, and she caught him staring as the wind waved each near the other, illuminating the contrasts. His attention was drawn to order the way most people were drawn to art, with appreciation and praise. He was attracted to interlocking forms of regularity and method. Neat rows of numbers in a ledger moved him, especially when they culminated in a balance that fit inside a single square. What Penny didn't know was whether all of this came naturally to him, or if he had cultivated it purposefully in reaction to something else.

Because he was also the man who used to tell Daniel stories at bedtime about fairies and ogres in the forest, elaborate tales springing from a mysterious well of imagination. Penny marveled at his ability to do this. She could only tell a story by reading it from a book, and she pulled toward Frank in these moments, drawn to his wild inventions, and most of all to his unmistakable love for their son in those early years.

Now it seemed as if his life's purpose was to stare at his phone, complain about jets, and catch a mythical rabbit in the garden. "And what will you do when you catch it?" she'd asked him. "Kill it, I suppose," he'd said, and she could not tell if he was joking.

A larger clump of scab had formed along the gash on his head, and the lesion was a deeper red, and more bloated than yesterday. Penny's sympathy for him waned.

"You should go back to the doctor, and if you won't go, then at least cover it up with a bandage." Her request echoed what she'd been asking of Violet—go see someone, get help. And what was the use of any of it? She handed Frank a cup of coffee and tried to remove the edge from her tone. "That wound is a little tough to look at."

"Thank you," he said, reaching for the coffee.

He smelled like smoke. She'd noticed it in the night, too, smoke and damp soil and cold when he'd crawled back into bed. He hadn't gone to the bathroom, he'd gone out into the rain. "Are you smoking again?" she asked.

"Yes," he said without hesitation, and his honesty surprised her, pleased her even. At least he was not pretending. And then she thought of Violet, her lungs. She glanced at the shirt in Frank's hand. "Are you planning on working today?"

He shrugged. "My head still hurts, but I can probably manage."

"Today? With Daniel arriving soon?"

Frank wiped his mouth as if erasing the thing he wanted to say, and replaced it with "If I hadn't been hit in the head, I'd be working like any other day, and you'd think nothing of me seeing Daniel for a bit when he arrived and then getting back to what needed to be done. But, I mean, depending on what he, what's going on there . . . Anyway, it's just because I've taken time off already with my head that you're now accusing me of putting my own needs above Daniel's."

Penny set her cup on the table. "I said no such thing." Had she? Her anger, or whatever it was, felt misplaced and right on target at once. "That's certainly not what I meant."

Frank stepped to the window that overlooked his garden. Spring had come early, with above-normal temperatures, and Frank had said the garden would yield so much more this year, but now he shook his head, and Penny understood that the white rabbit he'd claimed to see eating the first of the butter lettuce had apparently been at it again.

"I'm a bit on edge lately," he said. "I'm sure you've noticed."

Penny's voice retreated down her throat. She wasn't sure what he meant by *lately*. She held her chin and breathed in the scent of lemon on her fingers, which she tapped against her lips. When too much time had passed for her to respond, Frank held his hand up behind him as he headed down the hall. "Either way, I need to put some clothes on."

"It's OK," she said, feeling a tight sadness in her chest. "It's all right. You're all right." She sounded like Violet.

He was gone from the room, and the empty space felt wider, more open than before. Penny took a deep breath and raised her arms into a long stretch, which revealed how stiff her back and shoulders were, and she slumped forward into the ache. The need to weep filled her entire body, and the weight dropped her closer to her toes.

The house was spotless, the bread ready, everything dusted, and Daniel's sheets smelled like lavender softener. Penny, for one, would not be working today. If Frank wanted to crunch numbers, so be it, he could do all the accounting he wanted. But Penny wouldn't be handling calls or dealing with the reproduction rights for postcards today.

The sound of a baseball game coming through the vents confused her. Was Violet working? She listened for the creak of the floor, but none came.

She needed to be patient with all that was coming. She wouldn't make a scene today by rushing out to greet Daniel, either. He didn't care for that. She would wait until he was ready to come inside. He'd never been good at transitions. As a child he needed to be warned several times before departing a playground, just to get used to the idea of returning home. It wasn't that he threw a fit. Daniel was not a tantrum thrower. He was the opposite: a quiet child who turned his pain and discomfort inward, a child who was often looking down and swallowing back tears. At eight years old Daniel could sink into himself so deeply that it frightened Penny, and she would try to coax him free of it with distractions of food and toys, things that had surely ruined some part of his psychology. She worried then, as she worried now, that one day he might slip too far inside himself and stay away too long and never find his way out. She worried that whatever he had to tell them today had something to do with that.

18

"Y*ou ever get* the feeling that the world is trying to tell you something?" Richard had said to Violet during one of his "weather reports" a week before he died. "You know, like, Hey, buddy, take an umbrella when you leave the house." He turned to her with a grin, that way he had of stepping toward something serious, and then quickly pulling back with a joke as if he'd been read all wrong, but they both knew he had not, and that too was part of the joke. Seven days later he collapsed on the porch.

Violet stood at the same window where Richard had stood. The flicker was perched, half hidden, behind a droop of scant, scaly leaves of the cedar tree. He seemed to be watching her watching him. She admired his speckled feathers, tenacity, and swift swoop of flight. This bird was breaking her heart.

She recalled a speckled cattle dog she hadn't thought of in decades. Old and mean, corralling her to a path through a forest, a dog that was trying to tell her something, too, but only after he'd threatened her life. It felt similar with this bird. Pecking and pecking. "What is it you want?"

Lady Bird would have chased the flicker from the house, no question. She was a border collie with one white ear and one black, summer-sky-blue eyes, and a spectacular breakneck sprint. She was the fastest creature Violet had ever known, and the smartest that was not human, though her blue gaze, especially when focused on Violet, was as human as could be, embodied with loyalty and love, and Violet wondered if Lady

Bird saw the same look in Violet's eyes for her. Violet was now nearly as old in dog years as Lady Bird had been near the end of her life, though Lady Bird was blind and rigid with arthritis, and not nearly as bad-tempered as she had a right to be, especially after her white ear was ripped away in a fight with a raccoon a year before her death at fifteen. The ghastly howls in the woods still appeared in Violet's dreams, or what felt like dreams, moments when she drifted off in her reading chair in the middle of the afternoon. When she'd heard the yelps that day, she whistled and then screamed for Lady Bird, and when she didn't come, Richard set off to find her. When the dog finally appeared at the edge of the trees, Richard was cradling her in his arms, and her head was slick with blood. But when she saw Violet, she wriggled free of Richard's grasp and hobbled across the yard toward Violet with her head cocked to the side of her missing ear. Her good eye creased in worry as she approached, creeping low to the ground, as if apologizing for the trouble, the mess, the anguish she would have sensed rising in Violet's body when she dropped to her knees, held out her arms, and frantically looked the dog over. Lady Bird's blood mixed with Violet's richly red scars on her arm and hand, and the two of them blending this way, the way each had stood at death's door before being given another chance, seemed to bind them forever, like family.

Violet smacked the window, but the flicker had already flown away.

She looked around the loft as if remembering only now where she was. She would reclaim the day, get back to the painting in her mind where she'd left it, exactly as it was, exactly as it would appear on the canvas. She'd already calculated its dimensions in her notebook, imagined it into being.

Another baseball game, this one in the fifth inning. The announcer's voice had grown more urgent than it was at the start, and that was saying something.

Violet fastened the stray hairs around her face into the clip at the back of her head. Her indigo smock smelled of turpentine and sweat and of paint that reminded her of the purple Ditto ink from Francisco's homework decades ago. The fabric was dappled from earlier pieces, and Violet looked down, feeling outside herself, a witness to the possibility that the painting in Reykjavík could turn out to be her last.

And then, oddly, she just knew that it would not.

Who was it who once said that knowing you'll be hanged concentrates the mind wonderfully?

19

Millicent zigzagged through the rooms as if in search of something particular, meowing for no apparent reason that Penny could see. Was she ill? Here she was again, winding through Penny's feet. "Please don't die while Daniel is visiting," Penny said, and dumped kibble into her bowl. "We've got enough to deal with, sweet girl."

Millicent sniffed the food, and sauntered away when Penny tried to pet her.

The cat was twenty years old, having arrived within months of Richard's passing, and in this way served as a timekeeper of a most terrible thing. They loved her more than she probably deserved for a cat that clawed the edges of chairs and rugs, jumped onto the kitchen counter when no one was around just to see what she could knock to the floor, delivered dead mice at their feet, and deposited clumps of fur balls on the thresholds of rooms, as if to ensure they would be stepped on in the dark. None of them had ever owned a cat before, and if asked, they might have all said they were dog lovers instead. But Millicent arrived out of nowhere at the back patio door, getting everyone's attention with high-pitched, desperate mewls. Violet, Frank, Penny, and Daniel stood in a row from tallest to shortest, looking through the glass at this tiny orange ball with bright blue eyes. They were all reeling from Richard's death, and no one spoke, just stared with the dull grief of their bodies. Finally Violet stepped outside and scooped the tiny creature to her chest. "There now, little darling," she'd said. The cries immediately became purrs.

In the days that followed, Penny asked around town if anyone knew where the kitten might belong. It seemed hardly old enough to have been weaned. No one had an answer, but they kept Penny talking. They wanted to know how Violet was holding up without Richard. Penny didn't want to answer. She wanted only to talk about the kitten, to uncover the mystery of its origin, joking that perhaps it had slipped from the talons of an eagle that had snatched it from a neighboring community. "Cats know how to land on their feet," she said, which in a way was what she also thought of Violet, even as her pain was palpable in every room.

Frank, on the other hand, had not shed one tear over his father. Penny would have liked to tell people this when they were asking about Violet, because Frank could use the support. But she didn't say that, because she didn't know what it meant. It was a feeling more than a call to action. And anyway, the unexplained appearance of the cat reminded her of a children's story she used to read to Daniel, which was the whole reason she was thinking about Millicent now. The book was about a seagull dropping a large pail of orange paint onto a man's roof one night for reasons no one would ever know. This missing piece didn't matter to the story. When Penny joked about an eagle dropping the kitten from its talons, people didn't seem to know what mattered then, either. But in the children's story, the splatter of orange paint set in motion a change for the entire neighborhood, and afterward everyone became a little wild and a whole lot happier.

The fact that Millicent was still with them seemed a miracle, a part of their lives for two decades, which meant Richard had been gone for that long. Something shifted in the house the day the cat arrived, from the moment Violet fed her milk from a gold-rimmed teacup that had belonged to Richard's mother, to the moment Millicent insisted on sleeping in Daniel's bed —it seemed as if whatever gray matter the house had been infused with after Richard's death, this tiny kitten had found a way of cutting through and erasing the worst of it, one meandering strip and purr and ball of yarn after the next.

Penny believed something bigger than herself made an effort to tell people things—not God exactly, but something equally mysterious, vibrating between living things, but Penny didn't think she was very good at interpreting the messages. She'd never said this to anyone for fear of sounding idiotic. But she felt this thing when she walked among the trees, their rustling sounds and sharp green smells so decent and blameless and pure of heart, like innocent children wanting only to do and be what they already were. This was why she ended up in the yard when the earthquake hit. Whispering apologies across her sniveling lips as she passed in and around the trees. She couldn't stop saying it, hearing it, even as she covered her ears. An answer for what to do next didn't come from the trees, and it hadn't come to her still.

When she walked the beach beneath the vast sky, this *thing* was there, too, accompanied by the soft rhythm of the waves, soothing her with a kindness she couldn't explain and didn't feel she fully deserved, and sometimes she looked out at the ocean and thought of Virginia Woolf, whom Penny had read quite a bit of during college, a writer with a keen understanding of women and marriage and families, or so it had seemed to Penny before she'd embarked on her own marriage and family. And if Penny was remembering right, Virginia Woolf had kept a diary, too, right up until she filled her pockets with stones and slipped into a mighty river that led to the sea.

20

Violet *placed her* metal yardstick at the center of the canvas at the same moment someone hit a home run on the radio. She leveled it horizontally, the announcer yelled, the roaring crowd filled the airwaves, and Violet traced her pencil along the stick's hard edge, drawing a line from one end to the other, feeling as if she were doing something brand new. She slid the yardstick to the right, traced again, and moved it all the way to the left and traced again, until the painting had a single horizontal graphite line from one edge to the other.

She stepped back and examined its scale. Space evoked emotion in the same way an open landscape squeezed a heart. It set the mind to wonder, gave reverence to things beyond the self.

"Do you feel God in this house?"

The voice she heard was not her mother's. It was the *flat-footed preacher who'd been rejected by the war,* as he'd referred to himself, the man responsible for Violet finding her way to 1907 Blueberry Lane. It was Richard's brother, James.

Not long before Violet ran away from home, James had given her the novel she happened to have been holding when she fled. He never tried to touch her or slap her or yell in her face. He'd glanced around the living room in the house that Violet had shared with her mother and Annie Burke, as if he didn't know what he was doing there, and when left alone with Violet, he didn't slide closer on the sofa. Instead, he crossed the room to the window and, with his back turned, asked Violet what she liked most about her life. Nothing could have sounded stranger to her ears. When it finally sunk in that he was serious, the room shifted with the oddest delight. She fetched her sketchbook from beneath the loose floorboard in her room, and when she gave it to him, her hand shook, as if the pages were blasphemous, which could be said to be true: some of the ink drawings were of her own naked body before a mirror, her hip and thigh, a single budding breast, her long hair falling to her ribs. Most of the other drawings were of trees and shoes and kitchen objects, and even then, the way she saw each one was not considered natural but as if seen from the inside, where she rearranged the object before bringing it back into the light as something that seemed a bit more of the thing than it had been before. James's eyes widened with every page. He held the drawings one way, then another, to see what she'd done from different angles. He swallowed, and she backed away, expecting to be slapped, but he said, "No, no. It isn't like that." He closed the book, and he did not reach for the Bible, for a verse meant to diminish her sins. "You need to pursue what you've started here," he said, and when she asked what he meant, he said he didn't quite know, but he had seen this kind of thing with his kid brother. And what followed couldn't have been said in the way Violet remembered, because it came to her in images, like a painting or prose. He spoke of the West where cliffs broke off into the sea, and the land was evergreen and the weather mild enough for blossoms of every color to open year-round. He said it was as far as one can go in these United States, and that he himself was raised there. And then he slumped, as if becoming wistful at the mention. When he straightened he said he longed to see his brother, Richie, soon. "But I need to finish out this mission," he said, in a way that sounded as though he didn't want to finish it at all, and Violet remembered exactly how he said it, and a few other things, too, because she repeated the words for years, whispering sentences under her breath, or out loud to a forest, a meadow, creating echoes in a canyon, creating no sound at all against the noisy backdrop of the shipyards in Portland. Someday she would tell his brother how much he was missed. She would tell him that James wrote down his address in the sketchbook she'd left behind, but she'd memorized it immediately, in case she ever found herself at 1907 Blueberry Lane.

"Violet?" James asked all those years ago. "Do you feel God in this house?"

She was just a child. No one had ever asked her anything of the sort. "No, sir. I do not."

"Of course," he said. "How could you?"

She would tell his brother how he'd sighed and looked out the window as if searching for the next thing to say, which turned out to be "Do you like to read?"

This surprised her, too. "Yes."

"Here . . ." He reached into the case where he kept his Bible, and she prepared once again to be admonished for her sins, but he retrieved a dime-store paperback. "I think you might enjoy this. It's called *The Grapes of Wrath*. If anyone asks, you tell them it came from me, and the title comes from the Book of Revelation, chapter fourteen: 'And the angel swung his sickle into the earth, and gathered the vine of the earth, and cast it into the great winepress of the wrath of God.'"

Violet had now lived at 1907 Blueberry Lane for seventy-five years, and the book James gave her, though deeply yellowed, remained on her shelf. She wondered what he had seen in her, and at how his seeing it had set fire to it, fueled her to travel three thousand miles over the course of four years toward what felt, in the end, like destiny. Perhaps it was similar to what she saw in Quincy, a feeling for which she had no name. Spirit colliding with providence. Something would come from what Violet saw, though what it was, Violet couldn't say. When she imagined herself in the future, she felt pleased, looking back, at how everything had turned out.

Violet placed her yardstick two inches above the first line

and traced the pencil along the metal edge, and again traced its length until a second line was drawn across the horizon.

Her house was not the same house where Richard and James were raised, but the one Violet and Richard had built in its place, with tall ceilings and low eaves of refined wood and open spaces without clutter, a humbling aesthetic that both of them had craved. "My brother Richie likes to draw, like you," James had told her. "Stubborn, but a good kid. A really good kid. I hope the war ends quickly. His number will be coming up soon."

It was all Violet had to go on when she left home several weeks later, running from a different country preacher, the one who had done what he'd done to her before, and Violet ran like the devil toward the sense of an ending, a desire to head west, a singular bird knowing where to go and when.

And yet, how many times did she come close to never arriving at all? She recalled the train station in Houston where she'd disembarked, and afterward learned how to hitch a ride in a boxcar by watching others do the same. She recalled a rattlesnake sinking its teeth into her calf in a New Mexico desert, and acting fast in spite of her shock, spitting on a clump of dirt in her hand and slapping the paste onto the puncture wounds. She'd looked far in every direction, but didn't see any sign of a town. She believed the last thing she would ever see on earth was what she saw right then, and it brought into sharper focus the twisted branches of a mesquite tree splintering the indigo sky with silver bark. The ground was covered in pink Apache plumes. A pair of wild horses ran in the distance, their blond manes floating like ghosts above the dust in a world so beautiful it was more like a rendering, some exalted version taking the place of the real thing.

Violet had thought she would die that day, and she supposed this was the reason it was coming back to her now.

But of course, she had lived. Minutes passed, then an hour, and still her leg did not turn black, and nothing unusual came over her. She'd stood, looked around, and walked on, certain that the rattlesnake had bitten her, certain that its venom was deadly. And then it dawned on her that the scars had served as a layer of protection. The venom hadn't been able to penetrate the thick, disfigured skin.

Violet dropped the heavy yardstick. It clanged loudly against the wooden floor. Somewhere Penny was asking if everything was all right up there. "Fine!" Violet managed to say as she backed up and lowered her body into her reading chair.

Something else had happened that day. Something that, until now, had remained a quiet distance away, not so much gone, or even hidden, but lurking without a sound. Her temples began to ache as her mind defied what had been done to it, resurrecting images behind her eyes with such clarity that Violet began to sweat, just as she had sweat in the hot desert sun when a sharp, piercing pain struck her middle and brought her to her knees, where, within minutes, a child erupted from between her legs.

She had gripped the sand in her fists and shivered and swore as loudly as her voice could carry. It wasn't as if she didn't know what was coming. It was just too soon, the pain so piercing, and then this tiny girl appeared in the world, wet and blue, sliding through Violet's hands and onto the ground, and both of them covered with blood and sand and liquids that Violet had never before seen. The child was unmoving, no bigger than a small loaf of bread. And then a second wave of pain, a flush of what felt like another child exiting her body in the shape of a flat red organ attached by a rubbery blue cord to the baby's stomach, and then up around her delicate neck.

Violet was holding her pencil, though she'd only realized this when she snapped it in half between her fingers and was startled by the crack.

She knew once again that she'd buried the girl in the place where she was born, or was sort of born, not alive, but in the world just the same, and Violet had swatted away scorpions with the pea coat. She knew that she went on to follow a wide river whose name she never learned. But she didn't know how much time passed between one thing and the other. She knew she cupped river water in her hands and quenched a staggering thirst, again and again. She dipped her body in and out of the water over what must have been days. She knew that part of the time she was naked from the waist down, as there was no need to soil her clothes every hour of every day. She walked for hours this way, recalling the *savages* spoken of in church, feral people in faraway places for whom the preachers collected money so that they could travel across the world to save and clothe them. The wild needed taming. How else was the Lord to make himself known?

She arrived sometime later in a small desert town. The next day? The following week? Shivering, perhaps feverish, as she stared at a girl dangling a rag doll the size of the baby that Violet had left in the desert. The girl's mother was picking through apples on a stand until she spotted Violet reaching for the doll. The woman shrieked and whisked her daughter away, and Violet lifted two apples into her pocket and fled the town whose name she never knew, her body covered in filth, her bones heavy, as if they too were coated in grime.

21

The *crackle of* tires on gravel meant her only child had finally come home.

Even though Penny was expecting him, and she'd been watching through the window every other minute, it still gave her a jolt, a mix of startle and overwhelming joy.

Daniel didn't seem in any hurry to get out of the car. He sat behind the wheel, and though it was difficult to see him with the sun throwing shadows and sparks off of his car's white paint and windshield, Penny recognized the shape of his head, and the shape of what must be luggage, piled on the other seats. It seemed like a lot. Was he coming to stay?

A wave came over her like a premonition, a mild sense of unease. Like standing in two different moments at once. She had the urge to tell Daniel about wanting a dog. It made no sense, but she thought of a woman she knew named Susan who had a corgi named Cactus. Sometimes Penny didn't feel like talking, and she was sure this would surprise everyone who knew her, but she watched Susan and Cactus from the dunes where they couldn't see her, or she didn't think they could, and more than once she'd felt a yearning similar to what she felt during the year that Daniel turned three and Penny had wanted a second child—not quite, but similar. Back then, every part of her seemed to pulse with desire, a dizzying, overwhelming fever of need, and too often Frank had kissed her temple and rolled his back toward her and said, "Sleep well, Penny," before he slipped into a faintly snoring slumber.

What was taking Daniel so long? "Hey, Frank?" Penny called out. "Daniel's here!"

She stood at the bottom of the inside stairwell to Violet's loft. Earlier, there had been a loud clang against the floor, and Penny had stood here, calling up to ask if everything was OK. "Fine!" Violet had hollered back. But now, as Penny called out that Daniel was here, Violet didn't respond, and Penny guessed she was taking a nap or in the shower, and why was everyone acting like Daniel coming home was no big deal? There was no movement anywhere in the house.

Penny loved her son more than she had ever loved anyone or anything, and in this way she was glad she never had a second child. There was no one else with whom she was forced to share such feelings. That was how she'd always thought about it, but she didn't know. She'd only ever had the one.

22

Daniel *finally rose* from the car. Had he always been that tall, or was it possible that he was still growing? Nonsense. He was thirty-five years old, and he seemed to resemble Penny more than ever, and this caused a feeling in her heart like pain. It wasn't pain.

He stretched his arms above his head and drew what appeared to be a long and labored breath, as if gathering the courage to come inside. Penny sensed he could use a laugh. There wasn't enough laughter in this house. Part of the appeal of corgis was that they seemed to have a sense of humor. Maybe it was their large ears and short legs and long chubby back that waddled when they walked at their owner's ankles. Maybe the humor Penny saw came from the way they gaped at other dogs with such seriousness in spite of their own goofy looks.

Daniel closed the car door gently as if concerned he'd wake them in the house, and in truth Penny had not heard from Violet or Frank. The California sun had lightened his hair into the same strawberry blond of his boyhood, and he'd lost a little weight, but looked well. When she'd asked on the phone last week if his on-again off-again girlfriend Macy might be joining him, he'd said no, and then changed the subject to, of all things, Millicent. "How was she with the earthquake?" he wanted to know, which Penny found as endearing as it was strange. She didn't mention to him or anyone else in the house that Macy had called her cell within seconds of the quake, while Penny was outside with the trees—"Just to see," Macy said in a voicemail, which Penny had still not returned. "Just to hear your voice, Penny, and know that you are all OK." Penny couldn't tell Daniel that Macy called, because Macy called Penny's cell to reach her specifically, but Daniel had called the home phone to reach whoever might answer, and how could Penny say that as a fact and not an accusation about whom Daniel was most worried?

It was already late morning, and Penny caught a whiff of the warm, buttery scent of the bread. It churned the coffee in her otherwise empty stomach. If Daniel didn't get in here soon she would eat without him. She'd let the oven door hang open for warmth. Her hands shook from caffeine and adrenaline and nerves, but it felt a little chilly inside, and anyway, the windows were coated in steam, like winter, which she suddenly missed.

She opened the butter dish on the counter to be sure of what she already knew—that it had softened overnight. Even so, she ran her finger through the bright yellow stick and licked it clean, as a cat would. When she looked again for Daniel, she felt a little sick.

And then she hurried, arranging brie, Dublin cheddar, and thin slices of prosciutto on a cherrywood cutting board that Frank had made. Millicent came running, winding in and out of Penny's legs, more than once causing her to stumble. "If we could just get everyone to come running for Daniel the way you do for cheddar . . ."

When she peeked again, Daniel was on the mossy pathway to the porch, looking upward in the direction of the second-story windows. He waved, and from the smile on his face, Penny assumed Violet was greeting him in return.

Then the sound of Daniel's steps on the front porch, and a formal rap on the door as if he'd never lived here, and it stirred the feeling that the news he had come to share couldn't possibly be good.

Penny drew a few breaths of her own and then saw that

she had locked the door, and she fumbled to unbolt it, hollering, "Sorry, sorry," and finally swung it open. It was clear that Daniel was expecting his grandmother. The smile on his face held a second too long.

"Welcome home, honey," she said, and to her surprise he came forward for a giant hug, the kind he used to need as a boy after a long, difficult day at school, in search of mercy and relief. His smell, the feel of him—to hold one's child was to hold one's *child*, no matter their age—and for an instant Penny and Daniel were nothing but an alloyed bond of mother and son. "It's so good to have you here," Penny said, and just like that his arms slipped away and he stepped back, and the space between them filled with old grievances or something she could never quite put her finger on, nor force to go away.

"How's Grand?" he asked.

"She's, you know, she's your Grand."

"She looked a little pale from the window."

Daniel swiped his shoes on the mat, his eyes searching the hallway and living room, then he glanced behind him in the direction of the car. "I'll need to grab my things," he said. Penny felt him absorbing the house, adjusting to its order. His eyes appeared brighter against his tanned skin, and this too reminded her of when he was a boy and remained outdoors nearly all summer, sleeping in a tent with friends, building elaborate kingdoms with motes on the beach. A tug of emotion grabbed her throat, and she might easily have cried if not for focusing on her feet.

"You made bread," he said, smiling.

"I knew you were coming, so I baked it." Sometimes he liked to play along with a campy joke. Other times he seemed annoyed, as if she were being childish. Today he seemed somewhere in between.

"So, how's Dad's head?" Daniel asked.

"I don't think there's been much change."

"Well, he isn't really one to change," Daniel said.

Penny swallowed her mild irritation. "He's had a headache all week."

"Sorry," he said, glancing up the staircase to the second floor. "I was trying to make a joke." He glanced at the floor. No sooner did he say this than Frank appeared, still in his pajamas, squinting, strips of greasy hair flattened to his head. The scab of crusty stitches looked worse than ever, and Penny wondered if that was because she was seeing it for the first time through Daniel's eyes.

"Oh, son," Frank said. "Sorry. Give me just a second." He turned back down the hall.

"Are you talking to me, or the sun coming through the windows?" Daniel asked. "Did he mean me?"

"I don't know," Penny said, and hollered in the direction of Frank that she'd made more coffee.

"My stomach's upset," Frank said. "And I meant you, son, you. Sorry. This head . . ."

"Not drinking enough coffee is contributing to your headache."

"You've only said that twenty times this week."

"That doesn't mean it isn't true. You also need to eat."

"Tell it to the *yard*," Frank said, and Daniel turned to Penny, and she could not stop the heat from rising in her face. Why on earth would Frank choose this moment to mention her having run out into the yard?

She said, "When the earthquake . . . I ran outside, apparently, before I helped . . . I was in shock . . ."

"Sorry, guys, I'll be right out," Frank said before the bathroom door closed.

Daniel shook his head. "That cut looks pretty bad."

"I've told him."

"I'll get my things," he said.

Penny reached for her shoes, but Daniel raised his hand. "I've got it, Mom."

So she stood in the open doorway, silently fuming at Frank,

and watching Daniel as if she were the child and he the parent doing the adult work of making several trips to the car, retrieving more duffel bags each time.

"There's still a bit more," he said, stopping in the hallway as if to catch his breath. And then he took a single step, stopped again, and made no move to retrieve whatever else remained.

Penny nodded, but Daniel stalled, his expression changing, and she sensed he was about to tell her the thing he'd come to say. She wasn't ready to hear it. Shouldn't they wait until Violet and Frank were here so that Daniel wouldn't have to repeat himself, or so that Penny wouldn't be the one to have to tell the others if he didn't feel like explaining it all over again? Panic rose in her chest and then rang like the Emergency Alert System's tone between her ears. "I'm thinking about getting a dog," she said.

Daniel appeared mildly stricken. "What about Millicent?"

"She's twenty years old. I expect she'll die soon."

Daniel stuffed his hands in his pockets and frowned.

"That's not what I meant," she said.

"Where did Dad go?" Daniel rested a hand on the doorknob.

Penny glanced down the hall. "The bathroom?"

"There's something else I need to bring in. I was just waiting. I was waiting . . ." His voice trailed off, and Penny nodded repeatedly, but she didn't try to finish his sentence, didn't ask him to say more. She didn't make a single suggestion or try to offer him advice. Instead, she walked off in search of Frank.

23

Violet couldn't fully settle her dark thoughts back into place, but she was able to set them aside, like handkerchiefs folded into a drawer, even as she showered and fussed through her closet, deciding on a white linen blouse, capri pants, and red clogs. She would stand tall as she was and stick to the workaday tasks of the moment. She applied lipstick, venetian red, along with a smattering of garnet rouge, which she had not done, quite possibly, in years. When she saw herself in the mirror, her silver strands of hair, like tin-white streaks of electricity, contrasted with the warm reds, and she was relieved to be alive on this day, in this year, far away from the past. Her beloved grandson was home.

She watched from her window as he lugged his things into the house, and again, more bags to come, and she felt that something wasn't right. Her instinct was to go downstairs, but she'd promised Penny she would give them time alone.

Looking down on him in the driveway was like looking down from a great and disorienting height. The dizziness that had plagued her was not about to let up, though it wasn't the dizziness alone that she felt. No matter her resolve, she saw flashes of her former self trekking across the desert, a young girl cutting through a ranch with that old cattle dog snapping at her heels. He had smelled blood on her, and in the scent found weakness. She'd jumped out of the way of his bite and cursed him until her voice reached a pitch where it could no longer squeeze past her lips. Her body locked up in fury, and the dog backed away, stopped, and stared as if trying to understand how wrong he'd been about her. She threw him a chunk of bread she couldn't afford to spare. He swallowed it whole, and after that they looked at each other differently. Violet had walked on, and the dog trotted beside her for nearly a mile, as if making sure she was headed where she ought to be. She trusted him to steer her right, and when they came to a forest of ponderosa pines, he stopped. This was where he would leave her. He licked her hand in farewell, allowed her to scratch behind his ears, and then ran back to the place where he belonged.

Daniel waved from the mossy sidewalk, and Violet lifted her hand in return. She felt too much in the open, defenseless, like the lanky prey she once was. Back then, she was still learning that a dog could quickly be tamed, and blue rivers and purple mountains and meadows full of coneflowers and poppies could appear out of nowhere like a birthday surprise. There was nothing to prepare her for the magnificence she might find beyond a clutch of trees, or the downward side of a cliff, or when she stopped to rest in the shade and spotted a geode with cavities of purple or white crystals. She would come to understand it was the same with art, the way beauty arrived without warning, arresting her in place.

And here, now, was the strawberry-blond head of her grandson, like coneflowers in a field; it was a sight she could not get enough of. Every move he made seemed a gesture of love and grace. He was reaching inside the back seat as if trying to lift something out. When he finally inched his way free, it was clear he was pulling the bulk of something with him.

Heat rose to Violet's face.

Slowly, very, very slowly, pulling and pulling . . . and then . . . a sleeping child appeared in his arms.

A girl, perhaps three years old, with thin, dark hair down her back. She wore a yellow dress and blue Mary Jane shoes. Her tiny feet dangled against Daniel's thighs, as her arms rose to wrap around his neck. A canary, that was what she was, the smallest, lightest, most delicate yellow creature about to be lifted into the house.

Daniel pressed her to his shoulder, and she nestled her face into his neck. He balanced on one foot, kicking the door closed with the other.

Violet let go a gasp. Not a gasp so much as a squeak, which triggered a spasm so strong that, for the first time since she became sick, it felt as if she might not regain her breath. She hacked into a tissue, until the rust-colored flecks turned pink.

There had been no mention of a child. Not once. Violet's face was so hot she might have been feverish. Her temples throbbed. And by the time she calmed, her mouth tasted of copper and the wax of old lipstick on her tongue.

24

Penny *froze in* the doorway. Frank had still not come out of the bathroom. She was alone with what was happening here. And what exactly *was* happening? She didn't know, but felt the air expanding, the trees reaching for sun in the sky. "Frank? Can you come now, please?"

Daniel was retrieving something out of the back seat and then whispering sweetly, "We're here, we're here."

A small head with long brown hair appeared, an entire child, wrapped in Daniel's arms.

Frank's shoes clunked the wooden floor behind Penny, his footfalls vibrating the loose boards beneath her feet. From the corner of her eye she registered that he had dressed and combed his hair, and the air around him smelled of toothpaste and aftershave. His voice was low in her ear. "I'm sorry," he said.

"What are you talking about?" Penny seemed to glide onto the porch. Somehow she was standing there, and Frank was next to her, whispering in her ear as if completely unaware of Daniel and the girl.

After that, the world fell silent. Later, Penny couldn't recall the sound of waves crashing the rocks, of birds, of wind in the trees. But she could recite in detail the way her son carried a child into the house, those small feet bobbing against his long legs. He gently removed the hair from her eyes, and she nestled her face in the familiar comfort of her father's neck, and his large hand braced across the back of her small yellow dress.

Penny would always recall the exuberant, high-pitched mewling as Millicent swept past her legs to greet them, the first sound to reach Penny's ears. *Yes, yes, yes,* the cat seemed to be saying. But perhaps most vividly, and for the rest of her life, she would recall the moment she took her husband's hand, and the desperate feel that came back as he squeezed hers in return.

25

And suddenly everyone was holding a tumbler of lemonade with ice. Even the girl, though hers was served in a tiny Moroccan glass with a clear blue base and gold rim and no ice. The glass reminded Violet of the teacup of milk she'd given Millicent on the day she came to live with them.

They were seated in the living room, the girl wedged sideways on Daniel's lap, her shoes bonking the gray upholstery of the oversize chair, which everyone agreed was Francisco's chair on any other day. The sun flashed against the gold rim at the girl's mouth when she drank, and she seemed to have noticed, holding the glass steady at her lips, then dipping slightly for the flash, holding, and dipping and flashing, as a shy grin formed on her face. She was eyeing Violet and Violet was eyeing her. The urge to scoop her away from Daniel was overwhelming.

Francisco appeared stiff in the stiff-backed chair that no one ever sat in except for company, which they rarely had. The furniture was spaced too far apart for a conversation of the sort that it appeared they were about to have. The teak dining table would have been better to gather around, but it didn't matter. Penny had led them all here, where the faded red Persian rug in the middle of the room seemed to have become the focal point for everyone to rest their eyes when not staring at the girl.

Millicent came roaring in, as if to announce, once again,

Daniel's homecoming and the guest he brought with him, who was now glancing between Millicent and Daniel with a look of bewilderment and delight.

"Well, Daniel," Violet said. "This is . . . unexpected."

"I'm sorry . . . to shock you like this."

"Sorry?" Penny said. "Oh, Daniel . . ."

"There's no need . . ." Francisco said.

"To apologize," Violet said.

The sun now caught each glass of lemonade, as if everyone in the room were holding a torch. The soda bread and toppings were served on Penny's ceramic plates, and placed around the room for easy reach on the blond coffee and end tables, but no one was eating.

"So . . . who do we have here?" Penny said, in a voice reserved for children.

Daniel's arms seemed enormous, as if the girl against his chest was a toy. He pulled her closer and kissed the top of her head, and from the mouths dropping open around the room, the gesture had clenched every heart.

"Well, this is . . . do you want to say your name?" Daniel said.

Millicent jumped onto the chair with them, and the girl squealed and then rolled her eyes up to Daniel, as if waiting for him to answer on her behalf. When Daniel hesitated, she said, "Danny," though it sounded accented, something closer to *Dahny*.

Penny and Frank glanced at each other as if to ask if *Danny* was what the girl called Daniel, or if Danny was the girl's name.

Daniel smiled. "That's right. This is Danielle. But she goes by D-A-N-I, *Dani*. Her mother named her."

Everyone seemed to be looking at Violet now, as if for a sign of what to do next. Or perhaps they were taken aback by her lipstick and rouge. Or maybe they stared a second too long, because she was flushed. It was hot in there. The sun now entered through all corners of the room.

"So," Daniel said. "It's just . . . I'm trying to find a place to begin. It's a long story. A complicated one."

Everyone nodded like actors in a play. The only sound in the room was the girl's shoes bopping the chair, in between Penny's string of small sighs and Millicent's loud purring beneath the girl's long strokes down her back. The cat appeared young and rakish beneath her hand. "The cat's name is Millicent," Daniel said to Dani, and she whispered something near Millicent's ear that sounded nothing like *Millicent*. The more she turned to look at the cat, the more Violet saw how Dani's features held a striking resemblance to all the people she loved. There was Daniel in the shape of her chestnut eyes. Penny in her cheekbones. Francisco in the mouth and chin. But it was mostly Richard whom Violet saw—his dark, wavy hair and oval face. Except it went beyond his features into a realm of nuanced gestures. The shape and movement of eyebrows, the corner of a grin, the wave of hands . . . The likeness was uncanny, if not unsettling.

"I guess . . ." Daniel began, and Dani squirmed as if under the weight of so many eyes, and Daniel took her empty glass and set it on a coaster on the end table. Something unruly seemed to rise off of Penny, who repeatedly glanced at Francisco, while Francisco glanced at his shoes. His wound glared in the sun, and Violet saw the scene through the eyes of a child. It was a spectacle. *They* were a spectacle. Violet with her scars and old skin and protruding knuckles and wrists. Penny, a shaky, anxious wreck, though, to be fair, far quieter than Violet expected.

"Did you know about this?" Penny asked Violet in a whisper, reaching for her hand. Violet shook her head no. How absurd. "Of course not. I don't even know what *this* is," though she had a good idea.

Violet and Penny leaned back into the sofa, both crossing their legs, then crossing their arms, then cupping their chins in one hand, like some choreographed song-and-dance number from the 1930s. Francisco appeared to be holding his breath, and Violet wished he would let go, as he had in the kitchen, not with tears—unless he needed to, of course—but with whatever was just beneath his skin. Violet leaned forward and nearly said, *Let it go.*

"Son," Francisco said, as if reading Violet's mind, "this child, *your* child? Dani . . ." He drifted off, saying nothing more.

Violet was just glad to hear him speak, and she flashed on the times she'd stood over him when he was a sleeping child, and she filled with a sense of foreboding joy, her love so closely entwined with a fear that something terrible would come for him.

Penny stared at her husband, nodding in agreement, even as her mind seemed to have jumped ahead to something else. She glanced at the scars on Violet's hand and her ankle beneath the cuff of her jeans, and then her eyes narrowed as she studied Dani.

Just as Violet was thinking they were of the same mind, Penny burst out laughing. It was morbid for a child to be stuffed in a room of strangers, one with a stitched and infected forehead, one with a body full of scars, another visibly shaken yet laughing in a way that appeared unhinged. But Penny couldn't seem to stop herself, and now Violet began to snigger, too.

Francisco stared at the women with a look of concern.

Daniel stared with a look of disappointment, edging toward anger.

It seemed as if several minutes had passed, but that couldn't be right. People couldn't sit like that, together in a room swelling with a kind of agitated madness, with a young child so quiet on her father's lap, not knowing what was happening for minutes upon minutes, but that was how it felt, time passing, until Penny's laughter converted to a whimpering string of tears, and she held her face in her hands as if to help temper her emotions, but the room was already laced in some kind of agony.

"So," Violet said, "her mother named her . . ."

Penny's crying took on a fuller shape.

"Mom," Daniel whispered. "It's OK. Mom. *Mom*. Listen to me. Stop. Please. You're scaring Dani."

26

When Daniel first walked up the path to the house, the many worlds that made up who he was collided like fireworks inside his skull. He felt a headache coming on, and clenched his jaw against it. But as he thought of retrieving Dani, still asleep in the car, he felt a flicker of how much his mother must have loved him as a child, because now he knew what it felt like to kiss the top of his own child's head and breathe in her scent, and this was something his mother had done with him all the time.

The lilacs were in full bloom, and he knew that his mother would have clipped them for vases in the living room and kitchen so that the crosswind would fill the house with their scent. He knew before he opened the door that she would have baked soda bread, and that the house was going to smell like lilacs and warm, buttery bread, and this would put him at ease. He knew that his mother knew this, too.

When he saw her at the door it was all he could do not to fall apart. Her arms embraced him and he instantly felt that everything was going to be all right. He didn't have a clue how to be a parent. He didn't even *know* his own child. He'd missed all the stages that led up to who she was, and he'd pulled back from his mother in the doorway, not wanting her to see him cry and to worry any more than she already worried on any given day.

"You baked soda bread," he'd said, and his mother made a joke, but he was too distracted to laugh. He made a joke about his father, and it sounded crass the minute it left his mouth, and he'd wished he could take it back.

Now, in the living room, he stared at the bouquet on the coffee table when he spoke. "Her mother named her." His words felt as if they were launched into the house, back in time to the place where he'd grown up, and there was nothing he could do to make this moment any less surreal. He stumbled for what to say, in part because he couldn't get past how many times he'd thought within these walls of what it would be like to be grown and living on his own. All those years spent wondering about the person he would turn out to be—and now this was the person he turned out to be.

"Her mother's name is Arielle," he said.

Dani jerked her face upward at the sound of her mother's name.

Daniel offered her a quick, mollifying smile before continuing. "Four years ago, when Macy and I visited Aix-en-Provence?" He hesitated, hating to recall that trip. "We had a falling-out."

Within the long pause that followed, his parents and grandmother began to catch on, causing widening eyes, puckered mouths, and fidgeting of every kind. The movement was so kinetic that Dani must have felt it on her skin. She covered her face the way his mother had covered hers moments ago, as if trying to disappear. Daniel caressed her shoulder.

"I don't want to say it," Daniel told his family. He was overcome with thirst and drank down his lemonade, the taste of which also reminded him of being a child in this house. There seemed no escape. "Don't make me say it." He set the empty glass down.

Dani lowered her hands and smiled as if they were now engaged in a game of peekaboo. He was her father. A fact he still could not fully comprehend.

"There's no need," his father said, his voice warm with more sympathy than Daniel expected.

His mother eyed his father suspiciously, and then with a

look of remorse, as if fighting the thoughts inside her own head.

His grandmother seemed oblivious to his parents. Daniel met her eyes and felt a rush of emotion, a longing, as if he was again the child he used to be, safe in her care against his fighting mother and father. It was only now, as he gazed at Violet with what he knew must have been a love-filled stare, that he realized how much she'd aged in the time he'd been away. He second-guessed telling her about the other thing he'd come to say. This was enough for now, more than enough, certainly for today.

"We get it, Daniel," his mother said, and Daniel nodded as a thank-you, relieved that he didn't have to say out loud that the evening of his argument with Macy resulted in him sleeping with a stranger.

He didn't think he would ever tell them, under any circumstances, that the fight had to do with his grandmother. It seemed as absurd now as it did then. After visiting Cézanne's studio, one thing had led to another and the argument had stopped being about Cézanne and Violet Swan and art, and had become about Daniel being blind to the plight of women, especially women working in the arts, one of whom happened to be Macy. She was an illustrator whose work appeared on postcards and was framed in artisan specialty shops in Los Angeles, Portland, Chicago, and New York, and her signature itself, Macy Moore, was often written in as part of the work, too. But hardly a week went by when she didn't hear that a male illustrator was getting paid more than she was for the same work, or getting written up in *The New Yorker* for illustrations that were clearly influenced by hers, and she was right to feel frustrated, slighted, and angry. So when Daniel mentioned how it wasn't until he was standing in the middle of Cézanne's workspace, surrounded by familiar scents of paint and wooden floors, and felt the orange sun streaming through the large window, that he absorbed the power of all that had gone on there, and in turn began to feel the true impact of his grandmother's work, and Macy had said, "What do you mean?" and already he felt as if he had said the wrong thing. He was just thinking out loud. His thoughts weren't fully formed. "I mean, her talents and influence, the way the world sees her, what she offers, that sort of thing. I never quite saw her as, well, *her.*" Was that really what he meant? It was more of a feeling than an idea. Macy looked around with that nervous smile she had when holding back the thing she most wanted to say. "So, why did it take the details of this man's life and work for you to recognize the talent and influence of your grandmother's?" Before Daniel could think of a cohesive answer, her frustration burst forth in the form of "Never mind," and she marched off beneath the plane trees toward the Cours Mirabeau, where they were staying at a hotel, while Daniel wandered down a small side street and soon became lost.

Part of the problem with that conversation, he now understood, was that his grandmother wasn't like most artists, or other people for that matter, when it came to being seen. She preferred invisibility, wanting only for her work to be looked at, not her person. And even then, if it hadn't been for his grandfather sending photos of her paintings to a collector in New York all those years ago, Violet Swan might never have sold or signed a single work. She might have gone on to paint, of course she would have, but most likely she would have remained unknown, her life lived in the shadows. The fact was, she had lived in the shadows anyway, despite the fame. Everyone knew so little of her, and this drove Daniel a little crazy. He had the medium and the skill to offer up the full and true story of Violet Swan, but his grandmother continued to shut him down.

The idea first occurred to him the night of the argument with Macy, when he slipped into a corner bistro with red velvet curtains covering the bottom half of the windows—how his grandmother had always been a mystery, even to her own family, and he should make a documentary about her life. Yes! He knew what it was to be her grandson, and to some degree, what it was for her to be a mother to his father. But an awareness of her as a person and an artist in her own right had never fully penetrated his mind, and maybe this was normal, a learned way of seeing one's parents and grandparents as one grew up. But he was past growing up, wasn't he? He imagined all of this unfolding onscreen, and it filled him with an energy that signaled he was on to something, and right behind that excitement came a dull sense of dread. She would never let him do this. And so he sat at a dim bar asking for the cocktail of the house, feeling that his life was being thwarted in ways he couldn't fully explain or get past.

The brunette bartender suggested something called *tremblement de terre,* "earthquake," and oh, the strangeness of it struck Daniel now as he looked around his parents' living room where pictures had been thrown from the walls by the recent quake. The bartender had told him it was a drink served at parties for Toulouse-Lautrec, and Daniel said, "No, thank you," as he'd never cared for the man's work, nor had his grandmother, and the bartender laughed and told him the drink was quite good, and she was right. The beautiful red liquid in the delicate coupe glass with a gold rim was delicious and far more powerful than he was initially aware.

He drank another, thinking in a miserable way on the documentary he had just finished editing, about the life of a young politician who was making a name for himself. No one would ever see the conversations on the cutting room floor, the crass jokes, the side-eye glances at his female staff. The most telling expressions were cut in order to create a seamless illusion that what one was witnessing about this man was all there was to see. It was on film, after all, so no one could call it fake. The end result was the image of a fair man of integrity, working hard, stepping up, being fierce in the face of injustice, and winning over the world.

Daniel drank several *tremblement de terres* in great and surely unseemly gulps, fraught with bitterness over the fight with Macy, which seemed to have come out of nowhere. He was planning to ask Macy to marry him on that trip. He'd already bought the ring and tucked it into the pocket of his jeans.

"Her mother is French," Daniel said. "She's a bartender in Aix-en-Provence. Or was."

His grandmother's eyebrows rose in astonishment. He could hear the collective intake of breath around the room.

He looked down at his daughter, for his own comfort as much as hers, thinking of Arielle taking his hand when her shift ended, asking him to tell her everything about his life, and him telling about the people and the place where he now sat. He was the grandson of a famous abstract painter, Violet Swan. He revealed this to her in his drunkenness, and understood how drunk he was, because normally he protected his privacy as much as his grandmother's. Arielle's face lit up. She liked his American accent, and that he knew so much about art, which she said she was also kind of sick of talking about, having been born and raised in a place where all the *masters* had painted their *masterpieces,* and where she too was trying to paint, but was a bartender, a *barmaid,* as some Americans called her, but she had to live, didn't she? And here was the grandson of Violet Swan? She liked his college French, which was terrible and made her laugh. Her lips had a glossy pout, and her English was awkward but sounded sexy to his ears, and he was dying to kiss her, and then he did on the way to her apartment, a five-minute stroll along a narrow cobbled alleyway, where he briefly wondered if she was going to rob him, if he was one in a string of tourists she conned. Her studio apartment was a fifth-floor walk-up, a beautiful surprise behind a dingy door. It was spotlessly clean and stylish, with parquet floors and white walls. A black Le Corbusier chair—real or a very good knockoff, he couldn't tell—was placed by the large arched window, and stacks of books lined the floor and the shelves. The room smelled of burned coffee and ripe oranges that grew outside the open windows, and Daniel lay back on the firm bed with a white feather duvet, thinking how he wanted to stay there for the rest of his life. Arielle played a record he'd never heard, a woman singing sad French ballads, and they didn't tear at each other's clothes like in the movies; they were deliberate, easy, and slow.

"I never told anyone," Daniel said.

His family was quiet—perhaps speechless was more the word. They appeared united in whatever was going through their minds, and sat like a small platoon of expressionless soldiers, everyone on the same side in a way he'd never seen. "Not even Macy," he added. "*Especially* not Macy. But she, well, obviously, she knows now."

He tilted his head back and rubbed his eyes, pinched the bridge of his nose, recalling how he'd returned to the hotel at 3 a.m. reeking of perfumed soap, feeling Macy's awareness that something had happened and only he could say what it was, only he could relieve her of a maddening suspicion that he knew she continued to suppress for months, even years. Only he could assure her that she was not crazy, but he never did. "I want to marry you," he said while taking off his pants and pulling out the ring, catching his feet in the legs and falling over while the ring rolled under the bed. Macy yanked one of the pillows off and threw it at him where he lay on the floor. "Go to sleep," she'd said, or maybe it was hell she told him to go to. He had never been sure, because he was drunk and half-way under the bed, feeling around for the ring.

27

A *few months ago,* a man I didn't know knocked on our door in LA and told Macy he was looking for me," Daniel said. "By the time I came in from the backyard, he was showing her photographs of Dani and letters from Arielle. Macy immediately began packing her things."

"Oh, *honey,*" his mother said.

"It's OK, Mom. I'm fine. I will be. We're both . . . Listen, things haven't been that great with Macy for a while. I thought about asking her to marry me, in fact I started to ask her when we were in Aix, but everything went wrong, and now I'm relieved that it didn't work out. We weren't ever going to be happy. We weren't the greatest fit."

His father dropped his head and at once spoke up. "Would anyone like a drink? I mean a real drink?"

"Frank. It's a little early. Not even noon."

"Son? A beer?"

"No thanks, Dad."

His father walked over to the liquor console and poured himself a glass of brandy.

Daniel eyed his mother, who shook her head slowly, her expression flat, as if she had simply given up.

"Mom?" his father said, holding up his glass toward Daniel's grandmother, who raised a single eyebrow in return. "No, thank you, son."

"I don't know what to say," his mother said. "Can I get you anything, Daniel? Will she eat something? Will you eat something, Dani? There's some bread and cheese for you. Are you hungry?"

A lump lodged in Daniel's throat. It was such a small kindness, offering food to his child, but it moved him in a way he had no words for.

"It's French," his father said, returning to his chair, swirling brandy in the snifter. "Serving bread and cheese."

Was he making a joke? He wasn't very good at jokes.

"It is, Dad," Daniel said, and picked up the plate and held it to Dani. "We had a large breakfast. I don't know how much . . . Are you hungry, Dani?"

Dani reached for the bread. Everyone watched. The more she took, the more his mother appeared overwhelmed.

"I should have told you. I wanted to," Daniel said. "But let me . . . The thing is, up until the last minute I was still trying to make sure it wasn't some elaborate scheme. This guy at our door said he was a friend of a friend of hers, and I didn't know what to believe. So . . . first, well, I considered the timing. I mean, Dani *did* look related in the photographs, no doubt about that, and when I saw that she was born nine months after we returned home, things turned serious. And the fact that her mother had named her after me . . . I don't know what to say about that, except that right now her mother is in J-A-I-L for stealing from the bar where she worked, and from the customers, too. And there were drug charges as well. She was having a hard time raising Dani alone, all of which are reasons why she was trying to find me."

His mother covered her mouth.

His father swallowed his drink.

But his grandmother appeared vacant, as if her mind had stepped out and had yet to return.

"But it's not like our institutions here, where she is now. It's more rehabilitative. She's going to stay in there for at least a few years. This is not her first offense . . ."

His father looked as if he had a question.

"What is it, Dad?"

"Nothing. Go ahead."

"Are you sure?"

His father nodded.

"Well . . . for the past several months I've been waiting to find out if the story was true. First there was the DNA test . . . which, as you guys know, Macy and I gave each other as Christmas gifts several years ago. I never looked at it again after finding out that our family came from Great Britain and Ireland, which we already knew. So I closed my account, but of course the DNA stays in the database online. Whoever is a match with me will still show up in there, and the closer the relative, the easier the match is to explain." He hesitated, unable to look his grandmother in the eye. Again he wanted to talk to her, again he thought it best to wait.

"Anyway, Arielle took several tests with different companies on the off chance that I or someone related to me might have taken one, too. The thing is, she mailed in Dani's sample as her own, which, obviously, is how she confirmed me as the father." He jiggled Dani's shoulder as if to account for the outcome of everything he had said. Here she was, proof positive, the result of a one-night stand.

Millicent continued to purr as Dani stroked her head and behind her ears, and Daniel would have liked to close his own eyes like a cat and go to sleep.

"After paternity was confirmed, requests for a US passport had to go through, and that was a nightmare unto itself. Macy left me. Obviously. And I'm pretty much orbiting right now, trying to figure out where to land."

"Daniel," his grandmother said in barely a whisper.

"But Macy called me during the earthquake," his mother said, as if what Daniel just said couldn't be true. "She called me, and I never called back. I guess I must have sensed something. She must think I didn't call because I knew . . ."

His grandmother began to cough.

"She called you?" Daniel asked.

"Yes. She left a message on my cell." His mother glanced at his grandmother as she coughed. She looked back at Daniel.

"While you were out in the yard?" his father asked.

His mother acted as if his father hadn't spoken. "Why did you think you couldn't ask us for help, Daniel?"

The coughing worsened. His grandmother held a tissue to her mouth.

"Son, I understand," his father said above the hacking. "You must have felt ashamed . . ."

His mother frowned at his grandmother. And then his grandmother frowned at his father. She wiped her mouth with the tissue and slipped the ball of it into her pocket. "Excuse me," she said.

"Grand, are you all right?"

"*Violet*," his mother said, but his grandmother swiped the air. "I'm fine. Daniel, please, go on."

His mother let loose an air of exasperation between tight lips.

Daniel turned to his father. "Well, Dad, actually, I wouldn't say *ashamed*."

"No, maybe that's not what I meant. I mean, I just wish there was a way to understand why you felt you couldn't come to us."

"This isn't about you. I just needed to take care of this thing on my own, without anyone else's opinion or help."

"I didn't mean it like that," his father said. "OK, it's a little bit about us, but only in the sense—"

"Just . . . listen, Dad, it isn't about *that* at all."

They were never very good at being father and son. Ever since Daniel became a teenager, a dark tone drifted into the room when the two of them came near one another. Daniel had studied his father's traits of shutting out the people he loved, of stewing mysteriously around the house and out into his work shed, leaving others to guess the source of his moods, and Daniel worried he'd already inherited the things he detested, sensing too that there was something about himself that his father disliked, something that he could not change, and perhaps they were one and the same. "It isn't that I think so little of you, Dad. It's that I didn't think so highly of myself."

"Of course there's no shame here, Daniel," his grandmother said, which got a look from his father.

"Oh, son . . ." his mother started.

"Son . . ." his father interrupted. "These things . . . This is a difficult time, but we're here . . ." He looked away and then knocked back the rest of his brandy.

Was his father about to cry? Daniel had never seen his father cry, not once in his life. And now his mother seemed to have noticed and was quietly wiping her own wet face.

Daniel tried to get things back on track. "Listen. I don't understand why she didn't try to reach me here, at home, much sooner. Long before she found me in LA. She knew who I was. She knew I was the grandson of Violet Swan. It's not something I normally tell people, Grand, but I'd had a lot to drink."

His mother glanced down as if embarrassed by everything this implied.

His grandmother swiped the air. "Daniel, I couldn't care less."

"She could have just found me right *here*. The contact for acquisitions is online. Did any of you receive anything from anyone looking for me?"

His grandmother frowned and shook her head.

"Of course not," his mother said. "We would have told you."

His father said, "No. Nothing." He set his glass on the side table, rested his elbows on his thighs, and clasped his hands together.

Dani seemed to be studying the faces in the room, petting Millicent against Daniel's leg, and he thought that his daughter was something of a cat herself, calm and patient, her secret thoughts spinning. He had no idea if such quiet was normal for a child. He guessed it was not. "Anyway. Long story short, I went back to Aix, took one look at Dani in the neighbor's doorway across the hall from where she'd lived with her mother, and regardless of the DNA test, I knew who she belonged to."

Penny got up, and Daniel could hear her blowing her nose in the bathroom. She returned with a box of tissues.

"The first thing I said was 'You look exactly like my grandfather.'"

The room erupted with laughter.

Dani giggled, glancing from one face to the other.

His mother blew her nose and said, "Oh, Daniel. This is the best thing to happen. The best thing . . ."

His father nodded as a grin curled the corner of his mouth.

"The old woman who was looking after her until I got there stared at me with her powdered face, and when I started to choke up, I told her that Dani looked just like my grandfather, and she said, 'I do not think you mean what you're saying. Or is it that I do not understand?'"

The laughter continued, infused with a mix of relief and disbelief, and now Daniel had forgotten the rest of what he meant to say. His smiling daughter in his lap shifted his laughter toward a sting of emotion in his eyes.

Dani noticed, and her expression quickly fell.

"No, no. It's OK," he told her, as if they were back in France, where her fate was being decided in offices, over documents with a series of strangers, a frantic time that she couldn't possibly understand. "Everything is good. These are happy tears. Happy that I have you." He gave her a squeeze, and could only imagine what being brought here must feel like. To be so far from everything and everyone she had ever known. And everyone speaking a language she was still struggling to learn. It would have terrified Daniel as a child to leave home like this, to be taken so far away from his parents and grandparents. The only time he'd seen Dani cry, aside from in the courtroom, was sometimes when she first woke up, with a blank look right before the tears, as if she had forgotten where she was, or whom she was with, until she remembered.

His mother blew her nose. "Can I, I don't know, can I hold her, Daniel? Show her around the house a bit?"

"Of course, but she can be a little shy. She's normally a bit more talkative, but her English is still coming along. Apparently, her mother spoke some to her, too. She's three, and has only been with me for a couple of weeks. She may need a minute more to warm up to everyone, to being here . . ."

"*A couple of weeks?*" his mother said.

"When's her birthday?" his father asked.

"January sixth. I had just gotten home with her a few days before the earthquake. We were jet-lagged—"

"The Epiphany of Christ," his father said.

'What do you mean she's been with you a couple of weeks?" his mother said, an accusation rising in her tone.

"What's that, Dad?"

"Her birthday. It's the Epiphany."

Daniel was distracted by his grandmother's beaming face, as if whatever she had been puzzling through earlier was now solved. Her eyes were brighter than a moment ago, her face a tender gaze, and he guessed his daughter's resemblance to his grandfather had transfixed her.

"I know," Daniel told her. "She looks just like him."

"*Bonjour, Dani,*" Violet said. "*Comment allez-vous?*"

Dani twisted her body toward the sound of Violet's voice. Daniel's breath came up short.

"*Qui es-tu?*" Dani asked his grandmother.

"Your great-grandmother. *Je suis ton arrière grand-mère.*"

Dani studied her with a tilted head.

"Grand? I didn't, wait a . . ."

"*Notre jolie chat t'aime bien,*" his grandmother said.

"Violet?" his mother said, scooting to the edge of the sofa.

"How do you . . . Wait. You know *French?*"

"*Oui. Je parle français un peu.*"

His mother shifted her gaze between his father and his grandmother.

His father seemed the only one not surprised, but it was difficult to tell with him. He got up and poured himself another brandy.

"What the *hell*," his mother said, gripping her knees. "What the actual hell is it about this family?"

28

Penny couldn't help thinking how absurd the idea was that someone could write in a journal about such a thing as what had happened on this day, and that the act of writing it would reveal the bigger picture and underscore some sense to be made. Her palms and armpits felt clammy. Cool air from somewhere skimmed the back of her neck.

Try as she might not to laugh, she laughed. Try as she might not to get emotional, her emotions got the best of her too.

"Why did you think you couldn't tell us?" she'd asked, though it was not exactly what she meant. It was not an accusation that Daniel had done something wrong. It was more a question of why she and Frank couldn't seem to do right by their only child, let alone each other. How was it that they were not the ones he came to in this time of trouble? How was it that Daniel did not come to her, especially, when he needed help? He had gone from a boy who needed her for everything, who understood intrinsically that she would never turn him away, to a man who shut her out at one of the most difficult and confusing and important moments of his life.

It tore her up, the entire thing filled her with a hot, bewildering mix of disappointment and a raw kind of joy.

She got up to blow her nose. She came back with a box of tissues in case anyone else might need them, like Frank, who was drinking before lunch, and she'd wondered recently if he'd been drinking at random times when he seemed a little, what was it, soft? His eyes appeared to be welling, but Penny thought surely that was a mistake. She'd never seen him cry. Ever. This was not normal, and she knew this long before today, but it struck her suddenly, and hard.

A granddaughter. How was this possible? Of course she knew *how*, but still, *how*? In spite of how it all came to be, and how Daniel had decided to share the news, the news itself felt like the best thing that had ever happened to her. And surely Frank, too. There was nothing she could think of that could compare, short of giving birth to Daniel, but that was included in this—doubled up, a gift that kept giving. She had borne Daniel, and Daniel had shared in the birth of this girl. No wonder Violet felt so connected to Daniel. Penny seemed to have just now uncovered the most astonishing secret about family bonds. Her head zinged with giddiness.

And now, just as Penny was about to walk over to her grandchild, to hold the girl for the first time, Violet began speaking *French*.

"What the actual hell is it about this family?" Penny asked. She met Frank halfway across the room and took a sip of his brandy.

Instead of Violet explaining, she stood up and said, "So . . . she's *ours*. She's family. No more fuss. My goodness, what a day. I'd love to show her the upstairs. Can we do that? Let's do that." She turned swiftly toward the staircase, as if emboldened by a shot of youth.

Millicent jumped out of the chair as if she too were following orders.

Violet raised her glass of lemonade like a toast. "Go ahead and bring the food. Everyone."

"I think I'll stay here and clean up," Penny said, and regretted it immediately. She didn't want Daniel or Dani out of her sight. But she didn't want to go upstairs, either. She wanted to show Dani the rest of the house, *her* part of the house, where *she* lived, and the yard, the garden, the beach. She reached again for Frank's brandy and took another sip.

"I'll help you," Frank said, and now, even if she had wanted to change her mind and follow them upstairs, Penny felt obligated to remain with Frank.

But then, none of it mattered. Violet never made it more than a few steps. Her lips formed a pucker of confusion—what was she saying now? Was it French? *A . . . Da . . . Ada?* Her legs began to sway like long, S-shaped drapes, as if she were doing a tango, though not quite, before she landed on the floor.

PART THREE

29

Frank *understood he* could be awkward, even inappropri-ate at times, though he always figured this out after the fact. Like when Penny startled at the flicker and sat up in bed, Frank was startled too, but he just lay there laughing, his ac-tions not quite matching his intention, which was to let Penny know there was nothing to be afraid of.

Why did he do that?

But in this moment, Frank was quick on his feet, know-ing what needed to be done yet not quick enough to get it. His mother hit the floor before he could catch her. He'd been distracted by Penny. "I think I'll stay here and clean up," she'd said as their granddaughter—their *granddaughter*—was headed upstairs out of sight, and there was nothing that Frank could see that needed cleaning. Then she was taking another sip of his drink, and the feeling in the room was that something was about to happen, the air charged with cues, and Frank was ready, but not ready enough.

"I'll help," he said, which seemed a ridiculous way to brace himself against whatever was coming, but all he could think was that Penny shouldn't be alone. She never would have said she wanted to stay down here if something wasn't really both-ering her. And then, in the corner of his eye, the shape of his mother, the feel of a weighty silence, a signal that something was off, drew him away from the cluster of complicated feel-ings inside his chest. Yet he'd hesitated, softened by the warm brandy, staring at his wife and feeling the weight of regret.

And now Penny was yelling into a phone.

Daniel and Dani had disappeared outside.

Frank crouched near his mother, whispering in her face, "Wake up, Mom. Wake up now." His heart banged so hard he could feel the pulse in his eyes, and it occurred to him in a flash that maybe this was the start of a heart attack. "*Mom?*" He was sweating all over. His socks creaked with moisture in his shoes.

Something was wrong with him. A high-pitched ringing took over his ears. A blackout of sorts. He couldn't hear what anyone was saying. He stopped feeling his feet on the floor. When they had numbed him at the clinic, he felt more at peace than he'd felt in years. This was not like that.

The thought of his mother slipping away terrified him. A wave of sickness passed through his gut, and he called for Penny. He had spent his entire adult life calling for Penny, and what was he, some kind of child?

He lifted his mother's head onto his lap. Her skull was light as a pillow. He couldn't recall the last time he'd touched her with any sort of tenderness, and something inside him was starting to break. Her face was smooth and pale, and the soft skin around her mouth and eyes gently receded with gravity's pull, and she appeared younger than her years, even as her rouge was caught in the lines of her cheeks. He had known her since she was a young woman, younger than Daniel was now, and he was suddenly overcome with a feeling he'd had many times in his life, that he did not know her at all.

A small drop of what appeared to be blood dotted the corner of her lip as if she'd bitten her tongue.

Penny was off the phone and taking care of something else, always, anything, everything, without ever needing to be asked.

"Honey?" his mother whispered. Was she talking to him?

Through the window he could see Daniel in the yard with Dani, his son pointing out the garden to his daughter, pointing up into the trees, bouncing her on his hip across the lawn the way parents do when they are trying to distract their child from something bad. Oh, what he wouldn't give to have those pain meds again.

"They're on their way," Penny was saying. "You don't look well either, Frank. You're shaking. It's a shock, I know, but I think she's just fainted. Not enough oxygen to the head, she's all right, let me sit with her. Frank. Frank? Are you listening?" Penny cupped his cheek. "*Frank*," she said.

"I know, I know," he said, but he didn't know what he meant. There was a lot going on. And the worst of it was surely the fact that he should have — it was all fully, *fully* dawning on him now — told Daniel about the emails he'd received last year from Arielle.

And now the fighter jets roared over the house, so loud and close it felt as if the roof might shear off from its frame.

"Goddamn," he said, and shook his mother's shoulders.

"Stop it, Frank. Let her go."

What did she mean, *Let her go*?

"She's my mother," he said, flashing on his four-year-old self, and on his mother walking into this very room from the kitchen with a drink in her hand, and that old glazed look in her eye, and then boom, she collapsed. It was like having several mothers — one who adored him, another who was frightened of him, another still who didn't quite recognize his face.

Frank was just a boy, but his instincts had been to shake the life back into his mother, and that's what he had done, until his father shoved him out of the way. "It's just a little seizure," he said. "Give her some space." Frank had stepped back, and now his mother was draped backward over his father's lap, the weight of her head sloping downward like some Renaissance painting of the Pietà. His father was weeping onto the gold fabric of his mother's silk blouse. His father kissed her cheek, saying, "Violet, my love." Those tears, that whimpering, burned something deep within him, like disgust. His mother, dressed in high-waisted slacks like Katharine Hepburn, tall and commanding, except when she was not, and the entire scene imprinted on Frank's brain as if he were a bird bonding with its mother, establishing trust, which was to say, he couldn't trust his mother not to do this, not to leave him, couldn't trust his father to do the right thing when she did, to not become emotional, weepy as a *woman,* which was to say, Frank couldn't quite trust anyone.

"Is that you?" his mother whispered, and he gently set her head on the floor, let Penny take over. His hands were trembling and difficult to control.

It seemed as if all he had done was blink, and suddenly a young woman with short black hair and large tortoiseshell glasses was asking him questions about his forehead. "Can you tell me what happened to your head?"

Frank felt the crusty mound beneath his fingers.

A man with a blond buzz cut was peeling open his mother's lids. "Has she been sick?" he asked. "There's blood on her lip. Is that from you? Is that hers? Did she bite her tongue?"

His mind shifted back to his father's voice, *a little seizure, give her some space,* words his parents never spoke again. But Frank grew up thinking his mother had epilepsy, assuming she'd outgrown it, but how had he come to that conclusion? He didn't remember being told this. He'd gone to school with a kid who had fits in class, and everyone screamed to put a stick in his mouth so he did not bite his tongue or swallow it, and Frank did not know, even now, if that was actually possible, but he did know that the kid was epileptic, and he believed his mother was, too.

Penny was saying, "No, no. The earthquake. Stitches. Cancer—she has lung cancer."

Frank snapped to. "What now?"

Then his mother opened her eyes and looked at him with recognition and clarity, instead of coming around slowly and confusedly the way she'd done all those years ago, not recognizing her own son's face.

She was full of life, thrusting herself upright, and shocking them all by swinging her glass at the EMT.

The man jumped back and swore, gripping his bloody chin.

"Son," his mother said, and he leaned in front of the EMT. She clutched his collar and her eyes widened in panic as if enough air might not come, but it did, and she locked her sights on him, heaving and heaving, searching for something, inhaling deeply. "I'm so . . . glad you're . . . Son, son, son, do you remember Ada?"

30

How fated it all seemed now.

When Violet first saw Ada Dupré in Arizona, they barely spoke to one another, but it was enough to leave an impression on Violet. Then Ada disappeared without a word, and others in the restaurant where they'd worked together were concerned, but Violet was not. She had a feeling she would see her again, and she looked at it all as an interesting beginning, the start of something bigger to come. Several months later she found Ada in a boxcar on a California-bound train. Violet was sixteen, Ada was nineteen, and Violet loved her from the moment Ada helped heave her up onto the moving train.

But before Ada, there was a woman named Carol and her three kids. Everything about what happened to Violet during her time with them would forever shape her life, and forever shape her relationship with Ada.

Violet had come upon the children playing on a rope swing hanging from a sycamore tree somewhere near the Nevada-Arizona border, without an adult in sight. Two girls and one boy, ages three to six, and all too small to push each other on the swing. Trying left them spinning in circles, the rope twisting upon itself. "Let me," Violet said, laughing, and that was the beginning of hours of playing with the children, who then held her hands and took her home to their mother, Carol, telling her they had found their own babysitter at the tree. Carol worked as a barmaid in a town so small it was referred to only as Town.

Caring for those children proved to be one of the stranger pleasures of Violet's life. They barely spoke, rather yipped and bounded around the yard and house, and none resembled the other, like a litter of puppies. But they all carried the same stunned eyes that peered at the world with confusion and fascination, and Violet could feel their emotions on her skin, and she understood they could feel hers, too. They sometimes placed a palm on her face, or crawled unbidden onto her lap and lay a cheek against her chest as if to listen to the heart that cared for them. She had hoped that the kindness she'd showed them would last long after she was gone.

Carol never showed them affection, at least none that Violet ever saw, and a feeling like danger drifted through the house like rats living inside the walls, but the feeling mostly came off of Carol's boyfriend, Eddie. Violet told herself that the children would turn out all right, even if she never saw them again. Wouldn't they always recall her washing their hair and clothes, handing them clean bowls of dumplings, playing patty-cake, and tucking them in with stories about mother bears protecting their cubs and what it was like to ride a train through a bayou?

If only they could somehow forget everything that happened on her last day, when Carol still hadn't paid Violet after two months, as she'd promised, and Violet threatened to leave. Carol's answer to that was to swing a broom handle at Violet's head. When Violet ducked, the handle hit the edge of a doorway and snapped in half, the part with the straw flew off, and the broom became two sharp spears. Violet snatched up the sharp pieces and pointed one at Carol, and the children screamed and ran across the room in horror. Violet was taller than everyone in that house, and Carol was already wary of her height and scars. When Violet reached her hand into Carol's pocket and retrieved five dollars and some change, the children gasped but made no move toward her, and Carol silently put up her hands and let the money go. Violet shoved her out of the way and walked out of the house with a broom piece in each hand like a warrior, her sea bag of belongings over a shoulder, and for the first time in her life she felt the breadth of her body and strength, even as she was anxious for the children.

Moments later on the empty road, still agitated, and vowing that no one would ever hurt her again, she heard someone running from behind. She turned in time to see Eddie coming straight for her. Just that fast he had hold of her hair and was swinging her like a flimsy rag to the ground.

Violet filled with rage. Red, murderous, blistering rage. Fresh in her mind was the stillborn girl she had buried in the desert. When the nameless preacher had pinned her down in Georgia, he was quiet, shushing, as if trying to soothe Violet out of noticing what he was taking from her, and Violet froze in shock, sickened by the scent of his aftershave. She was not about to let this happen again. She slung her fists and kicked her legs. She screamed and clawed, but was met with Eddie's fists and elbows, his weight crushing her chest. The harder she fought, the more strength Eddie seemed to gain, calling her a monster and a freak, telling her *he would show her, he would show her, he would show her,* and he might have been saying it still, but by the time he tore her underthings from her body, Violet had evaporated into the desert air. She could no longer hear or feel what was happening, though it would seem as if her eyes had dilated and taken it in. Years later she would discover that some part of her knew quite well what had happened. Her body had kept track and was tallying the score.

By the time Eddie was gone and Violet came face-to-face with the pain that was waiting for her, she was astounded to find herself alive. She lay face-down in the road, for hours it seemed, though it couldn't have been that long. When people approached, they walked around her. A woman spit in her hair. Was it Carol? A child threw a rock at her skull. Was it one

of Carol's whom she had looked after? Her lids gently fluttered open and closed, and the day grew quiet, only the buzz
of horseflies and cawing crows, and Violet never knew the an-
swers to those questions. The sun was setting at the end of the
road by the time Violet lifted herself on all fours. Droplets of
blood from her lip and nose created a series of circles on the
ground, deep red suns against a yellow-red sky that was the
desert sand, and Violet could taste what she was looking at,
iron and dust, and it arrested something in her soul. Beauty
could be stubborn, even in the face of pain, in the face of the
worst kind of grief. She didn't want to succumb to madness
and discipline the way her mother had. She didn't want to
shut out the beautiful and good, the exaltation of the child she
once was, sitting at the kitchen table in the farmhouse, moved
to tears by a beauty she didn't understand and might never
understand, no, Violet would not exchange all of that for the
simple fact of being alive. Being alive was not enough.

Eddie had taken the money. He'd broken her nose and
torn pages from her notebook just to spite her. The pages
blew over the road as Violet located her balance, steadying
the ground beneath her feet. She lifted her belongings to her
shoulder that seared with pain. The temperature had dropped,
and coupled with all she'd endured, her body shivered with
nausea, agony, and cold.

There was no one on the road to see her take that first step
in the darkened hour. No one to stop her, either. By the first
morning light and for days afterward, she soaked her body in
icy rivers and lakes, and the cold eased the pain between her
legs. The weeks passed, and the limp became a walk, and the
walk eventually became the stride of a pregnant, six-foot girl,
trying to make her way to Nestucca Beach.

Which was when she met Ada . . .

"Violet? *Violet?*"

A man she didn't recognize was lifting her, trying to take
her somewhere she had no intention of going. Her face felt
wet. Was it blood? Her eyes stung. Was it her broken nose?

By the time she grasped that she was on the living room floor, and that the man in question was an EMT, and that her damp face was covered in the sticky sweetness of lemonade, she had already swung her fist and split the man's chin with the glass in her hand.

Francisco.

"Son." She had never smelled cigarettes on him before, but she smelled cigarettes now, and through the gauzy membrane that hung between her and the rest of the world, she believed her son had only recently taken up smoking as a reaction to something new, and she recalled the sharp feel of smoke in her own throat, and the way that first long drag always left her feeling lightheaded and giddy, but maybe that had to do with all the laughing she and Ada were doing, blowing smoke rings around each other's heads and speaking French.

"Do you remember Ada?"

31

The *moment his* grandmother fell to the floor, Daniel whisked Dani into the kitchen, and from there, out the back door.

"Let's go see outside," he'd said, his voice a new one, a cheery sort of panic. He carried her around the yard on his hip, pointing to what he saw, naming things for her as if naming them gave them importance—daffodils, cherry blossoms, and the small garden buds pushing through the soil. He pointed to the ocean in the distance and told her that soon they would go to the beach and build a *grand château* out of sand, which reminded him of his grandmother, and he hugged Dani closer, feeling her tiny bones in his desperate grip, and carefully easing off. She smelled like peach shampoo.

His grandmother had been breathing when he'd run from the house with Dani. She was alive, and mumbling something to his father.

And now a siren, that awful wail that only ever meant something terrible had happened, followed by that moment of suspension, of not knowing if the rescue had come too late.

Dani's eyes were huge, the red lights reflecting in the dark brown. She startled at the last horn of the siren, and her bottom lip quivered. "It's OK," Daniel said, bouncing her on his hip. "See the ambulance? It's just an ambulance. Can you say *am-bu-lance?*"

Daniel shut his eyes, feeling stupid and helpless, saw his grandmother falling, saw himself leaping up with Dani and rushing away. Recalled the ambulance that arrived too late to save his grandfather.

Dani pointed, sniffled, and said *ambulance* in French.

"Yes, yes, the same in English." He wondered if she'd ever seen anyone taken away in an emergency. Did she witness her mother being arrested by the police? Maybe that was why her lip quivered at the lights and siren.

He had no way of knowing what she'd seen or been through in her short life, and the thought crushed him. He knew only what Arielle had told him when he'd visited her in jail. "She's a very good girl. A funny girl. And smart. She's quiet but knows everything, *everything*, she watches what you do, so be careful." Afterward it seemed a terrible omission for her not to say what Dani's favorite food was, or toy, or story, or how she liked to fall asleep. A terrible thing for him not to have asked. He decided it was simply who Arielle was, and he wondered how much of her mother Dani had in her, and whether more, or less, was better, or worse.

His daughter didn't have enough words in any language to tell him the things he wanted to know, which was equally hard to think about, because he was sure her tiny body carried the feelings of her experiences, good or bad, even if they never shaped into ideas that could be expressed through words.

He pointed to the swallows on the wires above. "Look. Those birds came from California, just like us." Dani grinned. There was no way to be sure how much she actually understood.

The EMTs carried his grandmother out on a gurney through the front door and wheeled her into the driveway where Daniel and Dani could see. His grandmother was propped up, coughing, gesturing something to Daniel's father, who was following them out. "I'm sorry," she told him. Daniel was glad he hadn't brought up the DNA test. He might never know what it meant, who these people were that he was somehow related to, and at this point it seemed not to matter.

They slid the gurney into the ambulance. His father looked

as if he were arguing with one of the EMTs before he hopped up and took a seat near his mother. Just before they shut the door, his father waved at Daniel.

His own mother rushed out the back of the house toward him with her purse and keys. "Jesus, what a homecoming!" She laughed in the way of someone losing her mind. She touched Dani's cheek, smiled at her before turning back to Daniel. "Don't worry. Your grandmother is OK. I mean. For now. I have to meet them at the hospital."

"Are you sure? What do you mean *for now?*"

His mother nodded. "Can I hold her for just a moment?" She put out her arms and Dani leaned into them without hesitation. "Oh, Daniel. She's light as a cat." His mother caressed his daughter's back, inhaled, and raised her eyebrows. "And what is that . . . peach shampoo?"

Dani leaned into his mother's shoulder, her small hand caressing his mother's back now, and Daniel's throat tightened. He told himself not to fall apart in front of his daughter, unless falling apart was what he was supposed to do. God, what did he know about any of this?

His mother was already wiping the tears from her own face, and Daniel wiped his. "We're a couple of softies," she said.

After a moment, Daniel asked, "What do you mean that Grand is OK for now?"

"She's ill, Daniel. She'd like to tell you about it herself. I don't think they will keep her for more than one night, or that she'll *let* them. I don't think it's that . . . I don't think it's time yet for her to go. She just fainted from complications."

Daniel took a moment to let that sink in. Everything about this day was off, as if the earth had tilted a fraction, enough for minutes to feel out of sync, but not entirely out of whack. "And what about her speaking French? It was like she had a stroke or something. But I mean, that was *real* French. What the hell?"

His mother shook her head. "She's a strangely gifted person. I have no idea. I asked your father and he acted like everyone *knew*. I can't make sense of either of them on the best of days."

She glanced at her car, the ocean, the house, as if unable to move. But she quickly switched gears, telling Dani a story about a white rabbit that lived in the garden, munching on their vegetables, and how it was becoming so fat that soon he wouldn't be able to crawl under the fence and they would have to wait and see on which side it got stuck. Her voice cracked every now and then, but Dani was giggling in a way Daniel had never seen. Did she understand what his mother was saying? His mother had such a beautiful voice. He'd never told her that, and he didn't know why.

Dani's laughter was contagious.

"Oh, Daniel," his mother said, meeting his eye.

The urge to call Macy washed over him. He wanted to pick up the phone and say, *You are not going to believe this day*, and have her laugh with him, parse it all out with him, make it funnier and stranger than it already was. He had the urge to call old friends in LA and tell them the same, except they weren't exactly friends anymore. Since he and Macy had split, his friends split, too, as if Daniel and Macy had gone through a divorce and their friends had been awarded to Macy. No one could believe Daniel would do such a thing, especially not to someone like Macy, and Daniel was pretty sure that one of his friends was already dating her.

"I'm sorry, I have to go." Daniel didn't know if she meant him or Dani. She handed his daughter back with a look of agony. "I won't be long." She kissed Dani on the cheek. She did the same with Daniel. "What should she call me?"

"Whatever you want."

"What is the informal of *grandmother* in French? Like *granny*."

"*Mamie*."

"Oh. I like that. *Mamie*. OK. *Mamie* will be back soon." She squeezed Dani's hand and hugged them both.

"Call me the second you know something," Daniel said.

"Of course." She turned and headed down the driveway.

"Mom?"

She stopped and looked back.

"You have a beautiful voice."

"What?"

"I don't know why I never told you that before."

His mother stared. "Well. I mean, OK. Thank you, Daniel, for telling me now." She nodded and continued on, her head slightly dropped, her hand cupping her mouth. They watched until she got into her car and drove away.

Beyond the garden was the forest's edge, and Daniel carried Dani down the short, narrow path that was covered with pine needles and led to his old wooden swing in the large spruce. He and his father had built it when Daniel was a boy, using thick braided rope and a sturdy hemlock plank. It had softened over the years, now the white-silver of driftwood.

"Let me try first," Daniel said, setting her down to the side. He bounced his full weight on the swing. "I'm going to make sure it's safe." It appeared that it was, because just like that, Daniel was swinging. "You have to stay back," he said, climbing higher. He must have spent hours on any given day doing this one simple thing, and it amazed him now how differently he saw the world as a grown man, how fractured his attention had become, how generally dissatisfied he felt, or had felt, before Dani showed up and started rearranging his thinking.

He leaned back and gazed at the bright blue openings in the canopy of trees. He smelled the spruce and the damp ground encrusted with needles, the salty breeze whistling through the branches.

Then he turned toward the house, the familiar view as seen through the trees. He used to come out here to the swing to get away from his parents, and would tell himself that he would never be like them, certainly never be like his father. He would create a different kind of life, a different kind of marriage. His children would never have to endure the refrain of phrases—*you always, you never, I'm so sick of this,* you're *sick of this*? And then the awkward aftermath of inching back into each other's affections, which was often done using Daniel. *Maybe we should plant some carrots next summer. How about we grab dinner out? Did you hear about the meteor shower? We should all come out at night and have a look. How about an ice cream at the Little Grocer? Looks like you could use a new mitt.*

Dani jumped up and down, pumping her arms in the air. "I do it, *please!*"

"Yes," he said. "You want to try?" He slowed to a stop. Dani nodded so hard the weight of her head sent her stumbling forward.

He helped her wiggle onto the seat. She gripped the ropes and swung her legs out of sync while he pushed, her face beaming. "*Plus fort!*" she yelled. Harder. She wanted to go higher.

She leaned forward and back in an attempt to pick up speed. "You're a daredevil," he said. "You do *not* get that from me."

"*Plus fort!*" she cried.

"OK!" Daniel pushed, though not as hard as she wanted. "We're going higher," he said. "*Eeeee,*" she squealed, and on they went, passing into the afternoon, waiting for good news to arrive.

32

V*iolet could go* days or weeks without hearing news about the war, without feeling the dark blanket of worry and despair. She could go weeks without speaking to another human being, and when the world belonged only to her, she hopped trains between towns, walked alone on forest trails, down rocky desert roads, and the only other person she had an awareness of was the child growing inside her. She didn't remember when she'd had her last monthly. Her breasts ached as they had before, and pushed against her small brassiere. When no one else was around, it was only Violet and the child and the trees, cacti, and frenzied birds. It was snakes sidewinding her path, coyotes yipping in the distance. Most of all it was the world at large, a vast and shifting landscape beneath an ever-changing sky that Violet studied and felt in her skin, the churning patterns and palettes as alive as Violet walking the earth. She often stopped to translate what she saw into abstract renderings in her notebook, and because she had only graphite pencils, she wrote in the names of the colors where colors should be. Sage, blood orange, red desert rock, amethyst, peach, gold, and milky blue, rolling sideways off her tongue in the shade of a mesquite tree while she chewed the tree's pods, and then switched to reading a dime-store paperback she'd acquired along the way, or again, the novel James had given her, feeling luckier than the Joads making their way in the West, and more like the turtle in the story that had been flipped and righted itself. She didn't know how to feel about Rose of Sharon and her stillborn baby.

Violet had stolen a booklet on foraging in the Sonoran Desert from a train station news rack and studied how to follow the bees and butterflies. In between filching or bartering for bread and apples and cheese, she sucked on flowers and cactus fruits for free. The chuparosa was her favorite, with its tiny red blossoms filled with nectar that was sweet as sugar. She bit down hard and the unmistakable flavor of cucumber was released.

She stumbled into town after town, each one with the strange feel of the last, as if she was constantly arriving in a foreign land and needed to calculate how these people lived. She read the headlines at newsstands and observed the collective strain playing out in the eyes and mouths of strangers, which caused her own struggle to rise up and loom larger in her mind again, a shock after time spent forgetting, reading beneath a tree or scooping out the jelly meat of cactus flowers while butterflies rested on her shoulders and head. Towns were where she saw herself through the eyes of other people, and it seemed as if the world was put together by a series of dark curtains. No sooner did she pull one back to see where she was headed than another dropped down to take its place.

There came the day when she'd caught a boxcar headed south, and her plan was to hop off at the next junction for a northbound train. But the nearest stop turned out to be seventy-five miles farther south, and instead of arriving in California, Violet landed in another Arizona train station.

She was lightheaded with hunger when she climbed out of the shadows of the train, blasted by the sun ricocheting off buildings, cars, and gravel. The newsstand in the station was filled with stories about an invasion. At first Violet thought that the United States was under siege by the Germans or Japanese. She skimmed each paper and found that it was the Allies who had invaded France to fight the Germans. There were only a few people in the station, but each face carried the same weary look of fear.

In the restroom, near the sink, an advertisement was taped to the wall, a want ad for a restaurant. Violet ran her finger along the tiny print, noting the dirt under her nail.

WANTED

Single women of good moral character between
the ages of 18 and 30. Minimum 8th grade education.
Room and board, competitive wages, plus tips.

Violet studied her reflection. The juice from aloe leaves had protected her skin against the sun and dry air, but creases of dirt lined her eyes and forehead. She was deeply tanned and looked like her mother, eyes too old for the body that housed them, vacant behind a troubled stare. She forced a smile and recognized her father's face in her own. *It's a dandy, Violet!* And then a wider smile, and saw her sister Em.

Violet was tall enough to pass for eighteen.

For the first time since leaving home, she would steal more than one thing in a single day. Up until now she had limited herself. One apple, one loaf of bread, or one bar of soap. It was a way to keep penitent, even as it made no sense. But today, as she wandered through town looking for a victory garden where she might filch some greens or a tomato, her eyes filled with the vibrant colors all around—terracotta, turquoise, and red, and taking them in was a different kind of sustenance that filled her. In the middle of so much color stood a plain white house with a long front porch and dormer windows. It was set farther back from the street than the other houses, and nearly identical to the farmhouse of her childhood. Violet stared, feeling farther from home than ever. For some reason she recalled her mother and father taking her into town to see *City Lights* starring Charlie Chaplin. They had laughed in fits for days afterward. Her father imitated Chaplin, plowing behind their mule Dolly with an exaggerated side-to-side gait, pretending that Violet and her mother weren't watching from the shade of the lilacs at the side of the house, doubled over in laughter at his antics.

A flapping clothesline in the backyard of the white house caught Violet's eye. Long-sleeved dresses, children's pajamas, and kitchen cloths. Violet slipped onto the property in broad daylight and helped herself to a periwinkle dress, a pair of underthings, stockings, and a baby blanket that would make a good pillow on the road. They were still damp when she stuffed them into her bag.

She returned to the bathroom at the train station, stripped off her clothes, and washed her body and hair at the sink with her stolen bar of Swan soap, *Baby-mild for everything, and floats in the tub!* A woman entered, gasped, and bustled right out. Violet hurried, twisting her damp hair back into a bun, using a yellow ribbon she found in the trash days before. By the time she changed into the periwinkle dress and stockings, her hair was nearly dry from the heat. She wiped her shoes down, too, and felt clean all over, walking in stockings, everything giving rise to confidence, if not an appearance of moral character. She hid her belongings beneath the porch of an abandoned shack, plucked sprigs of wild lavender, and rubbed their oil on her temples and wrists and neck.

"What happened to your hand?" the shift manager, Dorothy, asked during the interview at the Shepard Inn. Violet's hand was the only place her scars were visible.

"I was burned in a house fire trying to save my sister."

Dorothy's eyes widened behind greasy glasses. "You *saved* your sister?"

"Yes. Thank heavens. Not a scratch on her." Violet glanced at her arm covered by her sleeve. The smell of roasted chicken made her woozy. "A small sacrifice."

"Well then. A young woman unafraid in the world is exactly

the kind we're looking for." Dorothy was, however, concerned about Violet's unseemly hand.

Violet glanced around the restaurant, gauging who was doing what. A man and a woman stood near the entrance, apparently waiting for someone to greet them. "Perhaps I could wear a pair of white gloves and seat the customers when they come in."

Dorothy reared back, impressed. "I like your style. Where did you say you were from?"

"Originally, Georgia. But my family moved west when my father took a job with the railroad. I've been living out this way for about six months now. I saw your ad and took the train into town today." It was as if she had taken on the voice and demeanor of a character in one of the books she was reading. A grown woman in the West, full of backbone and spunk.

"And how old are you? You're awfully tall."

"Yes, well, my parents are both quite tall. I turned eighteen in April."

"And no marriage proposals yet?" It was a serious question, though Violet had to control her laugh.

"No, ma'am. I'd like to work and help my family first before I commit to starting a family of my own."

"Well. Would that there were more young women like you, Miss Swan."

The contract stated that Violet would work ten-hour shifts, six days a week, and she would have a dorm mother to monitor that she was in her room by 10 p.m., no matter that an eighteen-year-old was a grown and legal adult woman.

Violet swallowed a sour taste in the back of her throat. She had enjoyed her freedom, but when she imagined sleeping in a bed with clean, stiff linens, washing her hair with shampoo, and getting plenty to eat, her eyes began to well. She looked down as she signed the form. "Allergies," she said. "These desert blooms."

She began work three hours later.

The uniforms were long black dresses with elaborate white aprons, like costumes. Violet agreed to smile no matter her mood. "Most of the girls practice in front of the mirror to be sure it doesn't appear forced," Dorothy told her. "You'll get the hang of it. And frankly, we expect you'll be happy here. These girls are thrilled to be out on their own, making more money than their mothers ever dreamed of."

It appeared to be true. Most of the women did seem to be enjoying themselves, their smiles genuine, if well-practiced, expressions of contentment. Violet watched the line of them smiling as they entered the dining area with plates stacked with food. Huge, matching grins, starched aprons covering their torsos, as if they themselves were the display of delicate desserts. But there was one woman, whose name tag read *Ada Dupré*, who repeatedly turned her head, so that her smile could slide off her face as if to take a rest. She was beautiful to look at: olive skin with a smattering of freckles, glass-green eyes, and lips naturally bright red. Violet knew they were natural because cosmetics were forbidden. Her hair was practically yellow, fresh and bright as a child's before age dulled the sheen. The more attention men paid to Ada, the more she sidestepped along. But Violet knew how the men felt. She had a kind of crush on Ada herself, a pull in her direction in a way she'd never felt before.

She and Ada passed each other in the narrow galley one day, and Violet introduced herself. Her forehead filled with heat and perspiration.

"And a pleasure to meet you, too," Ada said, unconvincingly. She turned and called to one of the cooks about an order, and Violet stood in awkward silence before walking away. Ada wasn't being rude. The way she acted came from someplace else, and though Violet didn't claim to understand what it was, she admired it just the same.

Ada's *r*'s dropped off the way Violet's mother's *r*'s did. The way Violet's must have dropped off, too, though she'd never given it any thought. She never spoke with Ada at work again, but a couple of times Ada smiled right at her as if something was understood between them. One month later, Ada didn't show up for her shift. Thirty minutes later, Dorothy came through the restaurant in a huff, saying Ada's dorm room was cleared out. "The damn girl ran off without warning."

The men in the kitchen touched Violet's waist as they squeezed past, often when she arrived for work through the kitchen door. She gritted her teeth and moved on. Sometimes male customers brushed a hand across her backside when she seated them, and when she took their coats, and when she leaned across to place menus on the table. She flinched and breathed through her nose, and the smile never left her face. She thought of James telling her she needed to pursue what she'd started. She thought of cliffs breaking off into the sea. Her smile was her currency, her ticket to the Pacific Northwest.

Within a week of starting work there, she had saved enough of her tips to purchase a small palette of paints by mail, arriving within days from Phoenix. After that, she woke each day at dawn and painted near the small dorm window in the light of the rising sun. She studied patterns of color. Not only what she saw and how to re-create it on paper, but also the mystery of how each shade made her feel.

After two months, Violet had collected four paychecks and filled several sketchbooks with experiments, as she worked her way toward an expression she had an instinct for, though not yet the skill. She might have endured the job a while longer, but after keeping an eye out for a doctor in town, someone who might help her situation, Violet had found no such person or office. In a town that size she didn't dare go asking. She suspected Dorothy would withhold her pay for lying. Violet was starting to show. Dorothy inquired about the "fullness in her hips." Violet promised to cut back on the pies.

She washed the periwinkle dress, underthings, and stockings she'd stolen from the line. She placed the clean, folded clothes on the front porch of the white farmhouse, and she whispered for forgiveness from the baby whose blanket she decided to keep.

A toddler peered out the front window, and Violet raised her hand in greeting. She was drawn to his wide, curious eyes and his small hand, waving. A woman appeared behind him, and the child was startled by the commotion, as was Violet, and then the front door swung open and the woman was yelling, "*Hey!*"

Violet ran and never looked back.

She stepped into a small dress shop and purchased a loose day-dress with a drawstring at the waist. The soft cotton print had penny-size circles of sky blue, white, and gray. The small buttons all the way down the front were violet. It was the prettiest dress she'd ever owned. She wore it out of the store and next went into a shoe store, where she bought a sturdy pair of leather ankle boots with laces, and she wore those out of the store, too. At the grocery she purchased two loaves of bread, two jars of blackberry jam, several apples, a twine of jerky, and a large bottle of root beer. And then she hopped a boxcar on the five o'clock train headed northwest for California. When it stopped after thirty-five miles, she hopped off and found another, but not until the next day. It wasn't always easy. The cars were often occupied by men in varying stages of drunkenness, and the cash she was carrying made her nervous. She fell asleep for several hours in the shade of an abandoned mining shed along the tracks.

It was two more weeks before Violet reached Los Angeles. A series of unavailable trains, wrong turns, and draining blisters on her heels and toes led her to eventually purchase a proper train ticket for the remaining fifty miles. In the hours of waiting, she washed her dress in the station bathroom, which dried quickly in the arid heat. She washed herself with a new bar of soap and boarded the train like everyone else.

Sitting near the window, she stared out at straw-colored hills and enormous white clouds and then watched her own reflection in the window. Her image was crisp in the light, as if she were looking in an actual mirror. Here was a woman with her hair pulled back, her face narrower, perhaps a little longer than it used to be, lips fuller than before. The neckline of her pretty patterned dress dipped along the bottom of the frame. Just like that, Violet had gone from an orphaned child to a grown woman on a train.

She arrived in downtown Los Angeles, weary and sore, her sea bag heavier than ever, and was shocked at how well-dressed everyone appeared. Men in fine suits and shined shoes, women wearing what Violet would call cocktail dresses, with green satin heels, and it wasn't even noon.

At a newsstand, she waited for customers to leave so she could strike up a conversation with the man working there. She flipped through a *Vogue* magazine. A full-page ad for Camel cigarettes had an illustration of a woman looking into a microscope, searching for flaws in the steel in a munitions factory. After a day's work on the war effort, she'd "earned the pleasure" of the "fragrant, blue-swirling smoke" of a Camel, as if the war were glamorous, exciting, full of possibilities.

"Are you going to buy that?" the man asked, not unkindly. There was no one else around.

Violet returned it to the rack. "Sorry. I'm wondering if you might have the name of a doctor, for . . . lady things. Lady . . . problems?"

To her surprise, the man nodded, nudged his glasses higher on his nose, and said, "Let me find a pen," as if he were asked this question every day. A radio was playing inside his stall. A baseball game full of cheering instead of news of the world, until someone mentioned Joe DiMaggio signing up last year to fight the war. Violet listened to the announcer through the crackling reception, while the man behind the counter searched for a piece of paper for his pen. His forthrightness about the situation put Violet at ease. As did the game. It reminded her of her father.

The man offered Violet a list of three names and addresses. "Go ahead and take the magazine," he said. "Don't worry about it."

"Oh, no," she said, but he had already come around and handed it to her.

She was at once grateful for his kindness and embarrassed by his charity. She thanked him several times, felt like hugging him, but restrained herself. She shook his hand and thanked him again.

When she walked away a wave of suspicion came over her. It all seemed too good to be true. But there had been no reason for her skepticism. The first doctor she visited, a haggard-looking bald-headed man with wire-frame glasses, took her in without an appointment. His eyes were made smaller by the spectacles, and his breath stank of old cigars, but he was clear on why she was there, and asked when her last monthly was. She gave him her best guess, and he frowned. "I can't help you, darling." He said nothing more after that, and left her standing on the black linoleum in the baby-blue room.

Violet stumbled outside and leaned against a prickly palm tree with fronds as high above her head as a hilltop. The air smelled like car exhaust. She wished the doctor hadn't called her darling.

The next doctor on the list was across town on the west side, a woman, whose receptionist told Violet on the phone that she couldn't see the doctor until the next day. Violet took the appointment and slowly made her way across town.

It was not until she smelled bacon and coffee that she stopped and saw her reflection in a restaurant window. She was larger and rounder than she'd realized. Perhaps the gradual change had made it less noticeable, or the view looking down was not as apparent as the view from the side. She was overcome with bone-deep exhaustion. All she wanted in the world was to rest in a soft bed and drink a cold glass of water. When she looked up and saw that the restaurant was actually the first floor of a hotel, she walked in and asked for a room.

It wasn't cheap, but it was worth every nickel. White tiled floors and walls, large windows with a view of a canyon and palm trees and sky.

Violet peeled off her clothes and shoes, peeled away the miles and days and months and years, as she bathed in a tub filled with complimentary bubbles. She floated in the hot water, dazed by comfort, as she flipped through the *Vogue* like a lady of finer means. An article by a woman named Dorothy Parker caught her attention, about soldiers coming home from the war. They were not the same men they were before they went away. These men had engaged in horrors that the rest of us would never know, and we needed to keep in mind that the confidants with whom they shared such horrors, their band of brothers, these men who had either witnessed the atrocities alongside them or died trying to overcome them, *they* were the ones, both living and dead, to whom the returning men would forever feel closest. Not their wives. "Say goodbye to the men you used to know."

The idea of this was as theoretical to Violet as it was an absolute truth. Somewhere in the world there was a man whom Violet had never met, a man fighting in the war this minute while she soaked in a tub, the mound of her belly full with another man's child, breaching above the bubbles. This fighting man would become Violet's husband, and he would have lived through dreadful things, and he would carry those things inside his body for the rest of his life, in the same way Violet would carry hers.

When she finished her bath, she laundered her clothing and hung the pieces around the room to dry. She opened the window for a breeze, letting the sheer drapes rise and fall while she slept naked between the crisp sheets.

The following morning she met with the woman doctor, who had bright red hair and a thick Scottish accent. She took one look at Violet, asked the date of her last monthly, and mentioned that there was a home that would likely take her and her baby in.

Another sidewalk beneath a palm. Another sting of defeat.

Violet calculated a better date for her last monthly before she met the third doctor, a short, soft-spoken man wearing a suit beneath his white coat. He was located down the street from the second. After a three-hour wait, he looked at the form she had filled out, and then he looked at her. He seemed skeptical of her claims. He tapped his chin as if thinking through his next move. "I need to examine you," he said, with such authority that Violet couldn't find her way to say no. "You need to pay up front." Violet nodded through her sudden terror.

She trembled on the examining table, though she could see that he was kind and gentle in his touch. He apologized for palpating her stomach and for sliding his hand inside of her, which made Violet yelp, not with pain but dread. No matter what he said to put her at ease, Violet couldn't stop shivering. She couldn't stop tears from seeping at the corners of her eyes. When he told her to please sit up and draped a cloth to cover her, he patted her knee, and she wiped her eyes briskly. "I'm sorry," he said. "You must have miscalculated. I can't help you, not when you're this far gone. You understand that if you were to have the child now, it would likely survive. It's a baby, nearly ready to be born."

He spoke to her as if she herself were a child, and of course she was. She nodded like a good girl.

He wrote down the name of a charity where she might be able to stay for the rest of her term if she was willing to give the child up for adoption. He handed back her money.

Perhaps it would have been the better thing to do, to stay in one place and give the child away and move on after that. But Violet could not stay still. She didn't understand her desire to keep moving, but the need overwhelmed her, drove her onward. With everything she had endured, this was one thing that she would not forsake.

She stuffed the money and the address in her sea bag, letting loose a whiff of paint from inside the bag, as if to remind her who she was and where she was meant to go. "Thank you," she whispered, and was again outside beneath the blinding sun. For hours afterward she continued to feel the doctor's hands.

She wandered another sidewalk in the heat of the day, her ears filling with noise. The entire city seemed to be moving at once, like ants, each movement a part to keep it whole. Even so, she looked the world over, fanning palms, lemon trees, single houses the size of ten back home and the color of worn, pale stones, with windows framed in black iron. Chartreuse bougainvillea arched over doorways. Eucalyptus trembled with steel-blue leaves like coins in the breeze. It was beautiful here, stunningly so.

Violet walked on until a different kind of glint caught her eye. A gold band on the sidewalk, reflecting in the sun. It was fake, a child's cheap toy, but she slipped it on the ring finger of her left hand with the thought that other people would feel better if she wore it. She considered the man she didn't know yet, fighting in the war. "Be careful," she whispered, and wondered if he might be sleeping now on the other side of the world, and if the sound of her voice might have slipped into his dreams.

She returned to the hotel and fell asleep for twelve hours. She woke and ate bread and ham and two oranges, until her fingers and the entire room smelled of citrus. She used the bathroom and wandered back to bed, thinking, *Just one more hour*. But one hour became two, and two hours turned into three days. The bill when she checked out took nearly all of her money.

Days later, with blisters from her boots, she waited behind a maple tree with her eye on an empty boxcar north of San Francisco. It was on its way to Oregon. The pleasant smells of the hotel room were long gone, replaced by sharp odors that lifted from her body in the breeze.

A storm was moving in, and if Violet didn't get on this train, she would spend another night in the dark and dampened shadows of the station. She waited for the whistle to signal the train's departure before she felt safe enough to come out and hop aboard. In the waiting, her life felt small in the best way, basic, in search of food and shelter like all living things. She pondered rivulets of rain on a fern, and drew shapes inside her head. The world at large seemed set on destroying itself while Violet considered what a mountain would look like defined by perfectly straight lines. Would it still set the heart to a furious beat, throw one's breath off rhythm the way it did hers when she imagined it inside her head? The feeling seeped across her chest in the form of joy, though lately she'd begun to cry without warning or clear cause. Her mother often wept when she was pregnant with Em. Tears dribbled past her smiling cheeks and laughter, which only added to the mystery of her emotions. How could her mother be feeling so many opposing things at once? Her father would hold her mother and tell her to remember how it was when she was carrying Violet. "It's too much love for one person to contain for too long a time." And that was how they knew that the baby would be coming soon.

This morning's newspapers, with their daily list of the town's dead, had caught Violet's eye. It was her birthday. She was sixteen years old today.

The whistle blew and the train began to roll. Violet came out from behind the tree and was trotting at the same pace as the train. Her breath was wispy and thin as she picked up speed. She felt larger than the day before, and was unsure how best to hop on, huffing and grunting louder than she meant to, and still the sounds released with every step.

And then a face appeared in the open door of the boxcar, a woman with a yellow scarf around yellow hair, dressed like a man in a blue button-down shirt and dungarees and leather boots. She scooted to the edge of the train car, jumped off, and ran straight for Violet. It was Ada Dupré.

Violet raised a hand and screamed, afraid that Ada was about to push her down. But Ada gripped her arm. "I can help, but you're going to have to give it all you've got, and if you don't make it fast, everything I own is going north without me."

Violet ran faster with Ada's encouragement, feeling an extra dose of strength as she gripped the edge of the sliding door and threw her sea bag inside. She leaped upward in the same moment she was shoved from behind. Her body rolled awkwardly across the metal bed, and she quickly sat up in disbelief.

The baby thrashed inside her, its angular bones poking beneath the fabric of Violet's dress. She caught a breath for both of them, holding her middle, while Ada sprung onto the train effortlessly, like a dance she had performed a thousand times.

"I'm Ada from New Orleans," she said.

"I know who you are. I'm Violet from Georgia. You don't recognize me?"

Ada studied her. "Where do I know you?"

"Arizona. The Shepard Inn."

"Oh, Lord. *That* place. You were an indentured servant too?"

Violet laughed. "For two months. I couldn't exactly waddle my moral character around after that."

Ada smiled. "I'm sorry I didn't remember you. I do now that you mention it. I kept my head down most of the time, just trying to *smile* through another day. And anyway, I guess you look a little different now."

In the silence Violet began to worry about nothing in particular and everything at once. She didn't know Ada and had learned not to trust people. She looked down at the ring on her finger.

"This is a fake," she said. "I don't have anything of worth."

"I see," Ada said. "Thank you for telling me. I was under the impression that you were rich."

Violet laughed nervously. "No, I just mean it's . . . never mind."

"My Lord," Ada said. Violet was reminded that she didn't pronounce her *r*'s. "Do I look like a thief?"

Was this a trick question? "No," Violet said. It was an honest answer. Ada didn't look anything like a thief. The bright yellow of her head against the constellation of glass-green eyes and freckles, the denim blue of her faded clothes, and her rich red lips made her look like a painting of a woman, too remarkable to be real.

"How old are you?" Violet asked.

"Nineteen. How old are you?"

"Sixteen. I lied to Dorothy, obviously."

"Everyone lies to Dorothy."

"Today is my birthday."

"Oh!" Ada leaned back. "Happy birthday, Violet. I would have taken you for older, though. And I don't just mean your, you know, condition."

"Everyone does."

"Well, never mind all that." Ada clapped her hands. "*Joyeux anniversaire!*"

Violet cocked her head.

Ada retrieved something fragile from what appeared to be a sugar sack. It was wrapped in a faded tea towel, frayed along the hem. She peeled back the corners and held up a large square of cornbread. "Happy birthday," she said. "It means happy birthday in French. Now break off a piece."

Violet gazed at the bread. "How do you know French?"

"It's my mother tongue. Really, what my mother and I spoke together. She died three years ago."

"Oh. I'm sorry."

"You look like you've lost someone, too."

Violet nodded. "My father and sister. And I guess my mother, but she's not dead. Just . . . lost."

Ada lifted the cornbread. "Then I'm sorry for you, too. Here. Don't be shy."

The smell of cornbread made the baby kick. Violet reached for the bread, choked back tears, and thanked her.

"Was your mother from France?" Violet asked.

Ada shook her head. "Her people came down from way up north, French Canadians."

Violet swallowed and felt the baby calm. "And how do you say happy birthday again?"

Ada repeated the phrase slowly, and Violet rolled it around inside her mouth with sticky crumbs. Ada corrected her several times until Violet got it right, and when she did, it felt like the most beautiful thing she'd ever said, words so soft and round lifting from her lips.

"What happened to you?" Ada asked, pointing to Violet's arm and leg.

"A fire. In my house when I was a kid."

"You're still a kid."

Violet chewed and looked away, embarrassed. Someone her age should not look like this, should not be a hobo on a train, should not be away from her mother, her home, and school.

"I guess," Violet said.

"Did anyone die in the fire?"

Violet lay her arm across her middle. "My father and sister. And our neighbor, Mr. Morgan."

"But you're alive."

Violet glanced at the ochre-colored hills, the rows of olive trees with their thin, silvery underleaves sparking the sunlight. Green spikes of cypress shot upward like candles whose tips glowed with the faintest orange from the sun so low in the sky. Maybe because it was her birthday, or maybe it was the kindness she'd been shown, either way, the gentleness of the moment reminded her of the early years of her childhood when she was happy and safe, the days before anything had gone wrong.

"Well, here we are," Ada said.

"Here we are," Violet said, aware of the storm closing in. "Sometimes it feels like I'm carrying an entire sea in here, like the tides pulling back and forth. I can feel that storm out there in a way I couldn't before, I mean, when it was just me." She looked down at her belly.

"Who put that baby in there?" Ada asked, and Violet looked up in a rush of anger that shocked her. The question seemed to have been asked the right way.

"A man I despised."

Ada pointed to Violet's ring. "Is that his?"

Violet shook her head. "It's just a piece of junk I found. Makes other people feel better when I have it on."

"Not me," Ada said. "Go ahead and throw it from the train."

Violet smiled. She pulled on the ring, but it wouldn't budge. "My finger's swollen. I can't get it off."

"When are you due?"

"I don't exactly know."

"Must be soon. You're big as a shed." Ada smiled.

Violet smiled in return. "I suppose I am."

"Don't have that baby on this train," Ada said.

"I'd rather not if I can help it."

"Where are you headed?"

"Portland, I guess. And then I'll need to make my way to the ocean."

"The ocean . . ."

Violet thought of the line from *The Grapes of Wrath* about the "high coast mountains" and "gray clouds coming in off the ocean." Was this the end or the beginning? She supposed it would always be a bit of both.

"I'm hoping to stay."

"What are you going to do with that baby?"

Did Violet already know? She thought she did. But she was thinking of the tiny girl left behind in the desert and was paralyzed by shame. If only she had clawed out the eyes of the oily preacher when he'd leaned her back on the sofa and slipped himself beneath her dress. If only she had screamed for her mother or old Annie Burke instead of going stiff and quiet as a deer. She knew that none of that mattered, but she still thought it. She knew that a woman could fight as hard as her body could throw a punch and claw to get away. She could scream as loud as was humanly possible and it would still make no difference. "I don't know. Or I think I do, but can't say."

"I understand."

"What about you?" Violet asked. "Where are you headed?"

"Portland. My cousins live there, Ann and Marie, sisters who work in the shipyard. They're the only family I have left. They say there's all kinds of work for women if you're interested."

Violet sat at attention.

"I hear they can't make things fast enough at the iron works and are always looking for help. There's a lot of talk up there about workers' rights. Something called Industrial Workers of the World. They're all about women's rights, too. Like contraception, for starters. I know you didn't mean to have that baby. That's not what I'm getting at."

"I know what you're getting at."

Ada pulled the pamphlet from a duffel and handed it to Violet. "Marie sent me this. She calls herself a Wobbly. Part of this outfit. I'm thinking of joining. You can read, can't you?"

Violet laughed. Of course she could read, but then her face fell because she knew how she appeared to the outside world. And how to explain that what she saw and felt on the inside was something completely different? Inside was a girl with a mother who offered Violet her attention and affection, gave her the gift of reading and writing before she was old enough for school. Inside was a girl with a father who bought her books he could hardly afford, taught her how phonographs worked, and sang songs of love and happiness and the joys of coming home. Inside was a girl with a perfect little sister whom Violet often rocked to sleep. Inside was six-year-old Violet who had never been burned, and held within her all the love and instincts of an artist and a mother toward all living things.

"Ann and Marie live in a place called Vanport," Ada said.

"The rent is cheap. You can put away some money. And you don't have to smile or dress like a meringue pie. It sits real low near the river, which I think I'll like. Kind of swampy. My cousins say it reminds them of home."

Violet thought of the drawings in her sea bag, the swamps, the stringy cypresses with claws for trunks. She thought of how it felt to look upon the scenery from a proper and comfortable seat on a train.

The storm was close enough to see the rain and sunshine at once, and the air took on a silver sheen, filling with the scent of fresh, green earth. "That's the devil beating his wife," Ada said, pointing to the mix of rain and sun, and Violet smiled, thinking of her mother saying the same all those years ago, before the devil became a real and haunting presence that lived in their house, and to whom her mother spoke just as often as she pleaded with God to make him go away. Shortly before the anniversary of the house fire, the Japanese bombed Pearl Harbor, and Violet's mother lost another layer of good sense. She was worse than Violet had ever seen. "Don't you *see*?" she said, coming for Violet. "Now these people have been burned alive in Pearl Harbor." Her mother struck her across the face. It was the first time, but wouldn't be the last. She was swept away by a feverish rage until Annie Burke came running in and calmed her with the prophets, and dabbed mint oil on her temples. In this way, Violet truly loved Annie, mean as she was, because Annie and her small country church had taken them in when the town turned against them for Violet's father having had an illegal still in the cellar that killed a good and decent man who'd lived *his* life following the law. Not to mention having killed an innocent child, too.

Violet finished the cornbread. She and Ada rocked in silence to the rhythm of the train. They scooted out of the way of the door, into the shadows, and Violet tried to ignore the wafts of urine and rot as the air stirred the corners.

After a time her body jerked, and she realized she'd fallen asleep sitting up.

"Here," Ada said. She pulled her bedroll toward Violet. "Lay your head down and I'll tell you a story."

Violet leaned over and felt the heat of the boxcar on her back, a pleasing, soothing warmth.

"My mother's name was Sarah Dupré, and I loved her more than God."

In the weeks that followed, Violet and Ada hopped on and off five more trains before arriving in Portland, and during that time Ada would offer Violet a thousand comforts, but the one Violet would hold most dear for the rest of her life was the way Ada helped her sleep by telling her stories of New Orleans, and of her mother, brothers, and friends, her singsong voice slipping in and out of French, the delicate sound evoking fairy tales and children.

33

*D*_{ani} *looked like* Little Red Riding Hood skipping around outside. The air had cooled in the woods, and Daniel had gone into the house for her red raincoat with the lining. For over an hour now she'd been taking turns running between the trees, into the yard, and back onto the swing, where she asked to be pushed higher and higher. Daniel checked his phone frequently, but there was nothing yet from his mom.

Then, from the corner of his eye he saw a figure lumbering up the driveway toward the backyard. A woman with a cast on her foot, limping with a cane. Her bright, wavy hair hung past her shoulders and flipped around her head with the breeze. She was wearing a long cream-colored sweater and leather ankle boots, and carrying what appeared to be a stack of books.

"Anyone home?" she called out.

Daniel recognized her as Quincy from the bookstore. "Back here!" He stepped into the clearing and waved.

"Oh!" She hobbled toward them.

"*Plus fort!*" Dani said from the swing. Daniel rushed back and gave her a push, and she giggled twice as hard, perhaps for the sake of an audience, but no matter, Daniel could barely stand what the sound of that miniature giggle did to his heart.

Now Quincy was laughing, too. She stopped within several feet of them and looked from one to the other. "Hi. I don't know if you remember me."

"Quincy. Of course I do." Daniel reached to shake her

hand, but she was holding the cane in her right hand, and when she lifted it, Daniel shook it instead, which gave them both a laugh. The books in her hand were for children.

Daniel was overcome with shyness, as if Quincy was a stranger and he was fifteen years old. They'd never spoken outside the store, and so here, especially with Dani, the interaction felt personal and strange. A ray of sun caught the necklace at her throat, a series of gray glass stones. Above them, her smoky gray eyes fixed on the two of them, one then the other.

She held up the stack. "I heard there was a little one around."

"How the heck did you hear such a thing so fast?"

Dani spotted the books. "Stop, stop!" She kicked and Daniel grabbed the rope and slowed her down. She wriggled off the swing.

"Small town," Quincy said.

"I'll say," Daniel said. "Dang."

"Dang," Dani said.

Quincy and Daniel eyed each other with a grin.

"I got a call from Violet. She asked me to come over."

"She *what*? When? She's at the hospital . . ."

"I know. She called me from your dad's cell phone. Her voice was pretty hoarse. She said, 'I'm on Francisco's cell in an ambulance, but don't worry,' she says, 'I would like it very much if you could take some books to the house for my great-granddaughter. As a favor to me. She's three.'"

Daniel shook his head. He stopped and pinched his nose between his eyes, then dropped his hand. "Thank you. I don't know what to say. This is Dani. My daughter. Her English isn't great."

"My pleasure. And that's the second odd thing I've heard today."

"It's a long story."

"Three years old," Quincy said, as if it were something particularly special.

Daniel nodded.

After a strained pause, Quincy gave him a knowing look. "Your grandmother is like no one I've ever met."

"She's definitely one of a kind. She fainted in the living room. I don't know if she told you anything else . . ."

"No, not just now, I mean."

"Well." Daniel didn't quite follow. "My mother thinks she's going to be OK. She's ill, she said. I don't yet know what that means."

Quincy glanced at the ground, then toward the ocean. "I'm sorry. She's one of my favorite people in this town. Or, I mean, any town with any people."

"I didn't realize you two knew each other that well."

Dani stepped close to Quincy and stared at the books.

"Oh . . . yes, I brought these for you. Some favorites of mine — Seuss, Silverstein, Sendak . . ."

"All the S's," Daniel said.

"Yesssssss."

Daniel could feel the enormity of his grin and tried to temper it. "That is really so generous of you." He glanced at her left hand and didn't see a ring. "Dani," he said, crouching, "this is Quincy. She brought you some books. Can you say thank you?"

"No."

"*No?*"

Dani shook her head.

Daniel tried not to laugh. "Why not?"

"I don't know."

Daniel smiled. "I think she's just trying out words. Is that a thing? I don't really know what I'm doing."

"I think it is. I'm not a mother, but I'm around kids in the store all the time."

"Thank you," Dani said.

"Ha. You're very welcome, Dani." Quincy flashed a smile at Daniel. "Would you like to sit on the grass and have a look with me?" Quincy summoned Dani to the yard where the view of the ocean was clearest. "Look at this. Look. At. This." She lowered herself onto the lawn, and Dani immediately crawled onto her lap.

It was still early, and the day already so many kinds of strange, and with so many hours still to go. "'Once there was a tree,'" Quincy read, and Daniel sat down beside her.

34

Violet *had handed* back Francisco's phone. "Thank you." Her voice was so hoarse it was barely a whisper. "Quincy said she'd take some books over. I can't bear for them to be at the house alone. And all because of me."

"Sorry for what, Mom?" Francisco asked.

"Sorry?"

"You said you were sorry when they put you in the ambulance, but for what? Fainting? Because that's just silly."

"No, I don't think so."

"You asked me if I remembered Ada. Do you remember saying any of this?"

Violet felt a surge of life at the mention of her friend. "It's been years since we spoke of her."

"I had the feeling you didn't want anyone to mention her. I thought it upset you."

"Yes. I suppose it did, it does, to some degree. She's been on my mind more than usual lately. I don't know . . ."

"I always liked her husband, John. Whatever happened to him?"

Violet felt the blood drain from her face. "What do you mean, what *happened* to him?"

"He just sort of disappeared . . ."

"He died in jail."

"What?"

"Why do you think it was hard for me to talk about her?"

"I don't recall anything like that," Francisco said. "I thought it was just because you missed her."

"I did. I do. But . . . how could you not *know* that?"

"I was just a kid when she died. Know *what*?"

"But you were *there*."

"Where?"

"In the room. When it happened. I thought this was why *you* never mentioned her."

"When *what* happened?"

The ambulance came to a halt. "Mom. *Mom*?" The EMTs jumped out, the back doors opened, and another fainting spell came over her. Soft as fleece, it lay across her arms and legs.

Shortly before the train rolled into Union Station in Portland, Violet's contractions tightened into a fiery band around her stomach and back.

"Do you think you can hold on?" Ada asked.

Violet told her between groans that she didn't even know what that meant.

Ada tried soothing her with lullabies, stories, and phrases in French, and Violet drifted in and out, encouraging her to keep going. The challenge of trying to understand what she was saying helped her mind float away from the agony.

The train slammed to an abrupt halt, and Violet cried out. Ada slowly helped her down and across the tracks. By the time they made it to the sidewalk, a cab driver had hopped out of his cab and was approaching, pointing to a clinic two blocks away. "Hey. Listen. I can give you a ride for free."

Violet whimpered at the thought of two blocks. She was overcome with misery, barely able to breathe. She accepted the idea that she would lie down and give birth on the sidewalk. It made no difference. She would die, and she thought it was just as well. But in the time it took to think such things, the cab driver and Ada managed her into the back seat of the taxi, and now they were out again, shuffling through the front doors of the clinic. The second they loosened their grip, Violet sank toward the floor.

Moments later, she seemed to be waking to a whole new level of pain, though she couldn't remember being asleep. She was propped onto a narrow, rickety bed, bare from the waist down, knees up, and a woman doctor was asking about the father of the baby, if there was someone the nurses should try to reach, and Violet screamed and Ada declared above the shrieks that the father was killed in the war. Violet imagined Eddie shot and stabbed and blown to pieces. Imagined him disintegrating into dust while she screamed, and Ada tried again to quiet her in French, which could barely be heard over Violet's hollering, which gave way to one long sustained holler, and that, too, abruptly ended when the newborn's kittenlike mewls broke into the room.

There was only the baby's pink arms and legs, the wet of her black hair and the side of her cheek, before the nurse lifted her away. When they tried to bring her back, Violet closed her eyes, refused to nurse her. Ada stood from the chair in the corner and insisted the nurses do whatever Violet asked.

Late in the evening, when Ada had briefly stepped out, Violet was roused by a nun in full habit, standing next to her bed. She spoke in low tones about charity and blessings, and Violet thought at first she had come to chastise her for her sins. Before she could tell her to go away, the nun thanked her on behalf of the family who desperately wanted her baby girl. Violet gripped her hand, kissed it, and rolled away in the bed with her eyes closed, listening to the nun's heavy shoes on the tiles, the final close of the door.

In the middle of the night Violet tugged the ring from her finger and flung it across the room, where it pinged against the tile floor in the dark. She recalled the glimpse of her baby, how even a sliver of her face was enough to see that she resembled Violet's father, whose face she last saw when he was headed down to the cellar with Mr. Morgan.

At daylight Violet woke Ada, who was slumped in a chair in the corner. She asked for paper and a pen to write a letter.

Dear Mother,
  I am well. You will see the postmark is from Oregon. I don't know if you are worried, but if you are, you needn't be. I have never been better. I will write again when the occasion allows. In the meantime, I miss Daddy, and I miss Em, and I miss you, too.

Always,
Violet

These would be the last words her mother would ever receive from Violet in her lifetime.

It was not until Violet's breasts had dried and softened, and she was working five shifts a week at Willamette Iron Works, settled into an apartment with Ada in Vanport, that she approached Ada in the middle of their workday to ask her to translate what she had said during Violet's labor. Somehow surrounding herself with work that sustained her life, and all the racket around them this time of day, made it feel safer, easier to approach the tender subject.

"*Tu es puissante et tu es aimée!*" Ada said above the noise. And then, as if she were suddenly too shy to translate it into English, she hesitated, looking around in a way that was unlike her. "It means you are powerful and you are loved."

Violet didn't ask if what she said was meant for her or for the baby. She thought again of the brief moment when she recognized her own father's face in her child's as the girl was taken away. She wondered what her new family had named her. She wondered what the child was doing now, and if some part of her would always miss the mother she never knew. She wondered if she would ever stop thinking of the girl, and if it was right that she ever should.

35

In the large, open loft, his little girl appeared to have dwindled in size, her footsteps so light they didn't creak the creaky floors. Her face was turned upward, eyes gazing all around with the purest expression of wonder.

Quincy looked around just the same, while her cast and cane clunked rhythmically through the quiet.

Seeing the loft through their eyes for the first time made it come to life even more for Daniel. Worn textures, neutral tones, and warm light. The smell of wood and acrylic paint and graphite pencils. Views so vast that to stare at them felt a little like falling off the edge of the world.

It was Dani who had asked to come up to the loft. After Quincy read all three books in the backyard, she asked about her *arrière grand-mère* and pointed upstairs, apparently remembering his grandmother's invitation before she collapsed on the floor.

"Touch?" Dani asked of the large painting beneath a dropcloth on the wall. "Not that one," Daniel said, tempted to take a look himself.

"Touch?" Dani asked of the books, and the plants, and the hand-woven pillows on the chairs.

"You may, you may, you may," Daniel said.

Quincy sat in his grandmother's reading chair and gazed around the room. He caught her swallowing several times. She had become very quiet, and he could feel her watching the two of them.

Dani stopped in front of the self-portrait that his grandfather had sketched near the bed. She pointed to it. "Mine?" she said.

Daniel looked at her, then Quincy.

"Mine?"

"That's, well, that's your great-grandfather. My granddad."

Dani stared at the drawing, hands hanging at her sides as if in deep study. She nodded at the portrait as if saying hello, or in answer to a question no one could hear except her.

Daniel and Quincy eyed each other.

And then, as if satisfied, Dani skipped away, spotted the vase of blue irises on the kitchen table, stopped, and pointed. "Iris," Daniel said. "They came from the yard. Aren't they beautiful?" he asked. "*Les fleurs sont-elles belles?*"

"Yes," she answered in English.

Daniel flashed on something his grandmother once said to him. He picked up the vase and held it behind his back, exactly as his grandmother had done, and he said, using her words, "Are they *still* beautiful?"

"*Oui,*" Dani said with a small laugh. Daniel pointed to his head. "Everything beautiful remains in here, even when you can't see it out here in the world."

He turned to Quincy. "My grandmother told me that when I was not much older than she is now. Hard to forget, even if I didn't quite get it, and I'm not sure she gets it either, though who can say? Two languages complicates things even further."

"You're lucky to have Violet in your life."

"Yes," Daniel said, slightly taken aback. "We all are."

"She reminds me a bit of my own grandmother. This grit beneath the kindness. Violet comes across so gentle and warm, which she is, but, I mean, there's so much more to her that's hard to define. Where did she come from before she was, you know, *Violet Swan*?"

"I'm embarrassed to say I don't know much. Only that she

was born in Georgia and came out here during the Second World War."

"Hmm," Quincy said, clearly dissatisfied with his answer.

The photograph that used to hang in the living room of Daniel's grandfather and great-uncle James now hung on the wall near the bed, by the sketch. It was crooked, and Daniel straightened it. The photo would have been taken in the early 1940s, he supposed, not long before his grandmother moved to Oregon.

"Who are they?" Quincy asked about the photo, and Daniel explained.

"And what was he like, your grandfather?"

"Oh . . . where to begin? He was kind and very gentle. He was funny in a dry way. His jokes often had this superior quality that I didn't always understand, but strived to. He used to lean into the banister on the front porch with a cigar in one hand and a whiskey in the other, his chin up, looking out like he was searching the ocean for ships, and maybe he was. He's sort of fixed in my memory this way, an image of a man, tall and serious, with a quick wit and gentle demeanor. But yeah, he kind of sticks in my head like a figure of a man smoking and drinking and contemplating the sea."

"A real Hemingway," Quincy said, which made him laugh.

"Except he wasn't macho or full of bluster or anything like that."

Daniel had other memories. Shortly before his grandfather died, he changed very quickly. Daniel had seen him in the rain, holding on to the eucalyptus tree at the edge of the lawn. His shoulders hunched and shuddering, his right arm flailing as he refused to have anyone come near. Then he tore off a tender branch and beat the bark with it until Grand made him stop by shoving him in the back, causing him to collide with the tree and fall down. He appeared to be drunk. Weeks later he tore the kitchen phone out of the wall and threw it across the room, where it cracked the plastic on Daniel's CD player on the table, which seemed a worse offense than the busted, flying phone. Everyone, including Granddad, tried for days to reassure Daniel that it was a terrible mistake. But Daniel was frightened of him after that, no matter the apologies. A week later his grandfather's heart gave out on the front porch. He collapsed with a cigar and a whiskey and a grave look in his eyes, fixed on Daniel's.

"I'm sorry," Quincy said. "Did I say the wrong thing?"

"Not at all."

Dani continued around the room, touching nearly everything, pecking in quick little spurts as if checking objects for heat.

"Can I tell you something personal?" Quincy asked.

Daniel liked her more by the minute. "Well, now you have to, right? In the spirit of curiosity and all."

Quincy smiled, and its effect took him by surprise. "Sorry. Yes, I suppose so. I was just going to say that when I was six years old I went live with my father. I didn't know who he was before that. He was a total stranger who showed up for me and my sister when my mother passed away."

Daniel felt his mouth slacken.

"Watching you brings it all back. I can see what it must have been like from my father's perspective. How frightened and unsure he must have felt. But also, I think you should know that there is something innate, something I can't put into words. I didn't know him, but I *did* at the same time. I felt safe with him. And at home."

Daniel lowered himself in the chair opposite Quincy. "I don't know what to say. I feel the same way about my grandmother. I've known her my entire life. She's the place where I feel most at home. But I can't say I *know* her, really know who she is, I mean, aside from being my grandmother, and the public persona of Violet Swan."

He had tried this conversation once with Macy and it didn't go so well.

"I was older than Dani when my father came for me and my sister," Quincy said, "and the complications were different than yours and hers, but still, it's good to see things from the other side. It never occurred to me, the full picture of the thing, until just now, watching you struggle with Dani—not *struggle* so much as reaching toward her and closing the gap. It's a beautiful thing to see."

"Well. Thank you." Daniel didn't know how to respond. An hour ago Quincy had been as good as a stranger to him. And now?

36

Life in Vanport was lively and loud, the opposite of Violet, and yet somehow she found everything she needed to make a home. The cheap public housing accommodated shipyard workers, transient laborers, single mothers, war brides, families of all kinds and sizes, and, as Violet soon learned, the majority of black residents, kept out of other housing in the city. Violet and Ada worked in the shipyard like nearly everyone who lived there, the two of them building flat-bottomed self-propelled boats called lighters, which transported goods to and from moored ships. They earned $1.29 an hour. It was 1944, and Violet was as good as rich.

Ada had been right about it being like Louisiana. There was even a small lake called Bayou, and a muddy stream called Bayou Slough. There was a Cottonwood Street, which reminded Violet of the South, and at all times of the day and night there was the sound of babies crying or babbling, children kicking balls, couples making love, men fighting. There were dances and card games and cooked meals that were eaten in and out of the apartments, shared in kitchens and on the lawns. Ada easily mixed with all sorts of people from all sorts of places. She shared suppers and dances and dirty jokes. Violet had seen her kiss men on the mouth. She had seen her do the same with women. Some evenings Ada would bathe, put on a taffeta dress and heels, and stroll around like the women in Los Angeles. Other times she wore trousers and boots and wool pullovers and every other word was a cuss. She read the newspapers every day, attended Wobbly meetings weekly. She babysat for women she barely knew, rocking and cooing their children. She'd play catch with the boys in the yard, and more than once stepped in with a baseball bat to keep a man from hitting a woman. She was every kind of person there ever was, and Violet loved the sound of her voice, her laughter drifting in from the next room.

Violet was nothing like Ada. She kept to herself nearly all the time, and Ada respected that, and told others to respect it, too. Twice a month Violet rode the bus into Portland for art supplies, hurrying past men on crutches and in wheelchairs, dodging women with strollers and children hanging on to strollers, and Violet couldn't help scanning the carriages, searching each small face for the familiar.

She visited the Portland Art Museum on Monday evenings, when it was free. The first time she saw the paintings of Cézanne and Picasso she didn't understand what was happening to her head. She had to sit on a bench in the center of the large room and pull herself together. It was like stepping inside another dimension, transcending this world for one she'd suspected existed but never had the proof before now. Her heart became the ghost of a heart, her mind unplugged. She left the museum feeling exalted and in love with every person she passed on the street.

When the work of a Portland artist named Mark Rothko was on exhibit, Violet was stunned by the mood and stance of the colors, the use of lines and shapes, which at first glance could have been mistaken as primitive or simplistic, but Violet saw them as she believed Rothko had meant for them to be seen—as complicated intentions of scale, vibrating with the force of life. His canvases were larger than most, and this appealed to Violet, too. The placard stated that Rothko believed that the larger the painting, the more intimate the connection with viewers, allowing them to step inside the work, rather than look upon its smallness from afar.

Those unnamed and inexplicable feelings that had been

churning inside Violet since she was a child began to make sense. Violet would be a painter—she *was* a painter. No other life would do.

She dressed every day the way Ada dressed at her most slovenly, in trousers and boots and woolen sweaters. The men in Vanport teased that she and Ada were lovers, which caused Violet to go red and reach for a cigarette. She had cut her hair in a bob at the chin, seemed to have finished growing at six feet, was as lean as she would ever be, and barely anyone spoke to her when Ada wasn't there. When Ada and her cousins were around, Ada spoke French, breaking into English for Violet's benefit, but Violet began to translate on her own. She absorbed the language the way she absorbed the rest of the world, with a quickened curiosity, and to the bone. Within a year, Violet was half conversing in French with the women. Within two, she was fluent.

While others complained that they felt walled in by the high levees surrounding the floodplain of Vanport, Violet felt content and contained, living as she did, so much of the time, inside her own head. Her abstract work resisted the daily racket of hammering and machinery, the dark, cold iron, the grease and steam. Everything that was part of the war machine was not part of Violet's work, except it was, of course, hovering just beyond the frame.

Two days out of every week, Violet turned back into the young girl in the farmhouse kitchen, her world made of color and composition. Back to when the worst thing that had ever happened was learning that beauty could break her heart. On those two days Violet exchanged one life for another, and sometimes late at night, if exhaustion had not gripped her bones, she painted long enough to uncover the way lines and a pale palette could evoke feelings in the viewer. One night she discovered how to make light appear as if it were shining through the back of the canvas and out onto the viewer's skin, creating an intimacy between Violet and the canvas and the world. She couldn't sleep, and at work the next day she nearly mangled her hand when she dozed and slumped over near a table saw.

Two years later, in the early fall of 1946, Violet arrived at 1907 Blueberry Lane—four years and two months after she ran free from Annie Burke's front door.

A heavyset woman was picking tomatoes in the yard of the modest, cedar-shingled house. She placed each one on the step nearest her, and gripped her hips and frowned at the car pulling in. Her gray hair was pulled tightly into a twisted bun. Even from a distance her character felt severe.

Aside from the red tomatoes and orange butterflies, the color violet was everywhere Violet looked. Drooping, cone-shaped blossoms of butterfly bushes at the corners of the house, rows of lavender lining the front yard at the street, and in the back, hydrangeas drooped under their own weight, as round and hefty as the woman in the violet housedress waiting in the front yard to see about this stranger.

Violet shifted the car into park, released the brake, and lurched forward as the car shut down. She'd purchased the used Ford for thirty-five dollars, but had been driving for only six months. All of her belongings were piled high in the seats. An easel poked from the back window. The Telefunken radio that Ada gave her as a going-away present sat atop a box in the passenger seat. Violet already missed her, though they'd said their goodbyes just hours ago when Ada helped Violet pack the car. When the war ended, Violet stayed in Vanport for the work, to save more money, and maybe she had stayed longer than she thought she would because of the girl, on the off chance that Violet might see her on the street, or, in a way that made no sense, in case the girl turned out to need her. But Ada had moved to Portland after talking her way into a government job, working with Japanese Americans recently released from internment camps. "They're more lost than we ever were," she told Violet over dinners, which they'd continued to share several times a month. "They were turned loose, right back into the same world that stripped them of their homes and livelihoods, and they have no idea who to trust. They have a stare like the walking dead." It was Ada with whom Violet had hunkered down when the news of Hiroshima and Nagasaki came over the radio. It was summer, the doors and windows in Vanport flung open, but the life-sounds of comings and goings suddenly muted, replaced by the crackle of radios erupting with urgent, staccato voices delivering the news. Anger and fear filled the air, and in the days following the two bombings, a sense of loathing weighed heavily over everything. It was with Ada that Violet had wept when the war was finally over.

A different kind of dread passed over Violet as she stepped from the car. She was out of place, and careful not to let the door slam, as the vehicle was slanted sideways in the crooked driveway.

The air smelled of thyme, rosemary, and lavender, soothing scents that Violet pulled through a long breath, her lips drawn into a tight smile. She had saved nearly everything she'd earned for two years in anticipation of this moment. Whatever wasn't needed for rent, food, and art supplies went into a bank account. She still owned the dress she'd bought in Arizona, but hadn't worn it since the baby was born. She could use some new clothes, she thought while standing under the gaze of this woman. Violet was dressed in blue jeans, rolled at the hem and dappled in paint. Her white button-down blouse with the sleeves rolled to her elbows was the only piece of clothing she didn't wear while working, and she'd tucked it neatly into her jeans, believing, until this moment, that she looked presentable. Her hair was freshly cut, blunt at the chin, but she knew already that this woman did not care for any of it, and Violet thought how badly she could use a cigarette just now.

"Do we know you?" the woman called out.

Violet walked toward her. "No, ma'am. Not yet." She recognized the look of grief in the woman's eyes as she came closer. Her lids drooped at the outside, and her smile was strained by the same weight. She reminded Violet of her own mother, that bone-deep vacancy of having lost a child. Violet had arrived too late. Richard was sent to fight, and had been lost to the war.

"My name is Violet, and I've come to say hello to your son, but I don't know if this is a good time, or . . ."

"Who?"

"Is James here? He sent me, but . . ."

The woman covered her mouth at the sound of her son's name. She dropped her hand as if in anger. "How would you know James?"

Violet had grown accustomed to accusations coming at her out of nowhere. "We met in Georgia. That's where I'm from."

Just then the front door opened and a young man, no more than twenty, stepped outside. He was wearing a white linen shirt, similar to Violet's, tucked into khakis. His dark hair was neatly combed. Violet was confused. She didn't understand how she could have misjudged his mother's face, the grief she had seen there.

"Who are you?" he asked, and the way he lifted his arm to grip the porch column and leaned into it, the way he looked across the yard at her, made her wonder what he was like when no one else was around. "Why are you here?" This self in front of his mother was not the self he showed to the rest of the world, and one day she would tell him this and surprise him with her clarity. The ocean glinted at his back.

"I'm Violet Swan," she said. "And you'll know in just a minute."

He dropped his arm. Even from where he stood, up on the porch, she could see that he was taller than her. And now he stepped down and came toward her, and she saw that she was right. He glanced at her scarred arm several times, even as she could tell he was trying to look away.

"You must be Richie." She rolled down her sleeves. "It's a bit chilly up here." She walked back to the car, grabbed the pea coat, and slipped it on. "Your brother sent me," she said, returning to where he stood.

"My brother has been dead for a year."

His words landed with a kick. Gravity sucked her several steps back. There was no place to sit, and no one was offering a chair on the porch, or even a front step. All this time she'd wondered if James had made it back yet, half expecting him to greet her at the door. Half expecting to hear that his little brother Richie had been killed overseas. But she was not, in any way, prepared to hear this. "I don't know what to say. I'm so sorry."

"How do you know my brother?" the man asked.

"It took me four years to get here."

"What's that?" the woman said.

Violet looked across the yard to the full view of the ocean. It had been at her back as she drove up the hill, and now with a single turn she was overcome by the magnificence of sky and water in nearly identical hues, meeting somewhere in the middle. It was too much at once, and she gritted her teeth against it, looked down at her scuffed boots splattered in paint, determined not to cry in front of strangers.

Then she glanced at the house, and at the man who must be Richard, and the mailbox that read 1907 Blueberry Lane, and she felt a path unfolding in a way she couldn't explain. Why *was* she here? What was so important that she had come all this way to say?

"He came through town with one of the revivals," she said. "He was kind to me. Like I said. He told me about his brother Richie, which I guess is you. He said you liked to draw. That's what got the whole thing started."

For a moment no one spoke.

"What whole thing?" Richard asked.

Violet felt the weight of the past four years. "I'll tell you about it. I will. But right now I'm looking for a place to rent. Could you point me in the right direction?"

"An entire place?" the woman asked. "Are you by yourself? What are you doing here?"

Richard glanced at Violet's car, the piles of things packed inside. "What do you have in there?"

"Paints, easels, a little bit of clothing. I have a dress I haven't worn in a couple of years and wouldn't mind wearing now." She had no idea what made her say this. What she meant was that it was suddenly warm inside her coat, and the dress would feel cooler, but she had sounded like Ada, bolder than she was.

Richard's mother took several steps toward her. "I'm not sure you belong here. This is a very small community."

"Come again?"

"I don't think you're going to fit in."

"Mother, for God's sake."

"Do not take the Lord's name in vain."

Violet made a visor with her hand. "The war is over, ma'am, and this is a free country, and I will live where I want to live, and do what I please."

Richard laughed, and his mother gasped and looked as if she'd been struck. She turned her back, stomped past Richard, and went into the house, letting the screen crack behind her.

"Sorry," Violet said.

"No. I'm the one who should be apologizing."

"There's no need. I had a righteous mother, too. Have. Still have. Maybe I do. It's been a while since we've been in touch. Anyway, I didn't need to be so rude."

He stepped closer and held out his hand, shaking Violet's firmly. "You said the right thing. And I'm Richard. Or Richie, if you like. Welcome to Nestucca Beach. There isn't much here. How long do you plan to stay?"

Violet studied his face. They were still shaking hands. "Probably the rest of my life."

Richard looked as though he was trying to figure out if she was joking. He let go of her hand and laughed with a full-bodied heartiness that gave Violet a rush, like knocking back a whiskey, stinging her chest.

"There's a place down on Main, which isn't much of a main street. A post office, the Little Grocer, a bakery, my dad's lumberyard, that's about it. The place I'm thinking about is above a small bookstore, so there's also a bookstore. A woman named Hazel owns the building. I can call over and see what she's got."

"Thank you. I like the light here. I mean up here. *Here.* On this hill where the sea grass and trees reflect the sky and the ocean."

Richard stood next to her, looking west. "It's part of what keeps me here."

"I really am sorry about James."

Richard faced her, taking a quick breath through his teeth, then nodding at the ground. "I appreciate that."

"Can I ask what happened?"

With this he looked back to the ocean again. "He was on his way home, made it all the way to Portland, and then, I don't know . . . I don't know what happened to him. But apparently he jumped off the Hawthorne Bridge. He was found two days later, a mile downriver."

Violet recalled the news story about a man who had jumped from the bridge and was later found, but whose identity she never knew. Perhaps his name was never mentioned, and even if it had been, she had never known James's full name, only his address. It felt like a dream she had long ago, a dream that meant nothing at the time, and now it was well past when she needed to understand.

"He had mailed me a letter and said there was something he wanted to say when he got home," Richard said, "something he needed me to understand about who he was. But he never arrived. Whatever it was, I would have understood. I miss him every day."

Violet wrapped her arms around Richard. The scent of his hair cream and aftershave would cling to her skin after they made love, and she knew this long before the fact. She gripped the stiff fabric of his shirt, which smelled of the outdoors, no doubt having been dried on the backyard line, rippling in the breeze.

Richard held her in return.

Violet saw the curtain move in the front window before it quickly snapped closed. "Your mother is watching," she whispered close to his ear, and he squeezed her tightly, rocking her gently side to side. It must have been a full minute before he let her go.

37

Penny and Frank sat together in an alcove set apart from the hospital waiting room, designed, Penny guessed, as a place to have private conversations about difficult things. But Penny and Frank weren't speaking, or touching, or comforting each other in any way. They were waiting silently for news about Violet.

Penny crossed her arms and stared at other people in the waiting room down the hall, solemn-faced, if not bored, and beyond them windows to the great outdoors, and not too far away was home. She had the urge to take off running down the hall and out the front doors. She wanted to be home with Daniel and Dani.

"What happened to the photograph of Richard and James that used to hang in the living room?" she asked.

Frank frowned as if thinking it through. "I don't know. I think my mother took it upstairs?"

"I noticed it was gone when I was cleaning up, preparing for Daniel." She paused, irritated all over again by Frank's and Violet's lack of enthusiasm for Daniel's arrival—and look what it turned out to be! "I always thought things downstairs belonged to us. That the first floor was our actual house, and everything in it belonged to us."

Frank stared at her. "What are you saying?"

"I don't know. It just bothers me that she took it."

"A photograph of her husband and his brother?"

"A photograph of your father and uncle."

Frank looked away and then turned back. "Tell me something, Penny—and I'm asking a real question in search of a real answer. Why do you dislike me so much? You and Daniel both?"

"Jesus Christ." Penny glanced toward the nurses' station. "Nobody *dislikes* you. All I was saying was that downstairs is supposed to be *ours*."

"It *is* ours."

"Well, it doesn't feel like it if your mom can just take things and put them upstairs like that."

"A photograph of her own husband."

"A photograph of your father."

Frank seemed to be seething to the point of alarm, as if he might stand up and punch a wall.

"What is going on with you?" she asked.

"Oh, I don't know, honey." His normally low voice rose several registers. "Maybe look around and see that you're in a hospital because my mother collapsed, because apparently she has lung cancer, which you knew about while I, her own son, knew nothing. Not to mention that you told me you were leaving me, even though you're still here."

Frank swiped his mouth and slowly let his hand fall into his lap.

Penny's face turned hot. She glanced down the hall. If anyone was listening, they didn't show it.

"OK. Look. First let me say that she didn't tell me, Frank. I mean, she *did*, but just this morning, and only because I squeezed it out of her. I caught her sneaking out to see Dr. Kath before you were out of bed. And then she told me, in so many words, you know how she can be, well, *evasive*, but I figured it out, and she said she was going to tell you. And then Daniel showed up. She couldn't exactly announce it then . . ."

Frank's eyebrows drew together as if he was waiting for more. "And I guess that's why you're still here, too. For Daniel."

Penny's mind went blank. The conversation they needed to have seemed locked away. For a moment she tried to retrieve it, but couldn't locate the first words to get there. And anyway, this was not the time or place to have it out.

"I'm sorry about your mom. I got the feeling she knew long before today and didn't tell any of us."

"I don't understand why she keeps everything to herself."

Penny burst out laughing.

"What," Frank said, "are you saying I'm like that? I would never keep something like that—"

"Maybe not *this*, OK, but if you add up the million somethings of slightly less importance, it's the same as one giant something of consequence, if you ask me."

Frank glanced away and didn't look back for a while, which was what he did when he knew she was right.

"I'm sorry, Frank. This isn't the time for these kinds of gripes. I know what I'm saying about the photograph sounds petty, but it doesn't *feel* that way. It feels like something bigger. I get mixed up trying to explain myself to myself, so I guess I can't expect you to understand."

"You never answered my question."

"What question?"

"About why you dislike me so much."

"It doesn't make any sense."

"Come on, Penny. You want to leave me and it has nothing to do with *disliking* me?"

"Anyway," she continued, "I just want to say that your mom has lived longer than most people. She's had a great life by anyone's standards. She's been luckier than most."

"Now who's avoiding the conversation?"

"This is not the *place*."

"Home doesn't seem to be the place, either." Frank shook his head at the floor. "I don't think my mom has been luckier than most."

"What do you mean?"

"She didn't seem so lucky when I was young. She wasn't well. I don't know. I feel like she's still that person, though, whoever that person was, feeling . . . unwell."

"What was wrong with her?"

"Something mental. Emotional."

Penny could not have been more confused. "You've never said anything of the sort to me in the forty-five years I've known you. And I've never seen something like that with her. Not once. In fact, she seems the complete opposite of that. Fully and altogether perfectly sane."

Frank shrugged.

"You can't just shrug, Frank. That's what I'm talking about . . . if you're wondering what's difficult for Daniel and me when it comes to you, it's that, the shrugging, the silence, the stalking off. No one knows what you're thinking or who you're pissed at or—"

"Who I'm *pissed* at? I'm not *pissed* at anyone."

"Ha!"

"Penny. Listen. I'm no happier than you. It's been a long time since it even occurred to me that I was happy, or might ever be happy again. So there. That ought to free you up to do whatever you need to do and get on with your life."

Penny's mouth went slack. It may have been an honest thing to say, but it was somehow hurtful, and she willed herself not to cry.

"Wait," he said. "That's not—I didn't mean it like it sounded. I'm not an asshole. I'm really not. I lo—" It seemed he was going to tell her that he loved her, but instead, he shook his head at the floor again and then looked up. "What I really want, and I mean this, is for you to be happy. And there is something I haven't told you that I should have, and I don't know why I was so stupid about it. I don't know, it's unforgivable, really, but you want to hear things, so I'll tell you."

"Oh, God, Frank. Have you been having an affair?"

Frank reared back. "What? The last thing I would do is go looking for another relationship to manage."

"Oh. I see."

"Come on, Penny."

"I get it. I'm a pain in your . . . something to *manage*."

"Penny. I swear to God. You don't know anything."

"Maybe that's because you never tell me anything. Like whatever you were just about to say about your affair."

"I'm not having an affair!" he shouted.

The nurse leaned over the counter and came into view. "Folks?" she said.

"Sorry," Frank said.

In the silence his hands began to shake.

"What is it?" Penny asked. "Tell me now and get it over with."

"I knew about Dani."

Penny went stiff as a statue. She understood the words he had spoken, but they rattled around inside her head. There was no place for them to land where they could possibly make sense.

"I received Arielle's emails," he said. "I thought it was a scam. At first I did. Then she started sending photographs, and I started to second-guess if it was real, and I just kept thinking, if I tell him, it's going to ruin his life. I know that sounds terrible, I know, but think about it. He's living with a woman we assume he's going to marry, and his life is his own, and I don't know what to say, all I can tell you is that at the time I felt like I was protecting him. I was thinking that Macy was going to leave him—and she did, so I was right on that count—which meant he was going to have to be a mother and father both to this child, and I couldn't bear thinking about his life taking a turn like that. I'd picture him going through all the things you used to do, like cooking and bathing and worrying and—"

Penny stuck up her hand. "Hold up. Hold it right there. Whoa, whoa, whoa. Where do I even start unpacking this? First of all, things *I used to do* while raising him . . . You're right. *I* did those things. Not you. And what exactly is your point? Don't answer. I'll tell you what *my* point is. Daniel had two parents, and you could have done way more of your share of the nurturing and everyday caregiving, but you took this hands-off, women's-work stance—"

"What the actual hell? That is *not* true."

"Really, Frank? Tell me, how many times did you take him to the doctor when he was sick? How many times did you change his diaper? How many meals did you cook for him? How many times did you pick him up and drop him off at friends'? How many times did you get up with him in the night?"

"That's because he always called for you!"

"Because he knew that I would come!"

Frank appeared stunned.

Penny burst into tears. It was as if years of resentment had pooled into a single moment, a dam let loose before anyone even knew it was cracked. "I'm exhausted. First taking care of Daniel, and in many ways, of you and Violet and Richard before he died. And then Millicent. It never stops. When I married you and we decided to have Daniel, I really thought I was getting an equal partner and that we would share in the caretaking of our child. I saw the example your father set—he wasn't afraid to care for others, to cook and clean and bandage Daniel's knee."

Frank appeared increasingly uncomfortable. Opening and closing his fists.

Penny looked at him. "What?"

"Nothing."

Her voice was a shouting whisper. "How dare you tell me not to worry about Daniel coming home. How *dare* you go on about how I needed to let him go, a man out in the world, which, by the way, is utter bullshit, Frank. You still live with your mother, for God's sake. Who are you trying to kid? And anyway, I *knew* it. I knew you were lying about something."

"I don't blame you for being upset—"

"Oh, very kind—"

"But to be fair, I didn't know if what Daniel was coming to say today was about Dani or something else. I didn't want you to worry, because all you do is worry, and it's exhausting, OK? There, I said it."

"What on earth? What do you mean he might have been coming to tell us something else? Like what? What *else* haven't you told me?"

"Nothing. I didn't mean it like that. I meant, I didn't know if Daniel knew about Dani. I had no way of knowing if this was what he was coming to say, and if it wasn't, I mean, if it had turned out to be something else, I'd already decided that I was going to tell him while he was here about Dani."

"When did you first hear from Arielle?"

"I don't know . . . A year and a half ago, maybe?"

Penny shook her head. "And when was the last time you heard from her?"

"About eight months ago. She stopped emailing after that."

"And it never occurred to you to share any of this with me?"

"I thought it might be a hoax. At first, I mean."

"But even *that*? You couldn't just tell me about it? Like, making conversation with your wife? You couldn't just share it with me and we could talk about it and decide from there whether or not we should tell Daniel? Because I *exhaust* you, Frank?"

"Yeah. You do."

"Well, you exhaust me, too."

"Great. We agree, finally, on something."

Penny glared into Frank's eyes. "This is pathetic, Frank. Absolutely pathetic. You have denied Daniel his own daughter, and you want to blame me for it."

"No. That's not what I said. I can never say what I mean with you. And anyway, I don't need you to beat me up over this. I'm doing a fine job myself. I took one look at her and it filled me with disgust. I know that you would have never done something like this. I don't know what's wrong with me. And no, that's not an invitation for you to tell me. Or worse, take pity on me."

"What's pitiful is that somewhere in your head you pictured Daniel being a parent to his child, and in your head that meant turning him into a caregiver, which, again, in your mind is something less than the man he was trying to be. Did I get that right?"

"No. I don't know."

"Pardon my French, but that is fucked up, Frank."

Frank rubbed his eyes. He dropped his hands and said, "I knew and I didn't say anything, OK. And then the emails stopped coming, and I thought, well, she's moved on and figured it out, or maybe it really was a hoax and it was good that no one took the bait."

"I really think you should stop talking, Frank."

In the quiet Penny continued to fume. She couldn't wait to get home and start making plans to leave, once and for all. She would find a new home in town, one that was all her own. She'd go back to being a real estate agent, and if Daniel returned to LA, then she'd split her time between here and there. Her mind was churning with plans, and already she felt lighter, more sure of herself.

Frank said, "I don't know what's wrong. With me, I mean. I know that something isn't right." He rubbed his face, dropped his hands into his lap. "I keep thinking about how Swan was my mother's name. Did you know that? I keep thinking about this lately, like it's some clue to something bigger. It's the name she was born with. My father must have been the first man in the country to take his wife's name."

Penny felt her jaw fall open. She snapped it shut. "How have I never heard this before?"

"Because it's embarrassing."

"It's *amazing*."

"I don't know . . . *what?*"

"It endears me even more to your father."

Frank sighed.

"You aren't nearly as enlightened as you claim to be."

"I don't know what I've been claiming."

"Your politics, for one," Penny said. "So incensed about inequalities. I think it's a little selective."

"I can't tell him about the emails," Frank said. "He'll never forgive me. He shouldn't."

"I don't see how you can hold on to that without it eating you alive."

"I don't know what's worse."

"I think if you told him the truth about this, if you apologized and were straight with him, it would probably bring the two of you closer."

"Ha. I doubt that."

Penny felt a warm seething in her chest and jaw, tried to temper it, and failed. He didn't seem to get how all of this worked. How people were supposed to open up to each other, and in the opening they became closer. They admitted their failings and were forgiven by the people who loved them.

"As soon as I saw her, I thought how much I wanted to tell her stories like I used to tell Daniel," Frank said. "And then, you know what else I thought? I don't know why, but I thought about how much I miss the lumberyard. And that's when I got up and made myself a drink."

PART FOUR

38

When *Violet returned* home from the hospital the following evening, it felt like the house from the future, the one that would carry on without her in it. The temperature had risen, summer was here, even as the calendar claimed it was still two weeks away. Heads of daffodils had wilted to the ground, and blush-tone peonies were floating like clouds in the warm breeze.

And then the rise and fall of a young girl's voice, exclamations and laughter from the adults corralling her through the world, one meal, one activity, one story at a time. The smell of sugar cookies, voices in the garden, the tick of shovels in the dirt. One evening, LPs spun on the turntable in the living room, old Motown records of Penny's: Al Green, Marvin Gaye, Gladys Knight and the Pips. Violet guessed that Daniel was playing them for Dani. But maybe it was Penny playing them for herself.

Before she'd been discharged, the doctors had shuffled around Violet's bed, looking her over, reading her chart as she lay like a lab specimen, a case study for their own purposes. She recognized the moment of obvious conclusion in their eyes, felt the pulse of their wavering when they believed they knew more than she did about her fate, and they were uncertain how to tell her.

"I've lived a long life," she said. "I don't mind what's happening, and you shouldn't either. It's probably good for you to get a look at the natural course of things."

Their eyes darted everywhere but on her, their smiles filled with nervous laughter, and it was then that Violet understood she was a failed experiment, someone who could not be saved, and therefore had no worth. She began to laugh, and laughter set off the coughing, and before she knew it someone was giving her oxygen. How quickly she'd been reduced to an old woman of no real consequence. It turned out she didn't care for that after all.

So she returned home to fusses over where best to sit, or what she might like to eat, and whether she wanted to be upstairs or down. Her own son had trouble looking her in the eye. It was everything she had tried to avoid by not telling them months ago.

Within days, Violet motioned to Daniel that she needed to speak to him in private.

Alone upstairs, he'd handed her a cup of ginger tea, sat across from her in what used to be his grandfather's reading chair.

"Listen, sweetheart," she said, "I was wrong about something. Or maybe I just wasn't ready to go along with you. I don't know. But I've given it some thought. There are a few things I'd like to tell you."

Daniel cocked his head. "OK."

Violet rolled her finger in a small circle, like film on a reel. "Not things. What I mean is, many things. My life. The interview. The . . ."

"You mean the documentary?"

Violet nodded. "I gave it some thought in the hospital . . . what you said about my legacy. And about gossip and speculation. And what would happen if you and your parents believed the things you heard."

"Your legacy."

"My legacy."

"And what about your privacy?"

Violet swiped the air. "I've lived an honest life. Stayed true to everything and everyone that meant something to me."

"But I'd have to ask hard questions, Grand, and you'd have to tell me the truth."

"Naturally."

Daniel laced his fingers in his lap. "OK. This is . . . I don't know what to say. Before I get too excited, I have to ask— how will everyone know that you're telling me the truth? I mean, that you're not just trying to create a narrative to suit yourself before you, you know . . . "

"Depart?" Violet chuckled. "Honey. Don't make me laugh. It stabs me in the ribs."

"Oh, Grand, no."

"Check the records of the state hospital, psychiatric ward, police and newspaper accounts from the early 1960s, and take a close look at that DNA test you took."

Daniel's mouth fell open.

"I know you found something on there that you'd like to ask me about. I could see it in your eyes."

"Jesus, Grand. How do you—"

"I'm a private person, but I'll always speak the truth."

"Wait, the psychiatric ward? Police? What's that about?"

Violet gazed at his beautiful young face, so expectant and warm. "I don't claim to know how these things work, but isn't all of this supposed to unfold on film?"

Daniel laughed. "You're already directing."

Violet felt the sadness in her own smile.

"All right. No more questions until we're up and rolling."

Violet's voice faded. "I'm tired, Daniel. And I've got work to finish." She glanced at the painting covered by the drop-cloth on the wall, the hours closing in. "I want to spend some time with my great-grandchild. What I mean is, we ought to get started soon."

39

The following day, Daniel drove to Portland to rent cameras and lights and nylon screens he called scrims and flags. During the hours he was gone, Violet painted without the radio on, listening instead to the house sounds, which no longer resembled sighing, as Penny had suggested, but the rise and fall of voices, as sentimental as Bach's violins. Penny, Francisco, and Dani. Once, when she glanced through the window to the yard below, the three of them were holding hands, Dani laughing in the middle as they swung her gently off the ground.

But on the first day of filming, Violet began to second-guess her decision. "How long will all of this business take?"

"We can try a couple of hours a day for as long as you want."

"What should I wear?" The camera was already rolling.

"Maybe you could start in your smock, so it feels authentic."

Violet frowned at the camera.

Daniel poked his head around. "What?"

"It's a film about me. Do you think if I'm not wearing the smock that people will wonder who the old woman is on the screen?"

Daniel laughed. "That's not what I meant."

"I'm just giving you a hard time," Violet said, but it was a *bit* of what she meant, and she caught a ripple of understanding in Daniel's eyes.

"I want to tell you everything, Daniel. And I don't know how it's going to come out. I mean, I understand you'll ask me questions, and I assume you're going to put this together in some form of a story with a beginning, middle, and end, but I think, for the sake of my memory, and the difficulty I have retrieving some things, which we'll get to, that you should just leave the camera going, unless I say to turn it off."

"I can do that."

"And also . . . There are some things that will be hard for you to hear."

Daniel stepped back, poked his head around again. "Are you *sure*, Grand?"

"Yes. And I'm sorry you'll have to hear them."

"Whatever you want to tell, I'm here. If it's too hard, or you change your mind, I can stop."

"Well. That's fine. I guess we should get to it."

Daniel moved from the camera to the lights and back, fussing with gadgets that Violet had never seen in her life. Her grandson was a director with a camera, and Violet was now a subject to be opened and consumed.

And then Dani popped into the room.

"Hey there!" Daniel turned as if he were planning on taking her back downstairs.

"Let her stay," Violet said, and Dani skipped toward them in bare feet.

Violet stood and crossed the loft to the smallest easel folded against the wall. Daniel slowly swung the camera to face her. She could hear the faint wheeze of her own breath. "I once had a sister named Emmylee," she said in a clumsy rush. "But we only ever called her Em. She's one of my earliest memories."

"You had a *sister*?"

The memory rushed in with the unmistakable smell of

burning flesh. The slow, stupefied awareness of her right side going up in flames. The birdcage. The snow.

"Here." Violet reached for the easel. "Help me with this, will you, Daniel?"

Daniel rushed over and placed the easel where Violet pointed, near the window.

Violet reached for the roll of butcher paper fastened to the wall, tore off a piece, and clipped it to the easel. "Dani?" she said, and the girl looked up with a face so open and pure she might have been a flower.

Violet offered her a cup of colored pencils.

Dani stared at the paper, took the cup, and slipped free a yellow pencil.

Violet smiled down on her and began talking again as she returned to her chair. "I used to think about Em when I rocked your father to sleep. His breath reminded me of hers, the ginger crackers and milk. It squeezed my chest so hard I'd have to shift your father from my arm to my shoulder, and rub his back to erase . . ." Violet sank back into her chair and glanced toward Dani.

"Erase what?" Daniel asked.

"The resentment toward a boy in my arms who'd done nothing wrong. Whose only fault was that he had been born to me."

Before Daniel had a chance to respond, Violet said, "I see the shock in your face. We're just getting started, honey."

"I *am* a little shocked."

"Well. One thing at a time." Violet tilted her head toward Dani, who was drawing a giant yellow circle. The sun? The top of a tree?

"What happened to her?" Daniel asked. "Your sister."

"The same thing that happened to me, with these scars." Violet lifted her right arm.

"The fire?"

Violet thumbed a streak of paint in the fold of skin on the back of her hand. "It's not what you think."

"How so?"

"It wasn't the Christmas tree like I told everyone."

"Oh."

Violet felt her mouth go dry. She was taking too long to speak.

"So, it wasn't the tree . . ." Daniel said.

"The tree *did* catch fire, I mean to say, but that's not what started it. The fire is what killed Em."

"Oh."

"Like I said, it wasn't the tree."

"Do you want to tell me more about it?"

"I've always wondered about this kind of nostalgia I feel for the world, what it was, exactly, that I felt for my family, for the people I love, if it stemmed from a part of me that already knew what was to come, and in this way was preparing me for it all along."

"I'm not sure I understand," Daniel asked.

"I once read a story about a bullfighter in Spain who, as a seven-year-old, used to hide behind his mother's skirt in fear of every little thing. The world terrified him. And then, ten years later, he was the best bullfighter in the world. A fierce competitor at seventeen years of age, completely unafraid of the very thing that could actually kill him, and not long after, it did. But he had spoken of these childhood fears, and he claimed some part of him must have known all along what he was headed for. And how was a young boy supposed to live without fear when something so fierce was waiting ahead to gore him?"

In the silence that followed there was only the sound of Dani's pencil scraping the butcher paper, *ship ship ship*.

"Does that story make you think about Em? About what happened to her?"

"It does."

"Have you ever told anyone about her?"

"No."

"Not even Granddad?"

"Well, yes. Only Granddad."

"So then . . . what happened?"

"She was such a tiny, beautiful thing."

Violet watched Dani at the easel. She had the attention and movements of an adult at work—observing her subject out the window, the flick of her pencil, and then the feathery marks as if she were shading something in. Violet eyed Daniel. Was she doing what it looked like she was doing?

"Her mother paints, too," he said. "I think she's imitating her."

Violet managed a nod, a small smile, paused with a kind of prayer inside her head that this girl should be allowed to grow into the person she was meant to be. That she be kept safe. That she follow her heart. "It must be hard for her to be without her mother."

Dani turned sharply as if she had understood. She turned back to the easel without comment.

Violet could see Daniel's Adam's apple bob in his throat. By her agreeing to make this documentary, he would be included. They all would. But he must have understood this from the start.

"Everything is hard right now, Grand. But I'm glad to be home. I want her to know you."

Violet felt a welling in her throat and face, and then her eyes. "I'm afraid all she's going to remember is an old woman hacking and wheezing and taking to her bed."

"Oh, Grand. Look around. You're everywhere in this house. Your work lives on in this world. And what about me? I'm a part of you that lives on, too."

Violet pulled in a thin breath that helped temper her emotions.

"She's drawing the cedar," Daniel said. "I'll be sure to tell her the joke about the bark a year from now."

Violet wiped her eyes. "I bet she'll get it, too, just like you."

Voices from downstairs began traveling up through the

vents. Violet and Daniel exchanged a look that meant perhaps they should shut the camera off.

"I think we should just ask your mom to put it back," Penny said.

"My mother clearly wants it upstairs."

Daniel started to get up.

"Leave it," Violet said.

"Are you sure? I'll need to get their permission."

"We'll cross that bridge. This is part of my life, too."

Penny said, "Well, like I said, I always thought of things down here as belonging to us."

"Why are you bringing this up again?" Francisco said.

"I don't know. It just bothers me."

"He was her husband."

"He was your father."

Silence.

Violet glanced at Daniel, embarrassed for having taken the photograph without asking. Of course Penny was upset, of course it bothered her that Violet could just go into their home and remove things on a whim. How would she feel if Penny had come upstairs and helped herself to a picture on the wall?

Daniel glanced toward the photo his mother was speaking of. He slid his hands down his face as if exasperated.

Then he turned to her, this beautiful grandson whom she hadn't seen in a year, and she had missed him so, and he was smiling that sweet smile he'd inherited from Penny. And here, his beautiful daughter, a small miracle who had traveled even farther than Violet to arrive in this place on the hill.

A rush of hot emotion warmed Violet's ears. Daniel would be here for the end, and Violet was glad for that, but she was so very sorry to have to let him go. If there was a God, Violet wanted it to be known that she'd like to take with her the image of him as a boy, with sun-bleached hair and a mouth rimmed in orange Popsicle, the sight of him bursting from behind a sand dune, happy to have been found. She'd like to take the towering cedar, and the bright green leaves of the white-barked alders, and the garden path lined in Scandinavian blues and yellows, with the crunch of pebbles beneath her clogs. She'd like the image of Francisco waving goodbye to her as he left for school, the image of the first time he brought Penny home to meet her and Richard. She'd like a tin of paints and canvases for all of eternity. She'd like earthly colors, smells, and sounds. And of course, she'd take a thousand images of Richard, but then maybe she didn't need to. Maybe he was already waiting for her in some other realm. Maybe Ada was there, too. It was something to imagine such a thing. Her heart beat faster, beautifully inside her old body.

She pointed to the photograph of Richard and James. "Do me a favor, sweetheart. Take that down when you go and hang it where it belongs."

40

His *grandmother closed* her eyes as if thinking something through, but then she began to doze. Daniel shut down the camera and lights, scooped up Dani and the photograph, and tiptoed out.

Every detail of the loft felt like a piece of her. The placement of every book and photo and tin can full of brushes felt intentional, every color and texture spoke of her universe, which was as much of a mystery to him now as it had been growing up. She'd had a sister. There was more to the fire than she'd said before. Her relationship to his father had not been easy from the start. All of this within minutes of speaking to her.

His mind flashed forward to a day when visitors would pay to enter her studio. What stories would they have been told by then? What exactly would they know? More than Daniel knew right now.

He stopped at the top of the stairs with Dani. "Let's take a seat for a minute," he whispered. "And then let's go to the beach."

Together they watched his mother slip clothes in and out of the washing machine in the laundry closet, the sound of the dryer spinning, all of it the same as when Daniel was a boy and would sit here with his grandmother on the other side of the door, his mother quietly lost in her thoughts, his father off at work, the house silent and calm, as if nothing had ever gone wrong . . .

His mother startled when she spotted him on the stairs. "What is it? Why are you sitting up there? Is Grand all right?"

"She's fine," he whispered, and took Dani's hand as they loped down with the photograph.

"How's it going up there?"

"Very well. Grand told me she had a sister."

Penny crossed her arms. "*What?* First the French . . . She *what?* Wait. Why are you holding that photograph?"

"She asked me to bring it downstairs."

Penny inhaled and covered her mouth. "Did she hear me? Could you hear our conversation?"

His father stepped out of his office. His hair was neatly combed. He was dressed like a professional businessman on a Tuesday. "Hey, you two." He bent down and gave Dani a high five.

"Five," Dani said, slapping his hand, which his father seemed to get a huge kick out of.

"God, Frank," his mother whispered. "Your mother heard me say that about the photograph. She told Daniel to bring it down. I'm horrified."

"Don't worry about it, Mom."

"It's going back where it was," Frank said. "No harm done."

"But it's not just *this*. What else has she heard? I didn't think sound traveled that well up there. And she can't hear so great, and she always has the radio on . . ."

His father took the photograph from him. "Thank you, Daniel. I'll hang it back up and we'll leave it at that."

"How embarrassing," his mother said.

"I think she agrees with you, Mom. That's why she's giving it back. Not because she's upset."

His parents exchanged looks.

"Not to change the subject, but my mother never had a sister, son," his father said. "And speaking French came from her friend Ada. Ada was from New Orleans or something, and I don't know what their story was, but they spoke French to each other all the time."

Daniel and his mother stepped back, shaking their heads. "You knew Ada?" Penny asked.

"Yes."

"How come you never told us that?" Daniel asked.

"I didn't think it was important, I don't know." His father shrugged. "It didn't seem to have anything to do with anything."

Daniel could see a wall of defense building inside him.

"Well, she told me she had a sister, and her name was Emmylee. They called her Em, and she died when Grand was seven years old."

"I don't know, son," his father said. "Maybe she's confused."

"But *I* know, Dad . . . And what do you mean, *confused*?"

"How can you be so sure?" his mother asked his father.

"She's my own mother. You think your mother could have had a sister and you not know?"

Daniel pictured his father as a baby, his grandmother as a young mother, shifting him uneasily from shoulder to shoulder.

"Why not?" his mother said, now filling the dryer with wet clothes. "Of course she could have. Who's to say I didn't lie to you about where *I* came from? It's lying. Lying is easy."

"That isn't funny," his father said.

"No, it's not," Daniel said. "Are you referring to me not telling you about Dani?"

"Of *course* not!" his parents said in unison.

"Your mother is trying to be funny," his father said, with less sarcasm than usual. He seemed to be enjoying himself, a little more at ease, and his mother did, too.

"*Funny?* I've never been accused of *funny*." They were saying the kinds of things they always said, but it sounded lighter, less accusatory, more like a kindhearted joke.

Daniel looked from his mother to his father for a sign of what had changed.

"Son, listen," his father said. "I think maybe, I don't know, not enough oxygen is getting to Grand's head, or the cancer, it can spread to the brain. She refused an MRI, saying there was no need, but that can definitely happen." He swallowed hard.

"You realize she can probably hear this entire conversation," his mother said, and then she slammed the dryer door, but to be fair, it wouldn't close otherwise. She shook her head.

"I think she's asleep," Daniel said.

"Why didn't she ever say anything about speaking French? I mean, you studied it in college, Daniel. Why didn't she bring it up then?"

"I don't know."

His mother turned to his father for an answer. He shrugged.

"Let's go," Dani said, and everyone looked down at her, leaning foot to foot impatiently.

"We're going down to the beach," Daniel said.

"Oh, that sounds like fun," his mother said. "Do you mind if I join you?"

Dani bopped up and down and took his mother's hand. "Yes, you come, too."

"Dad? Would you like to come?"

"I don't know. I'm so behind around here."

"Frank?" his mother said.

His father seemed to consider it for a split second. "Let me get out of these clothes."

Daniel gave a single nod, not wanting to say the wrong thing and ruin the fact that everyone was getting along. An effort was clearly being made.

He called out for Millicent on his way into the living room. "Let's see what she's up to," he said to Dani, and then they heard the sound of her paws pattering up the back steps and the cat door clanging open. "Oh, and the fire wasn't the tree like everyone thinks, either."

"What's that?" his mother asked with her head around the corner.

"I'll tell you what she said when we get to the beach."

Then again, maybe he wouldn't. His grandmother hadn't

asked him to keep quiet about what she told him, but he could see from this first opening of what she had to say that it might be best to wait and let them watch the film when it was done.

Daniel crouched to pet Millicent with Dani, his voice instinctively gentle around his daughter, and he recalled, when he was fourteen and teeming with a blusterous attitude, how he'd said and done so many stupid things. Would Dani do the same? He had been rude to his mother day after day, and then lain in bed at night recalling the things he'd said, and though they filled him with a bewildering remorse, he would get up and do the same the next day. He had avoided his father completely, had a difficult time even watching the man eat. But his grandmother had never been a target of his bad manners and brash behavior. Until one day he told her that her scarred hand, spattered in paint, looked like a Jackson Pollock painting. He'd said it with a cocky kind of pride, and his mother appeared to be impressed, but Violet had seen right through him, saw that he wanted only for her to know that he was familiar with Pollock's work, and what of it? "I never cared much for Jackson as a person, not to mention his work, and didn't care for the fact that the government was using him for their own purposes, while making him rich. He was a Communist, no less. Don't get me started. His wife's work was far more interesting than his. Her name was Lee Krasner, and I'm certain you've never heard of her."

The outburst had not only shut him up, but frightened him. There was anger in her voice, a tone he'd rarely heard. How was it that he'd never asked her to elaborate? He'd never asked about this painter named Lee, and what the story had been with Jackson Pollock. And as far as he knew, his mother had never asked to hear more, either.

41

Richard was sitting up front in the passenger seat of Violet's Ford when they pulled in behind the bookstore. Her palettes and brushes and the Telefunken radio were piled on his lap. The sight of her treasured belongings embraced by his arms filled her face with heat.

A short woman in pedal pushers and cat's-eye glasses stood at the edge of the lot, watching and squinting against the sun. She raised her hand in a wave.

"That would be Hazel," Richard said.

Violet stepped out of the car, and Hazel looked her up and down. She offered her hand, shook it, and said, "I don't rent to working girls, if you know what I mean."

Violet laughed out loud. "Are you trying to assure me that none of these women will be running about, or are you questioning my profession?" There was definitely something about being in this place that made Violet feel bolder, more settled in her own bones.

"*Hazel.* Jesus. Don't be rude." Richard was hurrying around the car to join them.

"I've had it happen, Richie, and I won't do it again. Jenny's got the bookstore running down here, a respectable business, and Will and Lissy have the bakery next door, and I won't have it on account of them, either. I won't have people coming around—"

"Hazel, she's not—"

"Well, what is it? Did you lose a husband to the war or something?"

Violet held the lapel of the pea coat. So far, the women in this town appeared to be . . . well . . . hard and pretty unfriendly. Maybe it was a matter of being proprietary over all they treasured. Violet flashed on the many small towns she'd traveled through to get to where she was standing right now. All the people who didn't care for outsiders, not even children, if they didn't know where they belonged.

"I understand your concern," Violet said, curious what it was about her that could be mistaken for a prostitute, or at the very least, someone whom others could not trust. She supposed it was the simple fact that she was alone in the world, as this seemed to imply that she was up to no good. "I did. Yes. I lost my father and my husband both to the war, ma'am." She glanced at Richard, wondering if he could tell that what she'd said wasn't true. A grin curled in the corner of his mouth.

"Oh," Hazel said. "Well. That being the case, I'm sorry for your loss."

"I have some money saved, and I want to live by the ocean. For peace of mind. I paint. I'm a painter. So I'll be doing that. And you won't hear a sound from me. I can pay you a year's rent in advance."

Hazel studied her with a different kind of earnest. "Well, now."

Richard stepped forward as if he were about to intercede on Violet's behalf.

"What kind of painting?" Hazel asked.

"Art. Fine art."

"You do portraits like this fellow here?"

Violet turned to Richard.

"I sketch. It's nothing. I'm sure what you do is far better than what I do."

The woman eyed them both. "I thought you two knew each other."

Violet started to answer, but Richard's face flashed deep red, and she hesitated, not wanting to embarrass him.

"I'm a family friend," she finally said. "It's just that we've been out of touch for a few years."

"She knew James," Richard said.

Hazel tilted her chin up, her lids a little heavy. "It's a shame what happened. I always liked that boy."

Richard glanced toward the ocean. Violet did the same. She would come to know how that vast swath of blue had the power to clear away grievances, or at least soften the edges that bound them so tightly in her chest. "Thank you, Hazel," Richard said. "He always liked you, too. And thank you for allowing Violet to rent your place. I can vouch for her character."

Later, after they were married, Richard would tell her he had been willing to say or do anything that day to be sure that she could stay.

The apartment walls were tacked with wainscoting that was originally white, but had faded to the buff color of sand. The bathroom window had a small view of the ocean, but only after the leaves dropped from the birch trees later that fall. The sky intrigued her, and this was the thing: even when the plumbing backed up, and the radiator rumbled and quit, and the windows rattled with drafts, and the fishermen down the hall came clanging in at all hours — the light was magnificent and ever-changing, so many hues of pink and charcoal and blue, depending on the day or hour or time of year. She would soon learn that in summer the western horizon became a streak of vermilion, redder than Georgia clay, and the days lasted from four thirty in the morning to eleven at night.

But that first winter, Violet fastened rolled-up towels to the windowsills and used tape to cover pockets of air along the panes, until the windows were dappled everywhere in small squares and strips of beige that matched the walls. She loved it there. It was the first place that felt like home since the fire, the first that was all her own, and though she missed Ada's companionship, the steady crash of waves reminded her of riding the train, and of that feeling that the world was still out there in front of them. The future was still unknown.

She had enough money for a year, perhaps two if she kept her expenses low, and in that time she would do nothing but paint. Her sweaters were moth-eaten, nearly all of her clothes spattered in acrylics. Her scarred hand and arm were often creased with streaks of her pale palettes, though she washed every evening before sitting down to eat. She lived off coffee and apples and walnuts and fresh fish, which came cheap. In summer she gathered pails of blackberries from the wooded area behind her building. She bought eggs from the small farm she passed on her afternoon walks. She painted every day until she was dizzy with exhaustion, though it was more like being drunk, overtaken by a warm and tender swoon. She painted in her dreams and, upon awakening, immediately re-created the visions. Some days began with her sitting on the side of her bed for hours, waiting for inspiration to reveal itself. And like a friend one could count on in times of trouble, lines and colors arrived without fail.

For the first two weeks there was no sign of Richard. Violet looked around for him every time she left the house. Then one day a basket appeared on her small balcony at the top of the stairs, tucked under the eaves, out of the rain, covered in a green tea towel. Inside, she found bread and a jar of home-made strawberry jam. A week later she found the same. It was always on a Saturday.

Early one morning at the beginning of December, Violet was having a terrible dream of being pinned to the ground, a heavy weight crushing her chest. She woke with the feeling that someone was on top of her, and though she soon realized she was alone, she must have yelled, then yelled again. When she turned she saw Richard on the balcony, in the blue-black dark, with a basket in his hand. His eyes were wide, startled, and she was certain he had heard her shriek.

She jumped out of bed, wrapped her sweater around her

nightgown, and opened the door to the bitter cold. "Richie," she called out as he snuck down the stairs. He turned at the sound of her voice, and Violet stepped out to gather the basket. "Will you have breakfast with me?"

He smiled and hurried back up.

"Thank you for the baskets. You're very kind. I've thought of leaving you a thank-you note. But I don't know. Something about the silence between us appeals to me."

Richard smiled, and remained smiling for seconds too long.

Violet tightened her sweater around her waist. She ran her fingers through her messy hair.

"It's the least I can do," he said. "You've got no one, and you're working all the time." His voice lingered as he looked around her room at the row of paintings on the floor, stacked against two walls, one where the dresser used to be. Violet had scooted it into the small hall adjacent to the bathroom, creating a corner where her easel was set up. Her paintings jutted out from the corner in a V, and she stood at its center as if she were the captain of a sailing ship.

"Do you mind if I take a closer look?" he asked.

"Not at all." Violet made them coffee at the stove. She unpacked the basket to find cinnamon bread and plums, which she sliced and served at the bistro table that barely fit their long legs underneath.

"I go to college in Portland," he said. "I'm studying art history, much to the dismay of my father, who owns the lumberyard in town."

"Oh. I see. Well . . ."

"One of my professors shared an article in class about a woman collector in New York who is looking to showcase the work of women, in particular abstract modernists. Her name is Betty Johnson."

Violet gazed at him over the rim of the mug at her lips. She slowly lowered it to the table.

"I'm no expert. But I like to think I understand what I see. Especially quality." He met her eyes without looking away.

Violet was the first to break the stare. The sun was only now beginning to rise, and she could hear the rattle of debris-filled gutters streaming rain down the side of the building.

"You're really good, Violet. I don't know what I was expecting, I mean, I knew without knowing. I realize that doesn't make sense, I just had this feeling when you pulled into my driveway. I don't know. I don't know. Never mind that. Is it all right if I turn on the overhead light to have a look?"

Violet stood and flipped the switch, recalling something she'd forgotten, when her father had electricity installed shortly before that final, fateful Christmas. She and Em had reached up and pulled the string to the bulb in the ceiling, again and again and again, amazed by the trick.

Richard's interest in her work made her nervous. She didn't like the attention. But she liked what he had to say, and she could talk to him about the work in a way that came naturally. She didn't know where his interest in her paintings ended and his interest in her began. For her it was one and the same.

They had breakfast, and when she dressed in the bathroom afterward, she was aware of his presence in the other room when her gown dropped to the floor, and heat moved through her body.

By the time she was in her boots, the rain had eased and they walked for miles down the shore and back, misted by an occasional drizzle, a gust that sprinkled sand into her hair and the curves of their ears. They smiled at one another beneath breaks of sunshine, and spoke of color, lines, and space. They spoke of the works they'd both seen in Portland and in books at the library. "What is it?" Richard asked as Violet's eyes welled with tears.

She stopped and tucked her hair behind her ear, out of the wind. "I never knew that people could talk this way to each other. I guess you're used to it, but I'm not. This is . . ." She flung her hands at her sides. "I don't know what it is." What she did know but didn't say was that in some strange way, it hurt to feel this good. She didn't understand any of what was happening.

Later that evening, Richard returned at her invitation, both of them still flushed and tired from talking and strolling for hours in the fresh air. Violet lit a candle on the small table and fried two pieces of cod from the market across the street. She tore off hunks of bread, set them on two plates, and added dabs of the brightest yellow butter she'd ever seen, bought from the woman who sold the eggs.

"I'm sure you're wondering what happened to me." Before Richard had a chance to respond, she lifted her hand. "Our Christmas tree caught fire when I was seven. The scars go from my shoulder all the way down to my foot. Just so you know."

Richard grew quiet and solemn. She imagined him picturing her scarred body beneath her clothes, and she regretted having said anything.

"I'm sorry," she said. "That wasn't quite the way to start out such a nice dinner."

"No, no, thank you for telling me. I *was* wondering, of course."

His hair was no longer neatly combed. It was shaggy, mussed on one side of his forehead, with small wisps at his ears.

"*Bon appétit,*" she said.

"*Guten appetit,*" he replied.

Violet caught his eye. "Were you there, in the war?"

He nodded at his plate and began to eat quickly.

Violet glanced through the window beyond him, to the charcoal sky. So this was him, then, the man she had thought of while she was soaking in the bathtub in Los Angeles, the man who would have come home a different person than the one who'd left for war. The man she was going to marry.

He smiled up at her, then down at his plate, then at Violet. "I will tell you about it sometime."

Moments later, a tender happiness began to blossom, delicate as blown glass, palpably taking shape between them. And again that feeling of hurt, with the good, opposing forces sitting side by side. What if this thing broke apart? What if it were suddenly taken away?

"I can't wait for you to meet my friend Ada," Violet said, and just the sound of Ada's name in her mouth put her at ease. "She's extraordinary. Not like anyone you'll ever know."

"I'm not sure I can manage two people like that in such a short amount of time."

Violet smiled at her plate. She was uncomfortable being placed in the same category as Ada. Embarrassed by the comparison.

Then silence, except for the tines ticking plates, swallowing, breathing, the wind and rain picking up outside. There was a weight to the world, an importance floating on the black-blue light of dusk.

"My mother used to call dusk the hour between the dog and the wolf," she said.

"Are you afraid of me?" Richard asked, and though it stunned her to hear this, it seemed right of him to ask. He had understood her implicitly from the start.

"No," she said. It was true, but she did not fully believe it before she said it. "Are you afraid of me?"

"Yes," he said, placing his fork on the table, glancing at her lips.

Violet was an eighteen-year-old woman, had twice given birth, and never once been kissed.

42

Daniel *startled from* a dream that was so real it took him a moment to figure out where he was. He jumped out of bed and glanced around the room. Dani was asleep in the spare bed near the window. The blanket pulled to her chin where he'd tucked it after reading her a story. He was in his childhood home, his childhood bedroom. The clock read 3 a.m., and something was wrong.

He had dreamed he was in the bookstore, talking to Quincy, when she leaned over the counter. Her blouse was falling open, the sun lighting the gray stones of her necklace, her collarbone. She moved closer and held the back of his neck and kissed him so powerfully that he leaped from one state of consciousness into another.

His eyes adjusted to the dark bedroom. He opened and closed his fists, feeling thirsty and agitated by something that had nothing to do with the dream. He needed a glass of water.

When he stepped into the hallway his bare foot came down on something wet. A fur ball stuck to his toes in the dim light. "Damn it, Millicent," he hissed. When he balanced his next step on his heel he felt Millicent's fur against his toes.

Even in the dark it was clear that her stillness was not sleep.

He sat near her, leaned his back against the wall, and stroked her fur. Her body was hard and cool to the touch. His throat tightened. She must have died hours ago.

And then the sound of small feet shuffling on the hardwood.

"*Oh*, Dani. Come here. Be careful. Step around. Sit with me. I'm afraid . . ."

Dani crawled onto his lap. He wanted to wake his mother. And suddenly, there she was.

"I heard voices. Why are you in the hall?"

Daniel drew her eyes to Millicent on the floor beside him. "I just found her."

"Is she . . . ?"

His mother lifted Dani up to her hip. "Oh, this is just, oh, Millicent. You sweet thing. I'm so sorry, Daniel."

"What's she doing?" Dani asked.

"She's . . ." his mother said. "Going to *heaven*?"

She looked at Daniel, and even in the dark he could see she was searching for a better answer. What *was* she doing? What was he supposed to tell his young daughter about death? What was she able to understand? Maybe there was a book about it. Yes, he would get a book, but then the dream rushed back, and it was all he could do to clear his throat. "Let's talk about it in the morning. I'm going to wrap her in something. I'll get a towel, I'll . . . I don't know what I'll do, but Mom, could you tuck Dani back in bed? I'm going to wake up Dad."

"You tuck Dani in, son. I'll wake your dad."

43

The sun had barely broken over the horizon when Frank, Daniel, and Penny gathered near the cedar tree. Dew on the needles filled the air with a pleasant acrid scent that Frank associated with nostalgia. Like songs from the 1970s that sent an ache through his heart every time they came on the radio, his youth seemed to crackle again on the air, memories shifting in and out of time.

Millicent lay nearby, wrapped in an old sweatshirt of Penny's. "It has my smell on it," she'd said. "Don't you think she'd . . ."

Frank had never seen Penny so distraught. She'd woken him by leaning onto the bed, sitting down, and giving herself over to a great fit of sobs. He'd sat up quickly, trying to understand. His first thought was that his mother was dead.

Just as he was starting to feel what it meant to lose her, just when the first splinter of grief entered his heart, Penny slowed between sobs and said, "She was lying on the floor, and there was a fur ball, apparently, that Daniel had stepped on, and poor Dani, asking where Millicent would go now . . ."

Frank burst out laughing. Jesus, it was the *cat*. His mother was *alive*. "Oh God, Penny," he said.

"Fuck you, Frank," she said.

And now he was lowering Millicent into the ground, and for everything he'd pushed away in the night, it came back to him tenfold. An image of the future appeared before his eyes, one where he lived alone, an angry old man whom people couldn't stand to be around, while Dani and Daniel spent holidays with Penny, who was thriving, all lighthearted and happy to be by herself. This future was coming for him, sharp as a hot knife through the chest.

He glanced at Penny wiping her eyes. Her hair fell forward over her shoulders when she reached up to rub the side of Daniel's arm. She smiled at Daniel, who smiled back, the tenderness between them palpable.

Frank grabbed the shovel and filled in the hole. The sound of soil dropping, every scrape of the metal against dirt, recalled his father's funeral, and how inconsolable his mother had been, how Penny had been the one to comfort her, too.

When he finished, he jammed the shovel upright in the ground, walked over, and kissed Penny on the mouth. It was not an erotic kiss, but it wasn't without passion, either.

Her eyes grew large.

"Jesus, Dad," Daniel said.

"I'm sorry about Millicent," he said, pulling away from Penny's lips. "I thought at first that you were crying because my mother had died."

"Oh!" Penny crossed her arms and took a step back. She let go a wet sound between her lips, like a raspberry.

"I'm going to go see if Grand is awake," Daniel said, walking away.

"And then you said what you said," Frank continued, "and it made me mad, and I didn't feel like explaining myself after that."

"OK."

He glanced at his feet. The yearning in her eyes was going to break him. And then, "Penny?" he said, looking up from the ground, but she had already turned away from him, and didn't stop walking at the sound of his voice. The kitchen door closed behind her.

"Penny," he said into the air—no matter, it was practice for when he would say it to her for real. "This isn't easy." He ran his hand through his hair. "I want to tell you some things.

I want to tell you what matters to me, or maybe doesn't but should. I want to hear what you think about it. I want to know a few things about you."

Frank sat on the ground next to the fresh grave, his ridiculous, hollow words dissipating in the air. He crossed his legs, propped his elbows on his knees, and held his head in his hands. "You may still want to leave me," he whispered, "but before you go, before you go . . ." He didn't know how to finish.

44

Richard had stopped by on a sunny Saturday before his Christmas break to photograph Violet's work. A buzz of excitement came off his body, and Violet absorbed it too quickly, too deeply, like a gust of wind. Each time he came around, Violet had to readjust herself. After so much time alone, it was a shock to be thrown into something so intense.

She stepped out onto the balcony to get some air, leaving him inside. Every now and then she glanced through the window to watch him clicking the camera and moving things around. Her life had changed so much, and was changing still. She was a woman on the verge. So much more was headed her way.

When Richard finished taking pictures, he hurried out, kissed her on the mouth, and told her he needed to get back to Portland to drop the film off to be developed before the shop closed. He yelled that he would be back in two days, when his break began, and reminded her he would be home for two full weeks. She was raising her hand in goodbye, laughing as he zipped around to his car. When he reached the car door, he turned and looked up at her from the street. "I love you," he yelled. Before she could tell him that she loved him too, before there was a chance to consider how this couldn't be possible when they had known each other for such a short time, when they had yet to see each other fully naked, Richard jumped into his car and drove away, leaving Violet on the balcony, wrapped in a whirl of emotion. He was not like other men who'd returned from the war, the way that article had said. Was he? It was true that she could feel a strange *other* in his silences, in the way he drank a whiskey and looked out at the sea. Even so, he never felt too far away from her, absorbed into his past, not yet, not in these early days.

Richard mailed the photographs to New York before Christmas.

Since their first day together, Violet had wanted to tell Richard about the child she gave away, if only to rid herself of the anchor that weighed at the center of her happiness. But how would such a thing make him feel? How would it improve his happiness, or hers? She thought of them both as having lived through their own wars, and they did not speak about these wars to anyone, not even to each other.

But she *had* told him about the girl she left in the desert, as a way to explain her body. How else to account for the tiny silver lines at the sides of her breasts and lower abdomen from stretching? It was a story connected to James, too. What had happened to her at the hands of the country preacher had happened shortly before she met James. She didn't know when she met James that she was already pregnant. She didn't know when James was encouraging her to become an artist, and when he told her to travel west and gave her the address on Blueberry Lane, that a child was already growing inside her. All she knew was that when the preacher who'd held her down before showed up again a week after Violet had met James, she had found the strength to refuse to speak to him, to refuse her mother's demands that all this man wanted was to save her. Even though she had no real understanding of where she was headed, she knew enough to know she would never be coming back.

She had wanted Richard to know that his brother, and all the circumstances surrounding those days, changed the course of her life, that she had arrived where she was today in large part because of James. And now that she was certain of Richard's love for her, she was certain just how much he loved and missed James. Telling him the story of the baby in the desert served more than one purpose. Telling him brought her and Richard closer together.

But she could not talk about the baby who had lived, who was living still, she assumed, somewhere in the world this minute. For starters, she didn't want Richard's pity, or worse, his judgment. This kind of thing could happen to a woman once, sure, a person could understand how this could happen once. But twice? This happened *twice*? She worried that even if it didn't change his feelings for her, he might want to find the girl, believing he was doing her a favor, even as Violet lived with the fear that the girl would someday find her. So instead of telling him, when he asked what was on her mind, when he could see she was mired in something heavy, Violet switched the subject to another thing that had also been on her mind. "My name is Violet Swan," she said, "and I don't ever plan on changing it."

"Is this your way of saying you will never marry me?"

"No. Are you asking me to marry you?"

"Yes."

On Christmas Eve, they told his parents in their small, overheated living room that they were going to be married. His mother set her sugar cookie back onto her plate. "I don't think . . . Are you sure? I mean, who am I to judge . . ."

His father, who was feeble for his age, ravaged a bit in the mind, offered a kind nod, as if unmoved by the announcement. And then he said, "I wish James were here to share the news."

The billowing silence smothered their happy news. And then his father said, "But I'm glad for you, Richard. Your mother and I are glad for you both."

"Yes, of course," his mother said, sounding miserable in a complicated way. And then her face and voice took on a new tone, as if she were trying to see what it would sound like if she really *were* glad for them. "I'd like you to have the chifforobe that belonged to my grandfather. But where will you live? I'll fill it with some nice things for you, Violet. Some linens and such."

"Welcome to the family, Violet," Richard's father said, and Violet did not feel any more welcome than the first day when she pulled into the drive. But when she looked at Richard's mother, she recognized the same expression she had seen in the women at train stations during the war, a look of abandonment.

Violet reached for her hand. "Thank you. That's very kind."

His mother patted the top of her hand and stood.

They married in a small chapel overlooking the Nehalem River. It was so cold in the spring that the rain kept threatening to turn to snow, but instead it went right to ice. Richard's father wept while hail pounded the roof, but his mother remained stoic, as if lost in a protective trance. Ada, whom Violet hadn't seen for several months, was there, dressed in a beautiful jade dress that matched her eyes. Her date was an architect named John Strout, a charming man whom they'd liked from the start.

And then Violet and Richard were off to the Grand Canyon for a honeymoon, where the landscape resembled Violet's scars, and Richard made her laugh by telling her about the map his parents gave him as a teenager.

It had taken many attempts over the previous weeks before Violet stopped thinking of Richard as the kind of man he was not. She had wanted him to touch her, and to touch him in return, but when they tried, she panicked, pulling the blanket to her throat. Her body was a foreign map of dangerous terrain. "It's all right," Richard would say. "When you're ready," he'd say, and make her a cup of tea, tell her they should take a walk, draw, read, or paint, expel their energy in other ways. But it seemed that the exhilaration of their honeymoon delivered her to a place of safety and joy. His body became a sanctuary, a place of pleasure and comfort. His hand between her legs felt good, felt right as anything she'd ever known, and she asked for more. And more. Her body was finally her own.

But two weeks of unbounded happiness in Colorado were quickly reeled in when they returned to find that Richard's parents weren't home. It was warm outside, and all the windows were shut. Flies had gathered in the kitchen.

The first person they ran into was Hazel, who screamed at the sight of them, cried that there was no way to reach them, and explained how Henry Daltry, who worked with Richard's father at the lumberyard, had seen Richard's father wander too close to the shore as a wave carrying a log clipped the backs of his legs and bowled him over. Richard's mother ran to help when another wave appeared and pulled them both out to sea before Henry could intervene. Hours later they washed up along the rocks of Neahkhanie Mountain. "They've been in the hospital morgue, waiting on you to . . . to lay them to rest."

For days, and then weeks, Richard said close to nothing, just drank whiskey on the porch and looked out at the sea, and Violet guessed that the place where he kept what had happened to him in the war was the same place where he was keeping his newest grief.

"Now we're both orphans," he said one day, perhaps already a little tipsy. Violet clarified that she never said her mother was dead.

"Where is she, then?"

Had he not been listening? She had told him everything. "In Georgia." She ended it there, not up to revisiting the topic.

Weeks after the funeral, a letter arrived from Betty Johnson in New York. Betty wanted Violet to know that she was traveling to Seattle and Portland in the coming months, and asked if she could meet Violet in Portland with Violet's work on hand.

In spite of his grief, or perhaps because of it, Richard could hardly contain his excitement. But Violet had already missed several weeks of work, from the wedding to the honeymoon to the funeral, to the distraction of Richard's moods. So she responded by thanking Betty for her interest, but wrote that she would not be able to meet her in Portland. She had not painted anything for weeks, owing to a series of events, and couldn't waste more time packing up and hauling her paintings over the pass and into town for someone who may or may not care to buy them. She invited Betty to come to the coast to see her work, apologizing for any inconvenience, and thanking her regardless of whether this arrangement would suit.

"Surely you did *not* tell her that," Richard said, though on some level he was clearly amused.

Three weeks later, Violet received a reply and told Richard, "Apparently, she was impressed by what I wrote. She says she admires my work ethic, and if the paintings are as good as they appear to be in the photographs, she looks forward to working with me in the near future."

Five weeks later, Betty rolled into town wearing a tight-fitting navy-blue dress and matching heels. She smoked non-stop, and the minute the sun sank low enough, she bought everyone a round of drinks and steaks at the Neahkahnie Tavern, where she offered to buy ten paintings, three of which were done on the linen canvases Violet had made from the fabric given to her by Richard's mother. But there were two paintings Violet refused to let go of: one titled *Grief,* the other *Love.* These were the first works that evoked her style of light and emotion. And these were the works that Betty wanted most of all. As a result, she paid Violet more than she normally might for the ones she took. "You're going somewhere," she said, pointing with her cigarette. "I see what you're capable of, and I can tell you right now, someday your work is going to be worth more money than either of you can imagine."

A year later, they had torn down the old house on Blueberry Lane and built their own. The idea of making the loft upstairs was entirely Violet's. John Strout, to whom Ada was now married, helped design the house.

When Violet told him that the only interior walls of the loft should be for the bathroom and walk-in closet, and they should have alder plank doors painted charcoal gray and hung on tracks for sliding open and closed, and that daylight should enter unimpeded from all directions, John stared at her as if he needed more convincing. He didn't care for the aesthetics, and asked, "Why do you need a full kitchen and bath up there? Is Richard to live downstairs while you live up? And what if your work doesn't continue to sell? Or you lose interest in painting, fickle as women can be." John winked at Richard, who frowned in return. This was the start of knowing that John could be the worst kind of man one minute and the best sort the next. He could talk about Violet's art in the same way Richard could, with a deep understanding and appreciation of her vision, and of other artists that Violet admired as well. He'd wash the dishes after dinner, whistling a tune, stopping to take a few dance steps with Ada. And then he'd make a crack to Richard about catching him looking at Ada's legs, or a comment to Ada about wishing he was more like Richard, bending to her needs. Then he'd laugh it off, apologize even, and call himself crass, the way he did after the remark about women being fickle. Nevertheless, Ada adored him, forgave him everything, and Violet understood John's appeal. It was difficult not to like someone so painfully handsome and bright. He could carry on conversations with enormous scope, from workers' rights to the state of affairs in Europe, to art, to husbandry, but perhaps his greatest charm was that he appeared to be listening with such interest when others spoke, it was practically like watching someone fall in love. In many ways, he was big enough to be a match for Ada.

"My work is paying your salary," Violet had replied to the comment about women being fickle. She was burning with rage that felt only slightly misplaced and even less embarrassing, and also satisfyingly on target. She walked out of his office, refusing to hear another word. She closed the door behind her and could hear John laughing and half apologizing, and she couldn't tell if Richard was laughing beneath the uproar, but he did not follow her out, and with this she had a bit of trouble for some time.

Once the house was built, the years passed, one into the next, in much the same way. During the day Violet painted in the loft while Richard sketched downstairs or outdoors, and evenings were spent having dinner at the Neahkahnie Tavern, where the fireplace roared in winter, French doors were propped wide open to the sunset in summer, and someone was always playing the piano in the main room. Artists rented cottages nearby, the rich on the ridge, the poor just below, near town. Betty came to visit every few years, and began to bring other artists with her. One was Lee Krasner, whose ability to work in so many different mediums Violet found remarkable. "I've only ever met or heard of men who do all that you've done," Violet told her. "And get three times the credit" was Lee's response.

Here was a woman living in the shadow of her husband's fame, and yet the oeuvre of her entire life was broad and impressive, from her art to her work in politics and education. She had studied at the famous Cooper Union and the National Academy of Design. She spoke fast, with the same New York accent as Betty. Her energy was electric, kinetic, her use of color fierce, and in this way, the opposite of Violet's pale, translucent light. Looking at Lee's work was like peeking inside Pandora's box. Dark aggressions gathered there, trapped in a single, mesmerizing space. It was impossible not to feel the lack of suffering when one looked beyond the frame.

Lee moved through the world as if unimpeded, just like Ada, with rigor and integrity, no matter what the world did or did not do for her. At dinner one night at the tavern, Violet caught a glimpse of Richard shying away from the conversation, sitting back as if bored, except when Lee confirmed the rumors about Jackson's affairs. "He doesn't even try to hide it," she said, and Richard crossed his arms in defense of something that Violet guessed had to do with finding his place in the family of these things. Violet was seven months pregnant and feeling fairly misplaced herself. But Violet saw something in Richard's eyes as he quickly looked away, looked back, and swallowed his drink. "What is it?" Lee said, elbow on the table, hand in the air, gesturing with her lit cigarette from one to the other. "You two look like you've seen a ghost."

45

Penny saw something move in the corner of her eye. She glanced up from tying her shoelaces on the back patio and spotted a white rabbit in the garden ten yards away, sitting on its hind legs, eating greens.

The back door creaked behind her, and she held up a hand to stop whoever was coming out. The rabbit continued to stare in her direction. The door settled back onto the latch.

Penny assumed it was Frank.

"I'll be damned," Daniel whispered.

When Penny turned and saw Dani with wide eyes above her red jacket, her hair pulled into a ponytail, which Daniel would have done for her, she felt as if she'd woken to another time and place, some alternate life she might have lived but never got the chance. Except now she had, and nothing about it seemed real. She looked at the rabbit and then at Daniel, with his finger to his lips. "Shh," he told Dani. "We don't want to scare him away."

"*Lapin*," Dani whispered, lowering herself into a little crouch, and Penny had a terrible urge to kiss her entire face, which she refrained from doing.

"Yes," Daniel said. "Look at that. A rabbit has come to visit. What should we name him?"

Penny recalled what the twins had said at the clinic about getting a dog to keep the critters from the garden. But what if she didn't want the critters to go away but also wanted the dog?

"*Chiot*," Dani said, and Daniel snickered into his shoulder.
"What does it mean?" Penny asked.
"Puppy," Daniel said, and turned to stifle his laugh.
Penny looked in the opposite direction and did the same.

She might not kiss Dani's entire face just yet, but she couldn't help running her hand through the length of Dani's ponytail. The girl smiled up at her with little pearls for teeth, and Penny made an effort not to show how hard these feelings were pulverizing her heart.

She turned to see Frank looking at her stroking Dani's hair, smiling, then pointing to the rabbit and smiling some more.

I see it, she mouthed with a grin. She recalled Frank's unexpected kiss, and felt herself blush as she turned away. Unlike the other day when they'd all gone off to the beach together, this moment felt a little less strained.

The rabbit seemed to have had its fill of the greens and hopped briskly beneath the fence and disappeared.

Frank stepped out wearing jeans and a black fleece, looking more relaxed than she'd seen him in years. He was carrying their wicker picnic basket, which had been around for decades. "What's so funny?" he asked, and she could see in his eyes that he felt left out.

"Dani called the rabbit *puppy* in French," Penny said, which set her and Daniel laughing all over again. Frank laughed too, but it didn't strike him quite as funny. Of course he had the garden to think about. "Shall we go?" he asked, holding up the basket. "I threw together a few snacks for the beach."

It was a small gesture, but one of the more thoughtful things he'd done in some time, and Penny didn't want it to go unnoticed. She also didn't want to draw too much attention to it and break up the joy she could sense everyone feeling. "Thank you," she said. He gave a small nod and faced the ocean, as if he were embarrassed by the sweetness of her tone.

As the three of them walked down the driveway, Penny glanced up to see Violet in the window, blowing them each a kiss. Frank waved and looked away. For several yards he kept his sights on the ground, until Penny stepped next to him.

"I wish Grand could come with us," Daniel said. "I loved when she used to take me to the beach. She'd point out all kinds of things that I never would have spotted otherwise."

Frank glanced at Daniel with a mild, faraway smile, and Penny wondered if Violet had ever taken him to the beach when he was a child. She guessed not, as Frank had never mentioned it, though that didn't necessarily mean it was true.

When they reached the site of the fairy fort, Frank stopped and turned to Daniel. "I think we should rebuild this with Dani. Set it up so that every time she passes it she'll feel something like you used to."

"Oh," Penny said, and regretted it immediately.

"Sure, Dad. I'd like that. Dani would like that."

They were quiet the rest of the way, as if everyone had become shy. This strange kindness, or whatever it was, clearly made them all uneasy, as if he or she didn't want to be the one to say the wrong thing and break the spell. They unfolded the blankets on the sand, emptied out the basket, and Penny and Frank spent the next several hours watching Daniel and Dani run around. Daniel was like a child again, re-creating castles and moats from his boyhood. Penny and Frank gazed at their son and granddaughter, drank wine, and commented on the waves and light and dogs running loose with other kids.

"There was something my mother said to me in the ambulance that still has my head spinning," Frank said, and Penny's reverie began to sink. "I've been waiting for her to take me aside and explain. She hasn't, and I'm hesitant to ask, not even sure I want to know."

"That sounds serious."

"She told me that Ada's husband John died in jail, and that I was in the room when *it* happened. But she wouldn't say what actually happened."

Penny leaned closer, offering him a look that said it was OK to go on.

"I don't remember it at all. But the way she made it sound reminded me of a time when she was passed out and my dad was crying over her."

Penny blinked rapidly. "I'm sorry. Can you start at the beginning?"

He took another sip of wine. "The other day, when she passed out, I was remembering a time, or thought I was, when my mother had what I thought were epileptic fits."

Penny's mouth fell open. "This is like, I don't even know. This is your mother we're talking about? Violet?"

"Well, now I don't know. I mean, the whole thing . . . I'm confused. I'm thinking she might have had some kind of shock treatments."

Penny reared back.

"She used to go to the hospital in Portland for several days at a time. I used to stay with Ada and John. When my mother came back, she'd act strange, tired and dazed. I don't really want to ask her about it. I don't think she wants to go there. But I'm kind of hoping she'll tell Daniel as part of this thing they're doing."

Penny shook her head. "This is . . . I'm just trying to wrap my head around it. I mean, I guess, if what you're saying is right, I don't know, Frank, maybe in this case you need to let it go for the moment. It's a lot to take in, and maybe this is why she's doing this project with Daniel. Maybe this is her chance to get it out?"

Frank pulled his knees to his chest.

"Daniel said he was going to tell me something about their conversation the last time we came down here," Penny said, "but he didn't. I don't want to ask and interfere with their fun. It feels so good to just sit here and watch the two of them play."

"Look, look, look," Dani said, rushing up to show Frank an ordinary rock. "Pretty," she said, and Frank declared it was the most gorgeous thing he'd ever seen.

And then, just like that, Dani said, "I'm tired."

Since when did a child admit to such a thing?

As they began to pack up, Penny could feel the fold of something new. She didn't want to discuss or even think about it, lest she cause the bubble to burst. It was the first time in ages when she felt better not saying anything to anyone.

On the walk home, she suggested they pop into the bookstore. "It won't take long. I already know what I want to get."

"Sure," Daniel said, with more enthusiasm than seemed warranted, and his tone revved up Dani, who was so tired she'd needed to be carried, her eyes bobbing shut with the rhythm of Daniel's steps.

And in they came, the four of them, stepping past the open Dutch door, their sun-kissed cheeks, a lightness to their steps. But this had nothing to do with the look on Quincy's face when she saw them. Her face was open and full of joy, but her sights were fully on Daniel. And his were fully on her. If there existed a gadget that could capture electricity between two people, it would have gone off full tilt between these two.

"Dani," Quincy said, "have you come for a book?" She continued to eye Daniel.

Penny glanced at Frank. He gave her a quick head-bob to say, *Yes, I see it too.*

Dani nodded with a serious face.

"Can I take Dani to the children's section?" Penny asked.

"Of course." Daniel handed her over, and as she wrapped the girl around her hip, she felt a familiar surge, like when she was walking among the trees.

She found a copy of the book about the big orange splot and brought it to the counter, and Daniel let out a gasp. "I've been thinking about this book. I can't wait to read it to her."

Dani wriggled to be put down, and Penny lowered her so she could see the books about gems and stars that Quincy had placed on the shelves below the counter.

Penny had planned to read the book to Dani herself, had been thinking about it for several days now, and stopped in to get it for that very reason. But of course her own father would want to read it to her. "Well, here you go. It's a gift from me."

Frank walked up with a stuffed white rabbit. "Look. I found Puppy."

Dani jumped up and down, reaching for it. Frank handed it to her, and Penny wondered, quite seriously, how a person was supposed to live with such things breaking one's heart all day long.

Daniel and Quincy wandered over to the corner, discussing novels. Quincy was saying, "I really think you'll like this one. The main character is struggling with what it means to come home again, well, and a whole lot more, but it's set around here, and you mentioned you like reading books that take place in the place you're in, so I'd consider this one for sure."

Penny wondered when and where these conversations had taken place. On the phone?

Dani roamed around the store with Puppy, singing to herself, showing the rabbit the shelves. She made her way to Daniel, who immediately picked her up.

"We need to get this one home," he said, a trace of regret in his voice.

At the register, Quincy inquired about Violet. "I know she can't really make it to the store these days, but I think about her all the time, not least of which because she used to live upstairs. It's like her presence is fixed around here."

Penny must have had a puzzled look on her face. Frank certainly did. He said, "What do you mean she used to live upstairs?"

Quincy narrowed her eyes as if she, or was it they, must have gotten something wrong. "I thought everyone knew that this was where she lived when she first came to town. No?"

"I never heard anything at all about where she lived when she came here," Frank said. "I assumed she rented a place at the tavern before it burned down."

"Oh," Quincy said.

"I never knew, either," Penny said.

"You?" Quincy asked Daniel.

"No. But I'll ask her to talk about it on film if she's willing."

Dani rubbed her eyes.

"We'll be home in a few minutes." Penny paid for the books and the rabbit, listening for any reluctance in the way Daniel and Quincy said goodbye, and finding it—that hesitation inherent in nervous attraction.

As they walked up the hill, Penny and Frank slipped back behind Daniel and Dani. She whispered in Frank's ear, "My God. Was there something in the air or what?"

"I'll say."

Penny hesitated. "But also, I mean, shock treatments on your mom, Frank? I can't stop thinking about what you said."

"I don't know for sure," he said, sinking back into himself, like a switch that caused her to retreat, too. For the rest of the way home she thought about that push and pull between Frank and Violet, that unexplained need for forgiveness that always hummed out around them.

46

Violet *climbed on* a stepstool in front of her canvas with a piece of sandpaper in her hand, something she had done hundreds of times in her life. She needed to give the surface of the painting a gentle scrubbing to create a more complex effect of the graphite lines and top layer of paint. But she stepped down off the stool in defeat.

A tumble would end everything prematurely. And the work was nearly done. But to finish it, she would have to ask for help. She lifted the dropcloth back over the canvas so that no one would see, and then she called to Francisco and Daniel from the top of the stairs. They came running as if to save her life.

Violet smiled. "I just needed a hand."

"Ohhh," they said.

"I need you to take the work off the wall and lay it on the floor so I can sand it. I don't want to lose my balance on the stool. See that the dropcloth stays over it, will you?"

She watched the men work together to take the canvas down, laughing in a panicked way as it slid one direction, then another, before they were able to lower it safely to the floor.

"Thank you both," Violet said, and they hesitated as if something more needed to be done or said.

"I'll need it back up on the wall in an hour or so, if you two don't mind."

As they walked away, nodding, Violet got the sense that she had given them some small thing, an uneventful moment that had put them in the same space at the same time, and managed to fill a tiny hole.

The temperature was rising, the hours of daylight remaining a bit longer. Summer was only a few days away, and Violet was learning how to ration her energy. She worked in intervals, resting in between, and when she wasn't doing either of those, she met with Daniel.

During the daytime, the conversation often hovered around art, how she'd taught herself to paint, developed her techniques and philosophies, recounted the early days of her success. She spoke of her relationship with Richard, of his love and support for her, and how she never stopped missing him, even now. It was pleasant, or more so, than the evening hours, when the shift in light seemed to summon things that happened to her as a child. Bit by bit, the details of her memories emerged, and bit by bit she shared them openly and honestly with Daniel.

She had not spoken to Francisco about what had happened with Ada, and she couldn't help but wonder how it was that he had not known. How many times had she wished she could go back over those minutes when Ada died, and do them just the slightest bit differently? When Ada offered to help Violet in the kitchen with the drinks, Violet insisted she stay put and listen to the music with John in the living room. "Dance with me," Ada said. "Why don't we just dance? Let the men get the drinks." But Violet had laughed her off, and in the time it took Ada to die, Violet was busy knocking over whiskey on the kitchen counter and floor. She and Richard were fumbling, trying to wipe it up, laughing at the mess, and that laughter was one of the worst things to recall, her own snickering punctuated by a drunken kiss with Richard, while in the next room John was squeezing the life out of Ada.

By the time Violet and Richard entered the room, Ada had slumped halfway from the sofa to the floor, and John stood over her body, staring at his hands in the air above his wife as if he couldn't believe what they had done. The backs of his knuckles were bleeding from Ada's nails. And there, to the side, stood eight-year-old Francisco, gripping the frame of a painting nearly half his size.

It was impossible to think of how differently their lives might have turned out if Violet hadn't told Ada she didn't need her help, and hadn't knocked over the whiskey in the kitchen, and instead returned to the living room three minutes earlier with a tray of drinks and good cheer. But who could say if John wouldn't have found another time to take Ada's life? Or perhaps thought better of his heavy drinking, and such a thought would have never occurred to him at all. Who could say what would have happened that night if Francisco had never come across the painting of Ada, hidden in the guest room closet where he was searching for the best spots to play hide-and-seek? Who could say if he hadn't brought it out into the living room, laughing at the naked breasts, how different things might have been? Perhaps Francisco would have grown up with more confidence and an open sort of kindness and more patience for things that frightened him, or that he did not like or understand. Perhaps he would not have grown into a man who shut out the people who cared most about him. Or maybe none of these things mattered at all. Maybe Ada was always going to die at John's hand, and Francisco was simply who he had been from the start.

"Who painted her?" Daniel asked after a moment of stunned silence. It was the right question.

"Richard," Violet whispered, feeling the red of the setting sun on her skin, the heavy weight of time pressing against the room.

47

Daniel *looked down* from the loft window with Dani on his hip. It was the middle of the week, and his father was unlocking his work shed and stepping inside. Daniel kissed his daughter's cheek, aware of the ordinary moment as his life with her began to take shape. He was already better at recognizing the things she wanted and needed. She no longer cried when she woke.

Moments later he heard the buzz of a saw, and looked over at his grandmother in her reading chair, fastening her hair into a clip. "What do you suppose that's all about?" she asked.

"He mentioned wanting to rebuild the fairy fort."

"Did he?"

"He asked if I wanted to help, so I don't know if that's what he's doing now or not."

"Well. Either way, this is good news. I'm happy to hear this."

"I can see him changing, Grand. There's something going on."

"I think your being here with Dani is changing everything."

"I don't know. I hope so."

"I meant to ask, was your mom OK with getting the picture back?"

"Yeah, but she was pretty embarrassed."

"I didn't mean for that."

"I know."

"I'll talk to her. How are they?"

Daniel and Dani rubbed noses and laughed. "They're right downstairs, you can ask them yourself."

"I'm aware. I mean, how do they seem? To you."

"The same? Maybe a little better lately. It's hard to tell with them. They're on some kind of rollercoaster that I've never understood. I can't tell if I'm unable to figure them out, even now, because I haven't seen them in a year, or if I got used to not being around people who can't stand each other and I have no idea what to make of them."

Would he edit that part out of the film? Should he?

He bounced Dani around the room on his hip. He was having a hard time getting started today. He didn't know how to approach his grandmother about what she had told him yesterday. Was his grandfather having an affair with Ada? And what about the DNA test? Did it have to do with this?

He stopped at the window with the best view of the ocean. "*Si belle*," Daniel said.

"*Qui?*" Dani said.

The saw continued to buzz in the work shed.

"It's really not that they can't stand each other, sweetheart," his grandmother said.

"What do you call it, then?"

"I don't know if it has a name. All I know is they're locked in the same old script. Repeating the same lines over and over. Of course, no one can tell them that. They certainly don't want to hear it from me."

"Or me."

"Or you. The young and the old. What do we know? Did I ever tell you about your father asking us to call him Frank?"

"I don't think so."

"It was around the time he turned twelve. He said everyone called him Frank now, and he wanted us to do the same. So Richard said, 'But that's a form of currency in Switzerland,' which made me laugh, and Richard laughed at me laughing, and Francisco stomped out of the room. He thought we were terrible parents."

Daniel flashed on the image of his grandfather painting a nude of his grandmother's best friend.

"Oh, I don't know about *that*, Grand. I've never heard him say a bad word about you in my life."

"Well. Just because your father doesn't reveal his emotions doesn't mean he doesn't have any." She cleared her throat. "Anyway . . . years later your father brought your mother home to meet us, and Richard said, 'Frank and Penny. There's quite a bit of tender between you two."

Daniel groaned. "Granddad, the master of the dad joke." He flashed on his father as a boy, running into a room with a nude painting, laughing at the nakedness, and in the next moment, his father would witness Ada's murder.

"Your mother laughed and said how relieved she was that he hadn't said, 'A penny for your thoughts.' I liked her from the start. I was so happy with your father's choice."

Daniel walked back to the other view. His father came out of the shed, brushing his hands on the seat of his pants before entering the house. "Do you think Macy was the wrong choice for me?" He wasn't sure why he said it. He felt a need to make quick sense of something and this was what popped into his head.

"Daniel, I'm sorry you've had to go through all of that. I'll be honest, I liked her well enough, I just don't think she was right for you."

Daniel nodded, walking around looking at the paintings and sketches, views from every window, the trees and sky, teaching Dani more words in English. She gazed at him with weariness one minute and pure devotion the next.

"The day is gorgeous, Daniel. You should take Dani down to the beach. We don't have to film today."

"I'm planning on it. I always forget how beautiful it all is until I return home. It never gets old."

"Can't say as much for the rest of us."

Daniel gave her a wry smile.

"It's a good place to raise a child."

Daniel kissed Dani's cheek and set her down in front of the easel. He took in a long breath. "I don't know. Being here, remembering all the things I loved about growing up, mostly makes me want to stay. But I don't know what's best for her. My parents . . ."

"I'm guessing wherever you're happy is where it's the best for her."

"Right now my entire life is in LA. I don't care much for the work I've been doing. Too often I'm forced to edit stuff that bores me, and even with the stuff I like, I'm forced to cut things that should probably remain, and having to leave things in that only serve to exploit or manipulate the viewer's feelings. It makes me feel like a fraud."

"But now you have this." She gestured her head toward the camera.

"Yes, thank you, Grand. This could be life-changing. In the meantime, I might not have a choice about staying or going as things shape up. I've had to turn down two jobs to come here, and as a freelancer I can only afford to do that so many times before people stop calling.

"If it's money you need . . ."

"No thanks, Grand. I'll be all right. It's my future I'm thinking of. I like LA. I do. I wish you could have come down to see it."

"I've seen it, Daniel."

Daniel looked at her. "That's right."

"It's been a while. I was sixteen years old."

"I'd say it's changed."

"Just a bit."

"What I was saying before?" his grandmother said. "I realize life is slow here, and of course that's the way we like it. It's quiet, and probably boring for most young people, or I imagine it is. It was never that way for me, or Richard. But I also know that it made you who you are, did it not? I'm biased, of course, but I quite like you, Daniel Swan." She glanced at Dani. "And there are people here who will love her unconditionally."

Daniel glanced at Dani, who was drawing again on butcher paper. His chest filled with emotion.

"What will her mother do when she's released? Will she come back for her?"

"No. I mean, I don't know. Maybe she'll come here to the States, to visit. But I have full legal custody. She has the right to see her. That's all. She's not a bad person, Grand. She wanted something better for Dani, and I think she wanted something better for herself. Arielle's own mother is in a nursing home, and her father doesn't have the capacity to raise Dani. He drinks too much and lives in a studio apartment. Arielle is an only child. And she *wanted* her with me. She wanted . . . I think she wanted her own life back, to be honest. I don't know. I don't hold that, or anything, against her. And she trusts me, which probably has something to do with you, me being your grandson, but that doesn't bother me."

"Daniel, I don't want to speak on things that aren't my business. But it's late in the day in more ways than one, and there's no need for me to be coy . . ."

"What?" Her face was so serious that Daniel sat next to her, took her hand.

"Quincy is here, too."

Later, Daniel would discover that this was one of those moments, unplanned, when the camera had the ability to capture a thought inside someone's head, to penetrate the eyes and see what was happening behind them. But the thoughts exposed that day weren't his grandmother's. They were his, on the cutting room floor.

48

They had spoken on the phone several times, ostensibly about books. Quincy called to say there was a book in the store on plants, and an old one on gems that had recently been reprinted, one that she herself had loved as a child and thought that Dani would love, too. The conversation stretched on, toward the book Daniel was reading, and one she had read and loved herself. Quincy shared more about growing up in Florida, and how she and her sister had left there to live with their father in Arizona. She told him about the time she learned to ride a bike, and how they'd cheered her on in the street as she went around and around, feeling her life changing in the middle of the change, which had only ever happened a few times in her life, and Daniel could not help wondering if it was happening to her here.

"My father used to make up elaborate stories for me at bedtime," he told her, which was something he'd sort of forgotten. "They would seep into my dreams, and in the morning I'd walk to school with my father's words and images still spinning behind my eyes."

"Do you think this had any influence on your interest in film?" Quincy asked.

"I'm sure it did, though to be honest, I'd never made that connection before now."

"I wonder what he would think if you told him that."

"I think he'd be shocked."

"I think he'd be pleased."

"Yeah. I guess he would."

"And your mother? What was she like?"

Daniel recalled his mother as if she were a ghost in a flurry, here then there, taking care of one thing, then the next. One memory rose above the rest. "I think she was always afraid of losing me. She used to sit by my bed when I was sick, and I'd wake in the night to find her slumped in the chair."

"Aw. I didn't have my mom around, so to me that sounds . . . comforting."

Daniel thought about Dani's expression when he had wiped her wet face while she reached for him. "It was a mix of things. I was always able to fall right back asleep with her there, but I also felt her fear, and in this way I wanted to protect her, this person who was meant to protect me."

"Hmm," she said, in a way that conveyed genuine interest. "Well . . ."

Daniel worried that Quincy was edging toward hanging up the phone. "I need to tell you something," he said. "I need to tell *someone,* and I can't tell my parents. My grandmother's stories are turning out to be way beyond anything I had imagined. I know there are no guarantees about how this film will turn out, or how well it will be received. But what she's telling me is changing the way I see her, the way I see everyone, really. It's impossible not to look at total strangers and wonder who they really are. I know it's going to change my parents when they see it, but I'm less sure about whether that will be for the better or the worse."

49

It was Memorial Day in 1948 when the Columbia River breached an embankment and wiped out the entire town of Vanport. It wasn't hard to do. The place was cheaply built on a floodplain and never should have been there to begin with. Ada was one of the government workers tasked with helping the survivors find homes. Her whole life had been dedicated to helping people find a place where they belonged."

"You miss her still, don't you?"

Violet looked away to the window, nodding at the trees outside.

"Something interesting about that whole business with Vanport is how life has a way of circling back in the strangest ways. Wood from the buildings that had been destroyed in the flood was reclaimed, and some of it found its way to Nestucca Beach. It's what the schoolhouse is built out of that you and Francisco went to. I'm sure your father thought I was crazy. But I used to touch the doorframes and walls, wondering if there was a way to tell which house that particular piece of wood came from, hoping I could feel a little of the past, and imagined it was possible that a piece might have come from the apartment where I'd lived with Ada."

"Wow, Grand. I had no idea. What was she like, your friend Ada?"

"She was every kind of person. It's hard to describe. I've never known anyone else like her. But the way she looked, she had such beautiful hands." Violet glanced at her own hands, then back to Daniel and the camera, the two of them now like one. "Her skin was flawless, like a bucket of olive-colored paint. And she had a delicate way of holding things — a glass, her gold pen. She had a simple elegance that you cannot teach a person. Effortless, graceful in the way she brushed her hair from her eyes — it drew attention without her trying. You simply couldn't look away when she was in the room. I wish *I* had painted her."

"Why didn't you?"

Violet tempered her expression, her emotions pushing up to the surface, causing her to squirm. "Richard was the portraitist."

Daniel leaned back from the camera. She could tell he was trying to be professional, trying to keep his mind on the job, but still, this was his grandfather they were discussing.

"I never knew about the painting until after she was gone."

"You had no idea he had painted her?"

Violet shook her head. "I can't say I blame him. It was art, after all. She had that perfect skin . . . It's just, I was mostly surprised that *Ada* never told me."

Daniel leaned around the camera and blinked as if focusing on Violet through the bright lights. "This might sound stupid, but I'm curious. What happened to the painting?"

"Richard got drunk and set fire to it in the pit out back."

"Jesus." Daniel shook his head.

"Unless I'm mistaken, and you're going to surprise us all and say that you've located the painting."

Daniel groaned, then laughed. "No, Grand. This is not reality TV."

"Well. People do such things and I don't care for it. I was saying, or about to say, your grandfather gave up painting after that. Done with the entire business, aside from sketching the dog."

In the silence that followed, Violet wondered if she was expected to speak. Then Daniel said, "What about my father?"

"What do you mean?"

"How did he cope with all of this?"

Violet tapped her fingers against her lips. "I don't know. I think what you see, who you know him to be, is how he's coped."

"I'm not sure . . ."

"There are worse ways to respond to terrible things."

"Are you talking about yourself or other people?"

"Both." Violet swiped the air, exhaustion settling in. "It's all behind me now, everyone is long gone, and somehow I'm still here."

"You are. And so is Dad."

Violet glanced at the floor. "It was unsettling, to say the least." She looked again at the camera. "To come upon that painting, to see Ada's face rendered in the way Richard had seen her, the way he'd imagined her, too, I suppose. Ada. Odd how everything about her was gorgeous and yet her legacy was gruesome and cruel."

"Did Granddad, you know, have an affair with Ada?"

Violet hesitated before answering. "The truth is, I don't know. I didn't know about the painting, so, well, like I said, I don't know. It came up later, naturally, and he denied it, but I don't know if I believed him. Ada was gone, and that was the bigger hurt to me, that I lost her, but I guess if they'd been having an affair, then Richard had lost her, too."

A long silence swelled between them.

"I'm sorry to bring this up, Grand. I just thought, well, I asked about it because you had mentioned the DNA test. You said you wanted to tell me about that. And I wondered if it had to do with Granddad. There are people on this site—and it doesn't make sense. I don't know how I'm related to them."

Violet needed to make a decision for all of time, right here, right now.

What good would it do to saddle some innocent woman and her family with the truth of how she came to be? Was it not possible to say she was born and given away because Violet was a sixteen-year-old girl, and leave it at that? They could think what they wanted of Violet in this case, they could, and it wouldn't bother her a bit. It was possible to talk about what she had lived through without connecting the two things as one. It was. Sometimes the truth was not only what happened, but also what one could make happen as a result.

"I had a daughter when I was sixteen years old. It was the right thing for me to give her away."

Daniel leaned back. "I see."

Violet wasn't sure he did. "Are you going to ask me about it? Don't you want to know?"

"Of course I want to know, it's just a little bit of a shock. What happened? Where is she? Do you know?"

Violet shook her head. "I figured you were going to tell me."

"I only know the names. Nothing more. Not yet. Do you want—"

"No. I'd like to leave things at that for now."

"What were the circumstances, Grand?"

"Let's just leave it at that."

50

T*he following morning,* Violet was weary before they began, and was wearier still when Daniel started off by asking, "What happened with the fire when you were young?"

Violet was stepping over the threshold of memory, a heavy weight in her bones as she plodded on through. "It was my father's still," she said.

Daniel leaned forward, elbows on his knees. "Say that again?"

"He had a copper still in the cellar."

"A *still*? He was what, a whiskey runner or something?"

"It was during Prohibition. No, wait, it was just about to end. I didn't understand back then that what he was doing was illegal. He'd been doing it for some time, which was how he bought our phonograph and records and the dresses for my mother. He had electricity installed in the house the year before, and indoor plumbing six months after that. It was our first Christmas, or was going to be, with colored lights."

Daniel kept his eye against the camera.

"It was a shiny copper contraption that smelled god-awful, but he gave so much of his attention to it, and this fascinated me. I didn't know it was wrong to have it. I didn't know I wasn't supposed to tell anyone."

"So, what happened?"

"Em and I were playing in the tree swing near the road on one of those strangely warm days that Georgia gets in December. Mrs. Morgan, our neighbor, was walking into town and stopped to say hello. I was a peculiar child. Peculiar as now, I suppose. Even then I knew this about myself. And it was confirmed by adults who said things like Mrs. Morgan said, when she leaned over to Em: 'You're the one who's like a flower. Look how pink and pretty you are. They should have named you Violet, and this other one here something else.'"

Daniel flinched.

"Oh, there are worse people in the world. I don't know if she was being mean on purpose or if she was a little off in the head. But the next thing out of my mouth seemed my only defense. I told her that my father had a pretty copper still in the basement and that only I got see it, not Em."

"Oh no."

"Yes. Mrs. Morgan slowly stood upright with her eyes on me. 'Is that right,' she said. 'Is that what your daddy does with all of the corn?' I told her it was, and I asked if Mr. Morgan had one, too. She said, 'No, but I'm of a mind he's going to like to speak with your daddy and learn all about it.'"

"Days later, it was evening and I remember lemon cake icing crusted on the corners of my mouth. I was messing with the Christmas tree. My father always put it up early, weeks before Christmas. It had a string of silver beads that I was fascinated with, and I was wondering how difficult it might be to get them off. And also whether my mother might notice if I did. I had planned to wrap the strand around my neck in a double loop, the way my mother wore a set of pearls. I wanted to be just like my mother back then. But of course, things changed."

Violet felt an unexpected rush of compassion for her mother.

"My mother was a lovely person. Once, she was. She taught me how to read. She loved me. She did."

Violet could hear her own words, and they sounded like she was telling herself this story at the same time she was telling it to the camera. The important thing was that it was true.

"The tree's needles pricked my arm when I reached between the branches, and coated my fingers with sap." Violet closed her eyes long enough to get a glimpse of her hand before the scars. "The tacky sap stuck my fingers and thumb together, and I pulled them apart and tapped them together again, thinking how I didn't want to stain my nightgown with that stuff, and that's when Em came in and asked what I was doing. I told her nothing, and she said our mama wouldn't like me to take those beads off the tree, and I said maybe she wouldn't know, and Em asked why I got to see the still and she didn't. In that minute I was thinking about what Mrs. Morgan had said to me, and it ate me up all over again, and I said, half jokingly, that maybe our daddy liked me better. Of course Em started to cry, and I felt terrible, and I told her how sorry I was, but she ran off. I didn't see where she went. I turned back to the beads.

"The next thing I recall was a knock at the door, and Mr. Morgan came in and spoke to my father in the hallway. I wasn't paying much attention. It didn't seem important. But then my mother came into the room saying she couldn't find Em. I said I didn't know where she'd gone, though the truth was I had some idea. But I was thinking about that sticky sap, and anyway I couldn't take the beads now because my mother was there, and then my father and Mr. Morgan walked past, so I turned for the bathroom to wash my hands, and my mother went into the kitchen to look for Em, and that's when the still exploded beneath the tree."

Violet could hear Daniel swallowing in the quiet.

"Apparently those things weren't safe to begin with. I'll never know for certain exactly what happened, only that the blast killed my father and Em and Mr. Morgan. And the townspeople despised my mother after that. The only people who would take her in belonged to the smallest-minded church in town. That's when my mother got religion something awful.

"She asked me while I was in the hospital if I had told the neighbors about the still. I said I had told Mrs. Morgan. I told her what Mrs. Morgan said, that my parents should have named Em Violet because she was so pretty, and named me something else, but she had no reaction whatsoever, and I felt cold beneath my burned skin.

"I'd grabbed Em's birdcage with her canary when my mother and I ran out the door. Looking back, I don't know how I had the mind to do that as we passed through the kitchen. I was literally on fire. But I do remember thinking how broken-hearted Em would be to lose her bird. I remember that. I remember the song it sang out in the snow, and I thought, *Wait till Em hears this.* It was eerie and beautiful."

For the first time in decades, Violet began to cry over Em. She held up her hand. "Sorry," she said.

"Should we stop?" Daniel asked.

She coughed into a tissue and shook her head. It felt good to say her name, to recall the love she'd had for her sister. And to hear that bird's gentle song trilling through her mind.

51

Summer had fully arrived, and with it, several days of June gloom. The marine layer covered the mornings in a cool mist, and by afternoon the heat of the sun burned it off, replacing the gray with a glare that reminded Daniel of Los Angeles, and he missed California, even as the warmth on his skin felt the same, and he missed Macy, though he guessed what he really missed was the life he imagined they would have, and not the one they actually did.

He could feel his parents anticipating his departure. Nothing had been said about what his plans were once the project with his grandmother was finished, but he could tell it was on their minds by the way they spoke of doing things with Dani in the future. *We'd like to take her to the merry-go-round in Seaside, the aquarium down in Newport, and what about a bonfire on the beach while the weather is still so good?*

There was also the matter of Quincy, and the complicated brew of feelings he was having toward her. Every evening at dinner, he wished she were there when he looked from his father to his grandmother to his mother, and he felt as if his mind was going to short-circuit. He didn't know how much longer he could hold in all the things his grandmother was telling him day by day.

Like today, she told him what had happened when she was fourteen, and again when she was sixteen, and she spoke of the guilt and shame: "How does that happen to a person twice? At least that's what I used to think. I understand now that it can happen that way, or worse, that it does . . ."

And then she asked him to turn off the camera, which he did. "I don't see any good that could ever come from her knowing. You understand? There will be no 'sins of the father' here, not as long as I'm alive, and hopefully not after my death. If anyone asks, then my dying wish, Daniel, is for you to say I told you that one had nothing to do with the other."

After that, he was allowed to turn the camera back on.

She said, "Not long ago I read something about how the cells of every child born to a woman remain inside the mother's body, and how each subsequent child carries cells from the child who was born before. Like Lady Bird and the cedar tree, my son carries the cells of his sisters in his body. What do you think that does to a person? Do you think they do anything, these cells? I don't know. It just makes me wonder at the world, at the things we carry."

And now here was Daniel at the dinner table, trying to behave as if the world had not changed.

"Can you pass me the salt?" his father asked.

Daniel slid the shaker across the table.

"What's on your mind?" his father asked.

So many things running through his head . . . Like when his grandmother said, "I underwent shock treatments, though Richard was against them from the start. He didn't want me to *change*, he said. I think he thought the treatments would make me dull, or damage me in some way. I don't know. But I was miserable back then. Perhaps it was what they now know is postpartum depression. Perhaps the misery lingered from things long before I had your father. I suspect it was a bit of both. Either way, I was haunted, especially around your father. It wasn't fair to him. The doctor promised the treatments would help. That they would make me a better mother to your father. And I was, eventually. I think I was. But I'll never know if the doctor was right, if the pulses to my brain had done the job, or if time itself and life here with your grandfather, and my work, had been what really cleared away the darkness."

And now his father was downright chatty, airy, wanting to make small talk with Daniel. It was an opening that Daniel would have liked to have accepted at any other time in his life. But not now, even as his father spoke about building the cubby house for the fairy fort, and a miniature garden for the rabbit, whom everyone called Puppy, and it made everyone at the table laugh, including his grandmother, and Daniel wondered at her lifetime of laughter, her work made of harmony and joy, with the things she carried.

52

On *the morning* of the day Richard died, he had stood at the window as if he were about to give a weather report. Instead, he said, "Dr. Kath's diagnosis makes perfect sense. Of course my arteries are blocked, of course my blood pressure is impossible to control. She called me a ticking time bomb, Violet." He laughed, but not like anything was funny. "Of course I am."

The week before that, he had ripped the kitchen phone from the wall and thrown it across the room, where it hit Daniel's CD player and sent everyone into a frenzied, splintered mess of fear.

"The surgery will help, Richie," Violet said. "People have them all the time."

He shook his head, and Violet didn't understand if he meant that she was wrong about that, or if he was implying that he would not have the surgery.

"Come back to bed. You seem tired."

"I am tired."

"But especially today."

"I am," he said, "especially today." And then he got dressed, put on his favorite sweater, the one that was her favorite, too, thick brown wool with chocolate-colored buttons, and he went outside, and the next thing she knew there was a ruckus in the yard, and she looked down to see him beating the eucalyptus with one of its own branches.

"I wish you had been able to tell his story, too," Violet told

Daniel for the camera. "I used to ask him, 'What are you look-ing for out there?' when he'd stare at the ocean. 'All the things I want to see,' he'd say. But what he meant was that when he looked at the ocean it helped to disappear the things he did not ever want to see again."

"Like what?"

"Like things from the war. The men he had killed, and seen killed. The worst of what humans do to one another he had been forced to do himself. It went against every bit of who he was."

"Did he talk about it with you?"

"Rarely. He told me that sometimes these things came back to him in his sleep, and it felt real, like he was reliving them. He was moody on those days, though I thought he hid it well."

"Did he share details with you? Do you want to say what they were?"

Violet sighed. It was not her story to tell. And yet, in some way, it was. "He said one of the worst things was when a Ger-man soldier stepped out from behind a tree with a drawn ri-fle. Their eyes met, and for whatever reason, the German, a boy—they were all just boys, Richard said—lowered his ri-fle and began to duck away. But in the next second, some-one from Richard's company shot the German in the head. Richard could never reconcile any of it. How could he? Boys, young men, ordered to kill each other by a group of men who would never hold a gun in their lifetimes.

"I think this is part of why he doted on your father. He doted on me, too, but I think your father, well, he was afraid Francisco would grow up and be sent to fight a war. He wor-ried all the time, as did I, that raising a boy was like raising live-stock, you take good care of them, keep them well fed, only to send them off to the slaughter.

"He devoted his life to me. And I think it's what he wanted. For him it was a way to give something back for whatever he had taken, which was too heavy for him to ever tell me the extent of. He didn't have to. I didn't need to know the details to understand. All I know is that he offered what I needed. I think the place where the two of those things met, the reasons, selfish or altruistic, come down at different places at different times, if not somewhere in between."

Violet thought of his face on the pillow next to hers, how grateful she had been for the many ways he'd saved her life, renewed it like the spring, again and again.

There came a knock at the door. Penny poked her head in. "Katherine is here for the family meeting."

Violet glanced at the chifforobe where she had kept Richard's sweater all these years, recalling how she'd slept with it for weeks after he was gone, breathing in the smell of his skin and familiar wool, the scent of the burned hole from his cigar, rich and visceral and sending her into a tailspin of grief, where she wondered, quite seriously, if there was a place in there where she could get him back, some bargain she could strike that she hadn't thought of before, a secret for reaching beyond the grave to retrieve what was rightfully hers, in the same way she had bargained for Em and her father and Ada. For a time she wondered: if she stayed inside the black nothingness, maybe it would take her to them instead. But then, what about Francisco and Penny and Daniel? "Come back," she had whispered for so long.

53

Violet thought of home like Dorothy cast into Oz, wanting only to return from the moment she was away. Back within the loft's bright white walls and its graphite sketches, old postcards from friends long since passed away pinned to the lath and plaster, a gracious, open universe with no demarcation of where the bedroom ended and the living room, studio, and kitchen began. Tall, rectangular windows, wooden rafters across the ceiling, embodied the sanctuary and grace she'd lived with for what had turned out to be most of her life, even as sorrow had sometimes followed her around like a tired child, asking to be lifted into her arms. Framed black-and-white photos of Daniel at the beach, Violet and Richard at the beach, and Ada in the shipyards, placed along the ceiling-high shelves with the novels and books on painters and textile makers that inspired Violet's work. But it was her iron-frame bed, the pale ginger quilt and cream-colored pillows, where she most wanted to be, looking across the room through the row of large windows onto hemlocks, junipers, the sky, the sea.

Ever since the earthquake several months ago, it seemed as if Violet had experienced some kind of magnification of all that had ever meant something, hurt something, alleviated something, troubles reconciled or not, and she guessed that this was how it worked when one got nearer to the end. One by one, like birds lighting on a wire, the memories had gathered, as if waiting to decide, as a flock, their next move.

And now she had come to the end, and truly there was

nothing puny or indecisive about it. The days were losing their shape as she lay among the pillows, opening and closing her eyelids, trying to make sense of the hour. She drifted toward her father, standing at the foot of her bed, miming like Chaplin, causing laughter to rise from her crippled chest. It no longer hurt to laugh. Her father patted her foot, told her the fire was not her fault. If it was anyone's, it was his. He'd been careless with the people he loved most in the world. Come home now, he said, and Violet said, *I'm already home.*

The world had offered her one more vermilion sunset, two more meteor showers, and several quiet rests on the front porch with her legs covered in a wool blanket, the air smelling of lavender and brine.

The flicker had gone away for weeks, and just this morning appeared again at the rain gutter. Violet had smiled as he thrummed. When he gets what he came for he'll move on. Had he gotten it yet? Had she?

Violet had believed when she spoke with Katherine that she'd like to die in her own bed. But when she sensed its arrival, she rang downstairs for Francisco. "I want to rest on the porch," she said, her voice barely a whisper.

Francisco seemed to understand that she was saying something beyond her words. "Here?" he asked, placing the chair in the spot where Richard had taken his final breath.

Richard on the porch that first day, God love him, that first glimpse and she knew, that first sound of his voice.

Who are you?

All he'd ever wanted her to be was who she already was.

Francisco sat next to her, holding her hand. He was a good man, she thought, looking out at the sea. Maybe she was seeing only what she wanted to see, but that didn't make it any less true. She recalled jostling him the first moment she held him, just to see that he was alive, his hands rising and falling on their own. Her love for him had frightened her. She would lose it someday, and it crushed her instantly, this boy made from her and Richard, this child made of the same stuff as the stars and trees and sky, her baby, the one she'd held on to her entire life, the one she was holding on to still.

The past was evanescence now, vaporous, not exactly gone, but no longer capable of taking a hold.

It seemed as if the house had come unmoored and was drifting out to sea.

54

Several weeks after the funeral, Penny brought the Tele-funken downstairs and placed it on the shelf above the spice rack. Mozart's Clarinet Concerto filled the room with a pleasant feeling, and Penny was thinking how events, at least in retrospect, seemed to lead to a place of purpose for reasons that weren't clear in the middle of the journey. Maybe people see what they want to see. Maybe everyone is caught up in someone else's idea of destiny. She didn't know, but it gave her a simple pleasure to contemplate such things without ever having to say these things out loud.

The first sentence she wrote in her new journal was a line from Virginia Woolf's final diary entry:

A curious seaside feeling in the air today.

Why had she chosen to write that? It turned out to be the same day Violet passed away.

Penny could hear the sounds of Frank and Daniel working in the shed, building miniature sets for the fairy fort, which they planned to put in place later today with Dani. The smells in the kitchen had been replaced by resin and sawdust, and Penny often sat in here when she wasn't working, to write in her journal and sniff at the old familiar scents.

She looked up as Frank appeared in the kitchen, wiping sawdust off his hands. His hair was dappled with it, and it lined his cheek. She thought he was coming to get something out of the refrigerator, but then he sat across from her, his face flushed and lean. He appeared younger, thinner in his grief.

His eyes were on her expectantly, as if he were gearing up to say something that had long been on his mind.

She closed her journal and wiped the sawdust from his cheek.

"You've changed," he said.

She looked down at her shirt and jeans. She smiled up at him. "It's the same outfit I had on this morning."

"Funny," he said.

"I'm funny now. I've changed."

Frank stared with all seriousness. "This isn't easy for me." He ran his hand through his hair and sawdust flittered and fell through the sunlight like gold. "I want to tell you some things about me. Things that happened to me that mattered, or maybe that didn't. What I think about now, who I want to be. And I want to know the same about you. You may still want to leave, but before you go, let me at least know you in the way I think I once did."

Penny leaned back in her chair. "Oh, Frank." It was like being on a date, the air tight with anticipation over who this person would turn out to be.

"Well, I'm serious."

"I believe you. Why don't you start by telling me something I don't know."

"OK. I stomped the shit out of that fort one day in a fit of blind rage."

55

How to explain the feeling of utter despair for a world that seemed oblivious to its own plight? Had his wife and mother not seen the fighter jets from the National Guard dogfighting over the ocean? Did they not feel the sonic boom when it rolled in off the water? What did they think it was for, fun and games? These were practice drills while the world was being taken over, one idiot at a time. The future was in the hands of people whom Frank would not trust to watch Millicent.

His mother and Penny had wanted him to stop watching the news, as if everything would magically improve if he weren't there to see it, as if his awareness of how the country had gone to hell would just disappear, and there would be no worry about the planet disintegrating, the extinction of resources, animals, humans, life of all kinds. Citizens of democracies around the world were using free will to vote in despots to lead them. How was Frank supposed to get up every day with the knowledge of what was happening and behave as if it weren't? His anger blistered him. How on earth was a person supposed to live a normal life?

He wrote emails to his representatives in Congress. Left phone messages on various lines at the White House, and more at the state legislature in Salem. He went out into the woods and he screamed. He took walks that only soothed the outer layer of his rage, and on one of them he let loose on the fairy fort for not doing a damn thing to make this life better. After that, he started sipping brandy throughout the day to help assuage the shame. No one seemed to notice, which sort of made him mad, too. He started smoking again, the first time since college, and even when Penny caught him, she didn't seem to care. She was pleased, he guessed, that he had at least told her the truth.

And then everything changed.

He saw the world through the eyes of a three-year-old child.

Weeks ago, an evening sunset was putting on a spectacular show of color, and everyone was out on the porch, including his mother, wrapped in a thick wool blanket, all of them ooh-ing and aahing through the screen door during Frank's evening news show. His blood pressure was rising, his irritation peaking at the way their joy was breaking over the opening monologue of the TV host. Frank was about to get up and close the front door when he saw Dani in the doorway, watching the screen.

Frank had no idea how long she'd been standing there. She looked frightened, if not confused. How much did a three-year-old understand? He had no idea. He hadn't paid close attention when Daniel was a boy. But now he guessed it wasn't that she understood the words or their meaning so much as she absorbed the sense of the thing, the spirit of it all, and goddamn if this thought didn't light a fire under him to jump up and turn the set off.

He picked up Dani, strode around the room with her on his hip. "No need to see that," he said.

"Why?" she said. This new phase had come on suddenly and attached itself to every situation, *why, why, why.* It kept everyone talking to her, answering the next question, and the next. Her language skills had improved remarkably.

"What happens when we die?" she asked.

Frank looked at the dark TV screen where mass shootings of children had just been discussed, and the president was saying words like *monsters, the mentally ill, handing out guns to teachers.*

Frank stared at Dani. How to answer such a question for a three-year-old?

"I don't know." He took the easy way out, that's how. "What do *you* think happens?" he asked, and waited for what would certainly be a nonsensical answer.

Dani looked at the TV and then at the windows that led to the backyard, where her father had whisked her away the day Violet collapsed.

"We miss them?" she said.

"Who?"

"The people we love."

Frank's heart clenched. His throat tightened. She had seen it from the other side, the side of the living, not the side of the dead.

"You're not like any other child," he said.

"I'm like my dad," she said, and smiled his own father's smile up at him, causing his heart to leap so hard he needed to sit down.

Epilogue

The old woman walked with the gait of his mother. Seventy-nine years old, and she could have been Frank's own mother had she had him at the same age that Violet had her.

The autumn leaves rolled out an orange path at her feet, and Frank stared and stared, her walk, her height, the shape of her eyes, her blunt-cut silver hair. It was nearly unbearable, frightening as a ghost to see.

Frank took Penny's hand on the porch. Penny took Daniel's. Daniel squeezed Dani's and pulled her against him.

And then, his mother's voice when she spoke. His mother, who had been dead for two years. Frank lifted his hand from Penny's and pressed it against his heart.

"Frank. It's a pleasure," the woman said. "Do we look like brother and sister?" she asked her daughter, coming up behind her, a round woman of lesser height, in her sixties, Frank guessed, who didn't resemble her at all.

"Very much," her daughter said.

"This is Georgia. I'm Elizabeth, of course."

Georgia didn't look like anyone Frank knew. *Georgia*. His mother would have gotten a kick out of that.

After a slow warm-up of introductions, questions about the house, about living on the coast, and the weather, Frank turned to Elizabeth, his sister, and said what was on his mind. "And have you had a good life?" He glanced at the spot on the porch where both of his parents had left this world, and maybe someday he would, too. His mother's death had changed him, and was changing him still. He asked more questions now, knowing he sometimes faltered. Penny encouraged him to keep trying. "Were your parents good to you?"

Elizabeth nodded. "I had a fine childhood. A happy one. Four siblings. I'm just sorry that I never got to meet Violet."

"So am I."

"I want to thank you again for reaching out and finding me," she said to Daniel. She turned to Frank. "And for your generosity toward my kids and grandkids. It's a lot of money."

"My mother would have wanted it that way."

"Well." She looked to Georgia, who smiled shyly. "Thank you," she said, looking around at everyone.

"I imagine it could not have been easy giving a child away," Elizabeth said. "At least I wouldn't think so, having had three of my own. I like to think she must have cared a great deal about me to let go of me like that."

Daniel turned his face toward the ocean. If Frank was not mistaken, he gave a slight wince.

"Yes," Frank said. "But it all worked out, didn't it?"

Penny leaned in as if to smooth the ruffled, awkward rise in the air. "It couldn't have been easy. A sixteen-year-old. My goodness. And a war going on."

"I'd say so." Elizabeth nodded. "Yes."

"And what do you do, or did you do?" Frank asked.

"I was a teacher. A mathematics professor at Portland State. I retired ten years ago."

"That's something. I enjoy numbers myself. I'm semiretired, but I used to take care of my mother's business, as you know from the outfit we hired that got in touch with you about the inheritance. I teach shop classes a couple of days a week now. At the community college."

"Oh. Do you make things yourself?"

This woman was his *sister*. He was not an only child and never had been. And now he was an old man in his sixties, and he was staring at a sister he never knew, and in the staring he felt one step closer to knowing his own mother. "Yeah. All kinds of stuff. Last week I made blades for a ceiling fan."

"Out of wood?"

"Yes, cherry. It's beautiful, if I do say so myself."

"It is, Frank," Penny said, leaning in, and Frank wished that his mother could have seen it. There was no one left who'd ever think to call him Francisco again, and he never thought he'd miss it, but he did. "We'll show you. It's hanging in our front room."

"What a crazy thing to have happen," Elizabeth said. His sister. His sister had said that, and she sounded exactly like his mother.

Frank looked around at his family, how much it had filled out in such a short time. Was this the last surprise?

We don't get to know everything, Frank's father once told him. But they might, *Frank* might, at least about his mother. They were waiting for Daniel to finish editing the documentary.

Snow had fallen for hours; flakes large as paper cutouts floating by the kitchen windows. It was early evening at the start of December, a blue light cast off the white into the rooms of Daniel's house. Nearly five inches on the ground, and no sign of letting up. Snowstorms on the coast were no longer rare.

Dani and the dog they'd rescued from the pound, an old black cocker named Steve, had been bouncing around the yard for nearly an hour with Daniel's parents and the corgi puppy his father had just given his mother as an early Christmas present. They hadn't named him yet. Their laughter was loud enough to hear inside the house.

Daniel and Quincy were preparing dinner—potato soup with fresh brown bread and a Caesar salad. Just being in the same room with her filled him with energy, like inspiration, unfolding and new. When Dani's laughter rose above the others', he and Quincy smiled across the island counter between them.

"Are you still nervous about Arielle's visit in the spring?" Quincy asked. "Silly question. I'm sure you are."

"I'm getting used to the idea. At the moment, Dani doesn't ask about her much, but I wonder if it's on her mind."

"It's on yours."

"Of course. Among a million other things."

"I think Arielle will be pleased with the life you've made for Dani. I think it's exactly what she'd hoped it would be when she wanted Dani here with you."

"Thank you for saying that," Daniel said.

"I'm sure it's true."

His grandmother had been gone for two years. Not long after she died, Daniel purchased a refurbished bungalow on the other side of the meadow, with the advice of his mother, who'd since renewed her real estate license. "It's got the original flooring and crown molding, and Daniel, the view, you cannot do better than this." The first winter Daniel read twenty books from the stacked shelves in the den. Dani learned to read board books. During the day when she was at preschool, he walked the hills when last year's snow was heavy enough to crack the branches. But most of his hours were spent editing the film, and in this way, he continued to have a conversation with his grandmother, her voice, her face, her stories filling his days. He'd gotten to know her as well as he might know anyone in his life. It was only in the past few months, as he'd finished the work, that he began to settle in to her absence, and to the grief.

Now the sounds of boots stomping in the foyer, dogs shaking fur, his parents wrangling the animals, drying them with towels, nylon jackets slipping off, the clang of hangers.

"What smells so good?" his mother called out.

"Come see!" Quincy said.

They were here to preview the documentary. The release was three weeks away, and Daniel was nervous nearly all of the time, not because he thought it might fail, but because the buzz at the film festivals had been overwhelmingly positive. "Don't be seduced by the noise," Quincy had told him more than once, which sounded just like something his grandmother would say.

Steve and the corgi pup soon passed out in front of the fire, and the smell of wet dog faded by the time everyone had gathered around the table.

"What about Randall?" his mother said, her nose still red from the cold.

"For the dog?" his father asked.

"Well, not a person."

"What about Fergus?" his father said.

"It would probably please the queen."

They all joined in the name game — Cooper, Copper, Blue, Tank, Diesel, Bubba, Winston . . .

"Winston," his mother said. "I like Winston. I think."

"What about two names?" Dani asked. "Like Copper Blue?"

"Oh?" Daniel's mother touched her shoulder. "Honey, I like that even better."

And then they ate in near quiet, the sense of why they were gathered suddenly weighing on the air.

By the time Daniel tucked Dani into bed, he was exhausted himself. "I want to hear one of Grandpop's stories," Dani said.

Daniel was glad for the reprieve. "OK. I'll send him in."

"When do *I* get to see it?" Dani asked, for the twentieth time, about the film.

"When you're a little bit older. The day will come, I promise."

They were so at home now that it seemed as if Dani had always been there. Daniel no longer worried over having missed her early years.

He kissed her forehead as he always did, thinking how quickly time passed when you loved someone. And he stood feeling the force of responsibility that anchored that love.

"What do you think she's doing now?" Dani asked. It was a

game they played with people and animals that were not there, imaginary or real. She was asking about Violet.

"I think she's painting," Daniel said.

"I think she's wishing she could see the film."

Daniel laughed. He kissed her forehead again. "Goodnight, little mouse."

"Goodnight, Papa. Don't forget to send Grandpop in!"

"Of course."

In the den, Daniel pointed a thumb over his shoulder. She wants you, Dad. Story time."

His father jumped up with the energy of a young man.

"Don't be long!" his mother said, smiling, clearly pleased. He could have taken as long as he wanted.

When at last they gathered in front of the large TV in the den, Daniel stood before it as if on a stage and said, "I've decided not to preface this with anything." He picked up the remote. "I think the story speaks for itself." He glanced at Quincy for support, found her smile, a gentle nod. She had not seen the film, either.

The title, *Pale Morning Light with Violet Swan,* opened the credits, with *Le cygne* playing on the soundtrack.

The first scene was Violet in her reading chair, dressed in her smock and jeans, dappled in her signature palette. She gazed directly at the camera, her face serious and kind in the warm light.

Everyone in the room turned to one another. "I'm going to tell you some things," she said. Oh, how they missed Violet Swan.

And here she was, speaking in a whispery tone about drawing at the kitchen table as a child, the love for her parents, the confusion of what had appeared on the page beneath her pencil. "It was odd, but whatever it was, a *gift,* I suppose, all of it, the whole wide world, moved me to tears."

She spoke about the fire that changed the course of her life. "Who can say if I would have ever found my way here without it? Who can say what would have become of any of us? My father was a whiskey runner for a time. Who can say what he might have done if Prohibition never happened."

She spoke of running away from the revivals and the traveling preachers. "They were con men, you understand? They took things from people. One in particular took something from me."

Daniel could see his father becoming restless. His mother held his hand.

"I ran away when I was fourteen years old. Off into the woods, crossed the state line into Alabama. I was pregnant and didn't know, or sort of knew but not fully understood. That preacher . . ." Violet shook her head in disgust, and Daniel did not turn to see anyone's expression.

"But the opaline streaks across the heavens, the flock of cerulean warblers migrating through the forest like pieces of moving, frenetic blue sky . . . that's when I finally wept the way those country preachers had always wanted. That's when I felt something holy."

Her work appeared on the screen, one painting after another, a series of soft pale colors and simple lines. Daniel could feel the room, the entire house, relax. A flow was set in place, a meditation that allied Violet and her work, accompanied by her favorite music.

Violet's voice was markedly strained, though it seemed fitting as she spoke of sober things—war and a stillborn child she'd buried in the desert. She gently whispered about the sky and trees and colors of the desert and mountain meadows. She whispered about the sea.

Her hands shook, and in the shaking one felt the courage it had taken to have a camera on her. Her coughing increased, and even as Daniel shortened each instance through editing, it was clear that the cough was worsening over time.

She spoke of arriving in Nestucca Beach. "'How long do you plan to stay?' this handsome young man asked me, and I

looked at him, quite seriously, and said, 'The rest of my life.'"
She wiped her eyes. "Richie," she said, though it was barely
audible.

She spoke of living above the bookstore, selling her first
paintings to the famous Betty Johnson, meeting other artists, choosing to live away from the art scene in New York, to
remain on the distant coast in isolation. There was the Vanport flood and the reclaimed wood used to build the schoolhouse her son and grandson attended. And of the painting in
London, *Until Kingdom Come*. Of this, she pointed her finger at the camera, which Daniel had moved in close until her
eyes were clear and large when she said, "To that critic—listen here. The inspiration wasn't something haughty, like you
made it out to be. It wasn't about a disdain for religion, it was
about being small and petty, about wanting something better
for my son and daughter-in-law, which perhaps, by the time
you're seeing this, they may have gotten a hold of." She looked
down at her hands in her lap. Chopin, Nocturne in E-flat Ma-
jor, played in the background.

Daniel couldn't help but glance at his parents. Their damp
eyes glistened in the blue light. "My God," his father said.
"*Daniel . . .*"

It was clear to everyone that Violet had unlocked something inside all of them throughout her life, doors swung open
to another kind of being, and now, through her death, and
with her final words, the family continued to step over another threshold. All the gentle, awkward ways they maneu-
vered in and around each other, trying to be better, learning
to do things the right way, putting Dani at the center, like a
compass rose.

And then Violet spoke of Em, her face wistful, turning
away. "Such a tiny, beautiful thing. I've missed her every single day of my life."

Daniel thought he might have to stop the film. His father
was clearly upset, trying to stifle his tears, wiping his wet face,
clearing his throat. "I'm sorry," he finally said, and when he

saw everyone looking, he threw his hand in the air as a gesture that they needed to finish watching. "Come on, now. Please. I'm *fine.*"

But then Violet was speaking about Ada, and what had happened at the hands of her husband, John. "We all liked him. He was so charismatic, which made things worse, of course, the fact that we didn't see what was behind it, that we couldn't protect her from him. He had us fooled, and Ada had never been anyone's fool. That's how good he was with his con." Now Violet wept, for the first time in the film. "What was worse than losing my best friend was the fact that my son, who was just a boy, had found the painting and brought it out for everyone to see. He was laughing, I remember so clearly the sound of his laughter in the next room, and I had thought to myself how lucky we all were, to have lived through so much, to have come to this moment in our lives of such goodness and joy, and I was no longer needing the treatments, the worst of everything seemed behind us then, and when I walked back in the room, Ada was slumped on the floor, and my poor son . . ."

"Do you want to stop for the day, Grand?" Daniel asked from behind the camera.

"No. I want to say that my son was standing there, trembling. And after that, well, what was he supposed to think about the world? About art? About men? It was a wonder I did not kill John myself. In fact, Richard had to pull me back. I had run into the kitchen for a knife."

"No. Is that *true?*"

"It is. Richard stopped me. Grabbed my shoulders and kept saying Francisco was there. 'Don't do this. Don't make it worse.' Then John ran out the door. He was caught later, down the street, by the police. I was overcome with a terrible headache. I used to get them. Like small seizures of some kind. I guess I passed out, and don't remember a whole lot after that."

Daniel paused the film. "Dad? Are you all right?"

His mother had her arms wrapped around his father, his face down in his hands. He patted her to let go, nodded, and again the gesture in the air with his hand. Daniel could feel the emotion his father had stifled over a lifetime, all the pain he'd endured and stuffed away, pooling in one place.

"Can I get you something, Frank?" Quincy asked.

"No, thank you. I'm OK. Come on now. Everyone stop fussing. Daniel, please let it play."

Daniel hesitated, clearing his own throat, before continuing.

Next, the screen filled again with Violet's work, mixed with clips of people in museums, their heads tilted in contemplation, hands over their mouths, a young woman seeming to stifle her emotions. "It's like the light shines through and gets on your skin," a man said. "I don't know why, but it makes me want to weep," a woman said. "I mean, in a happy way, I don't know, I feel happier than I did when I walked in here. Just staring at the lines, the pale blues, I don't know. How does she do that?"

"Everything about the shipyards was hard, loud, dirty," Violet said. "It was like I lived the inverse during my days off, learning how to paint. I went to the Portland museum on Mondays when it was free. I saved every penny." She laughed. "I swear, I barely ate. My clothes were moth-eaten. But I knew what I wanted. I knew what my life should look like, and where I belonged. It came to me through the canvas. In every way. It came to me there."

And then, with a sharp turn of an edit, as if to show that all of life could never be so dreamy all the time, Violet suddenly said, "I had a daughter when I was sixteen. And it was right of me to give her away. She was mine. Just mine. I guess I believe in magic." Violet laughed at herself, and the scene cut to the fairy fort, to Dani's small hand placing the miniature chairs at the table.

"*What?*" Penny said.

"Daniel!" Frank said. "I thought you just found this out a few months ago. You've known about Elizabeth for *two years?*"

Daniel hit pause.

"How on earth have you kept this from me?"

"Dad, do you want to finish the film?"

"Frank, please," his mother said.

"No, this is huge. Daniel, how—"

"She didn't want me to tell you before now. In fact, she didn't want me to tell you at all. She meant for it to come out in the film, so she could tell you herself. But the film took longer to edit than I'd expected. And I didn't think it was right to wait so long. There was the matter of the estate. She hadn't thought it through."

"But two years, Daniel? That's still a long time . . ."

"It's still not as bad as you keeping Dani from *me*, Dad."

His parents gasped.

Quincy covered her eyes and shook her head.

"How did you know about *that?*" his mother asked.

"I found the emails when I was helping with Grand's estate."

"Oh Jesus." His father scooted to the edge of the sofa. "Oh no. Oh son. I'm sorry, that was wrong . . ."

"I know, Dad."

"It was terrible of me. I should have never—"

"Oh, for God's sake," his mother said.

"I'm going to start the film now," Daniel said.

"All right," his father said. "I'm sorry, son."

"I *know*, Dad. It's a shitty deal, but I know."

Daniel backed up the film a bit to let everyone recover and fall back into the work.

In the final moments, Violet's last painting filled the screen, and the tension in the room evaporated. The sight of it was like the sun itself warming the air. Her voice off camera now, her face never to return, just the work, like clues to the person she had been. "It's called *Pale Morning Light with Violet Swan*," she said. "Like the dawn of a new day. Each one is an offering, take it, it's yours to do what you want with it."

The camera floated languidly over the canvas. "You see the lines of a grid," Violet said, "one for each person I've loved. You see the spaces in between . . . That's where the beauty is, step back to understand the scope, come forward to see the details, the grit of imperfection masquerading as perfection. And this in the corner . . ." The camera floated to the bottom right corner to show a small, faded grid, a pale rusty red that appeared to extend beyond the edge of the frame. "This is me," she whispered. "I've never included myself in my work, not directly, but this here, this color, the compressed lines, the grid different from the rest? Like a hand, you see. It's damaged, but still reaching."

The camera retreated until the painting again filled the entire screen with its gossamer light.

And then Daniel's voice-over began.

"My grandmother died not long after telling me about the ochre-colored hills she'd once seen from the boxcar of a train. There were rows of olive trees with thin, silvery underleaves sparking the sunlight. In the distance, spikes of green cypress shot upward like candles, their tops glowing orange from the California sunset. She said perhaps she was thinking about it now because of the kindness she'd been shown that day, and here at the end, she felt only kindness for the world in return. Was that it? *Kindness*? she wondered. Perhaps it was simpler still. She was reminded of when she was a young child and could hear her sister in the next room, laughing with their father. And when she gazed at a Dutch-orange bread box until its color came alive in her hands. It was a time before tragedy came for everyone and everything she loved. Her mouth full of lemon cake, her mother's soft hem swishing vanilla through the air. 'An ordinary happiness runs through me,' she said, patting my hand. 'This is everything beautiful, this is *love*. Are you listening? Do you hear?'"

Acknowledgments

Violet's paintings were inspired by the great works of Agnes Martin, whose life, art, and writings continue to be an inspiration to me. Diving into the depth of Agnes's life and work has proved to be life-changing.

Many thanks to Jane Comerford for writing *At the Foot of the Mountain*. As it turns out, the history of Manzanita, Oregon, which is the real setting for this novel, matched my imagined history of a coastal village founded by artists in the early part of the twentieth century. Life continues to imitate art.

In the course of writing this novel, I became the owner of my local, independent bookstore, Cloud & Leaf, and would like to thank the community and all the visitors for their continued support. What a pleasure to engage in a different kind of creative process, to play a role in the exchange of ideas and to share the books that move our hearts and minds. The nuances of these exchanges, and the bookstore itself, gallantly seeped into Violet's story.

Grateful thanks to my agent, Larry Kirshbaum, for years of support and unwavering faith in me and my work. Every laugh and every prayer did the trick. I could not do this without you. Your kindness and friendship is appreciated more than I can ever convey.

Thank you Nicole Angeloro, the best editor a writer could hope for, never failing to keep me on course with thoughtful insights and humor and a sharp wit to match. What a pleasure it is to shepherd books into the world with you. And thanks to

Larry Cooper for the finest of fine manuscript edits, the clearest of clarity, gunk removal, and shine. I also want to thank the entire team at Houghton Mifflin Harcourt, who do what they do behind the scenes to make it all look easy. I am so grateful for your support.

Art invariably arrives in the world with the help and encouragement of others, which I have found in Sharon Harrigan and Holly Lorincz. Their close reads and sound advice, for my work and life, have been instrumental in keeping me afloat. Thank you both so very much.

And thank you to my talented sons, Dylan Brown and Liam Reed, for the honor of accompanying them through their own creative lives, as they continue to support me through mine. This is a book about motherhood as much as anything else, and, as always, you were never far from my thoughts in the course of its writing. I haven't always known what I wanted in this world, or what to do with what I'd been given, and at times this has brought about some havoc. But without question, I've always wanted to be a mother to the two of you. You will always be the best thing I'll ever have a hand in making.

And last, I am tremendously grateful to Robert Kelleher, whose grace and love for this world and for me and my work, and for my sons and his daughters, in the face of the darkest challenges, is a steady inspiration to all who are fortunate enough to know him. What a life we've made in our home by the sea. My love, such things are possible.